THE SHOP ON HIDDEN LANE

TITLES BY JAYNE ANN KRENTZ

THE LOST NIGHT FILES TRILOGY

Shattering Dawn
The Night Island
Sleep No More

THE FOGG LAKE TRILOGY

Lightning in a Mirror
All the Colors of Night
The Vanishing

The Shop on Hidden Lane
Untouchable
Promise Not to Tell
When All the Girls Have Gone
Secret Sisters
Trust No One
River Road
Dream Eyes
Copper Beach
In Too Deep
Fired Up
Running Hot
Sizzle and Burn
White Lies
All Night Long
Falling Awake
Truth or Dare
Light in Shadow
Summer in Eclipse Bay
Together in Eclipse Bay
Smoke in Mirrors
Lost & Found
Dawn in Eclipse Bay
Soft Focus
Eclipse Bay
Eye of the Beholder
Flash
Sharp Edges
Deep Waters
Absolutely, Positively
Trust Me
Grand Passion
Hidden Talents
Wildest Hearts
Family Man
Perfect Partners
Sweet Fortune
Silver Linings
The Golden Chance

TITLES BY JAYNE ANN KRENTZ WRITING AS AMANDA QUICK

The Bride Wore White
When She Dreams
The Lady Has a Past
Close Up
Tightrope
The Other Lady Vanishes
The Girl Who Knew Too Much
'Til Death Do Us Part
Garden of Lies
Otherwise Engaged
The Mystery Woman
Crystal Gardens
Quicksilver
Burning Lamp
The Perfect Poison
The Third Circle
The River Knows
Second Sight
Lie by Moonlight
The Paid Companion
Wait Until Midnight
Late for the Wedding
Don't Look Back
Slightly Shady
Wicked Widow
I Thee Wed

With This Ring
Affair
Mischief
Mystique
Mistress
Deception
Desire
Dangerous
Reckless
Ravished
Rendezvous
Scandal
Surrender
Seduction

TITLES BY JAYNE ANN KRENTZ WRITING AS JAYNE CASTLE

It Takes a Psychic
People in Glass Houses
Sweetwater and the Witch
Guild Boss
Illusion Town
Siren's Call
The Hot Zone
Deception Cove
The Lost Night
Canyons of Night
Midnight Crystal
Obsidian Prey
Dark Light
Silver Master
Ghost Hunter
After Glow
Harmony
After Dark
Orchid
Zinnia
Amaryllis

THE GUINEVERE JONES SERIES

Desperate and Deceptive
THE GUINEVERE JONES COLLECTION, VOLUME 1
The Desperate Game
The Chilling Deception

Sinister and Fatal
THE GUINEVERE JONES COLLECTION, VOLUME 2
The Sinister Touch
The Fatal Fortune

SPECIALS

The Scargill Cove Case Files
Bridal Jitters
(WRITING AS JAYNE CASTLE)

ANTHOLOGIES

Charmed
(WITH JULIE BEARD, LORI FOSTER, AND EILEEN WILKS)

TITLES WRITTEN BY JAYNE ANN KRENTZ AND JAYNE CASTLE

No Going Back

THE SHOP ON HIDDEN LANE

Jayne Ann Krentz

BERKLEY
NEW YORK

BERKLEY
An imprint of Penguin Random House LLC
1745 Broadway, New York, NY 10019
penguinrandomhouse.com

Book design by George Towne

Library of Congress Cataloging-in-Publication Data

Names: Krentz, Jayne Ann author
Title: The Shop on Hidden Lane / Jayne Ann Krentz.
Description: New York: Berkley, 2026.
Identifiers: LCCN 2025023622 (print) | LCCN 2025023623 (ebook) |
ISBN 9798217187348 hardcover | ISBN 9798217187355 ebook
Subjects: LCGFT: Fiction | Paranormal romance fiction | Thrillers (Fiction) | Novels
Classification: LCC PS3561.R44 S486 2026 (print) | LCC PS3561.R44 (ebook) |
DDC 813/.54—dc23/eng/20250626
LC record available at https://lccn.loc.gov/2025023622
LC ebook record available at https://lccn.loc.gov/2025023623

Printed in the United States of America
1st Printing

The authorized representative in the EU for product safety and compliance is Penguin Random House Ireland, Morrison Chambers, 32 Nassau Street, Dublin D02 YH68, Ireland, https://eu-contact.penguin.ie.

For Jim and Wendy
and Steve and Michele
and Don and Joan.
I am so grateful that we are family.
I love you all.

PROLOGUE

SHE CAME OUT OF THE TRANCE ON A CRASHING WAVE OF ADRENALINE THAT FLOODED HER veins with a euphoric sense of relief. Once again, she had survived the treacherous crossing that separated the dreamstate from the waking state. For a wild, glorious moment she was a sorceress, a queen, a goddess. There would be a price to pay, but the ice fever would set in later. In this moment she could almost fly.

She took off her mirrored sunglasses and waited for the artist's reaction.

He screamed.

She winced. "Please don't do that. It's very unnerving."

It was midnight and the alley was heavily shadowed but in the light from his phone she could see the artist's face. His handsome, dramatically sculpted features had been transformed into a slack-jawed, wide-eyed mask of horror.

"No," he gasped. He stumbled back a few steps, both hands stretched out in front of him. "Stay away from me. I know what you are."

"You said I was your Muse."

"You're a succubus."

He whirled and fled to the mouth of the alley and disappeared into the foggy San Francisco night. She listened to his pounding footfalls until they faded away to nothing.

Another failed experiment. This serial dating project was becoming very depressing. She was starting to doubt Aunt Bea's assurance that sooner or later the right man would come along.

She dropped the small set of chimes and the little mallet into one of the pockets of her long, puffy coat. The adrenaline would wear off soon. She needed to get back to her apartment and make herself a cup of Bea's special herbal tisane. It would ward off the worst of the ice fever.

Clapping a gloved hand over her nose and mouth, she willed herself to ignore the stench of urine-soaked bricks and made her way toward the entrance of the alley. She sidestepped the dark psychic stain that marked the spot where the murder had occurred.

She heard the scurrying of small rodent claws in the dense shadows and picked up her pace, careful to avoid the detritus of used needles, empty liquor bottles, and garbage. She always wore a pair of sturdy leather boots when she went out on dates in dark alleys.

Safely back on the sidewalk, she moved into the glow of a streetlamp, took out her phone, and used the app to call a car service. She confirmed the booking and glanced up. At the edge of her vision she glimpsed the dark silhouette of a man. He emerged from the fog and came toward her, moving too quickly. She did not need to see the glint of the knife in his hand to know that his intentions were not good.

Irritated, she waited until he was closer and then she turned, locked eyes with him, and smiled.

"I'm not in the mood," she said.

The would-be assailant froze. A heartbeat later he uttered a choked scream, turned, and ran.

At least he hadn't called her a demon. Maybe he didn't know fancy words like *succubus.*

At the intersection a car turned the corner and coasted slowly to a halt in front of her. She checked the license plate and confirmed that it was the vehicle she had booked. A woman on her own at midnight in the city could not be too careful.

She slipped on the mirrored sunglasses before she opened the door and got into the back seat. If the driver wondered why she was wearing shades in the middle of the night, he kept his curiosity to himself.

She fastened the seat belt, sat back, and concentrated on analyzing the disastrous evening. She was forced to admit that she had to take most of the responsibility for the failure. She had misread the artist. Live men were a lot harder to read than dead men.

Sometimes she was tempted to abandon the dating project altogether, but Bea insisted that she keep trying. *"Harpers don't give up."*

Bea had evidently given up, though. She was in her late forties now and, while she had plenty of friends in the small community of Mirror Lake, she had never found a life partner.

Perhaps the venue had been the problem tonight. Murder scenes were not particularly romantic. But there was no other way to run the test on potential lovers.

She would ponder that issue later. All she wanted to do now was get back to her snug little apartment and brew the tisane. Once she was sure the fever was under control she would enter the artist into her log of failed experiments. The list was growing uncomfortably long.

The first image of a demonic female figure wearing mirrored sunglasses and holding a set of chimes arrived by encrypted text three days later. The words *YOU ARE MINE* accompanied the sketch.

ONE

"I CAN'T BELIEVE MY AUNT IS HAVING AN AFFAIR WITH YOUR UNCLE." SOPHY HARPER stared at the rumpled bed, shocked to the core. "He's a *Wells*."

"So am I," Luke Wells said. "We can discuss the feud between our families some other time. In case you haven't noticed, we've got a situation here. There is every reason to think your aunt and my uncle are in serious trouble. Someone died out there in the front room of this cabin."

He was right. She pulled herself together.

"It wasn't Bea or your uncle," she said. "I'm sure of that. The energy of the stain is quite different from the energy in this room." She shuddered and tried to ignore the evidence in front of her eyes. *What on earth were you thinking, Aunt Bea? Seriously? You've been sleeping with a Wells?*

The offending couple had disappeared, but the evidence of their intimate relationship was unmistakable. Sophy recognized the fluffy pink robe dangling from a wall hook as the one she had given Bea on her last birthday. The book on the nightstand was the novel Bea had raved about in a recent email. And the toothpaste tube next to the second toothbrush on the vanity in the small bathroom was neatly rolled up from the bottom—the way Bea always rolled toothpaste tubes. Sophy refused to open any drawers for fear of finding a vibrator or sex toys.

She pushed her black-and-crystal cat-eye glasses higher on her nose and gestured toward the tumbled sheets. "How long has this been going on?"

"I have no idea," Luke said. An ominous impatience infused his dark voice. "Furthermore, I don't give a damn. I thought I made it clear we need to move fast. I hired you to read and clean the murder scene in the front room, not take to your fainting couch because you've been scandalized by your aunt's behavior."

She turned away from the bed. "Don't try to tell me you're not more than a little stunned yourself. Aunt Bea is a Harper. I can't believe she would allow herself to be seduced by a Wells."

"Maybe you've got it backward. Maybe your aunt seduced my uncle."

Sophy stared at him, momentarily too flabbergasted to respond.

"You said your aunt texted you that she had been called away on a psychic consultation?" Luke said.

She was sure she heard a sarcastic edge on the words *psychic consultation,* but under the circumstances she told herself she would rise above it.

"That's right." She composed herself. "It's not the first time she's traveled on short notice. She asked me if I would come up here to Mirror Lake to look after the shop while she was out of town."

"So, you packed a suitcase, left San Francisco, and drove two hours into the northern California mountains to look after a shop that does very little business at this time of year?"

"If you're implying that I know more about what happened

here than I'm telling you, you can go jump in the lake. Yes, I agreed to keep an eye on the shop. As it happens, it was good timing. I needed a break."

"From your library work?" he asked a little too smoothly.

"No, from the crime scene reading." She winced. "I enjoy the library work, but the readings get to you after a while."

And so did the failed experiments. She was still recovering from the succubus incident. A woman could only take so much.

"I understand," Luke said quietly.

Startled because he sounded as if he did understand, she shot him a wary look. But his expression gave nothing away.

"Never mind," Luke said. "You can wring your hands later." He went through the doorway into the small front room. "We need to figure out what happened here. You confirmed we've got a murder scene. The Boss says you're a housekeeper. You can read 'em and clean 'em. Time to go to work."

She disliked the nickname. Not only was it an insult to real housekeepers everywhere, it did not begin to describe her psychic talent. But once again she reminded herself that she had to focus.

The Boss, she knew, was Harry Wells, Luke's paternal grandfather. Harry was currently CEO of Wells, Inc., a sophisticated technology firm that specialized in cutting-edge security devices.

The alarming evidence in the bedroom aside, the Harpers and the Wellses hadn't been known to socialize for four generations. They did, however, keep an eye on each other from a distance. Given the pact that bound the families and the decades of distrust between them, they did not have any choice. As a result, she was aware that the Wells family had settled on Luke as the heir to his grandfather's position at the company. Evidently no one else in the clan wanted the job, including Luke's father and his uncle, Deke.

She had first met Luke Wells about twenty minutes ago when he had arrived on the doorstep of the Shop on Hidden Lane. But in addition to his future role as the head of Wells, Inc., she knew a couple of other things about him. According to the rumor mill in the psychic community, insiders called him No-Talent Wells. It was said that every generation or so the family produced a member with no measurable psychic abilities. Evidently that individual got stuck with the job of running the highly profitable company.

No-Talent Wells. Talk about unpleasant nicknames. She could almost feel sorry for Luke. Almost.

Focus, woman. Like it or not, Wells is right. Bea might be in real trouble.

She followed Luke back out into the other room, where his hellhound companion, Bruce, was busy exploring various scents. Man and dog went together, she thought. They both looked dangerous.

Dark-haired, with a lean, sleekly muscled build, an austere profile, and amber eyes that gave new meaning to the term *old soul,* Luke had the vibe of a CIA assassin—cold-blooded, stern, and judgy.

Admittedly, she had never met an assassin. She had stumbled over the tracks of a few serial killers in her crime scene reading work, but no actual assassins, at least not that she was aware of. She didn't know if the CIA employed professional assassins, but she had a good imagination, and she was pretty sure that if they did, Luke would fit the profile. The fact that he was wearing a lot of black—black leather bomber jacket, black pullover, black trousers, and black boots—enhanced the impression.

Bruce suited the part of an assassin's dog. He was a dark-furred, lean, sleekly muscled beast of indeterminant breed. His amber-gold eyes were disturbingly similar to Luke's—sharp, smart, and a little feral. He should have been named Anubis or Cerberus. Who called a dog like this one Bruce?

Yep, Luke and Bruce made a good pair. A couple of hellhounds. Luckily, she was good with dogs. Unfortunately she could not say the same about men.

"Give me a minute," she snapped. "I need to get a sense of the atmosphere in this space before I can begin the reading."

Walking with ghosts was always a grim business, and murder scenes were the worst, especially at night. She dreaded the work but she was stuck with a psychic talent for it. In addition, she felt a moral obligation to use her abilities when called upon to do so. It was, however, a hard way to make a living, because business was not brisk. Few police investigators took psychics seriously. Most cops assumed she and others like her were frauds. Investigators who did believe she was the real deal rarely had a budget that allowed for hiring psychic consultants.

She had vowed to cut back on the pro bono work but that was proving difficult. Turning down the handful of clients who trusted her to help solve horrible crimes sent her on a very unpleasant guilt trip.

She paid the rent with a real job, one she loved. She was a librarian who had found her niche consulting for private libraries and collectors who specialized in books and materials that dealt with the paranormal. Granted, that meant she often did business with what most people would call eccentric clients. But she and her sister, Chloe—also a librarian—had been raised by their aunt. Bea was a librarian and a professional psychic consultant who operated the Shop on Hidden Lane. Sophy and Chloe had grown up in a business that thrived on eccentric customers. They knew how to deal with them.

"The sooner you get started, the sooner you can go back to selling crystals, wind chimes, tarot cards, and the rest of that tourist junk in your aunt's shop," Luke prompted.

Sophy shoved her hands into the pockets of the ankle-length puffer coat and glared. "Pro tip, Wells. Insulting my aunt's business is not a smart way to establish a professional working relationship based on mutual respect."

"I'm not here to establish a relationship of any kind."

"Oddly enough, I got that impression."

"I want answers. I have one priority, and that is to find my uncle. My grandmother told me that you agreed to take the job. I'm paying you what I suspect is double the going rate for this kind of work."

"Triple, actually. Special price for a Wells."

"Figures. I expect results."

"As if I had a choice," Sophy grumbled. "Your grandmother said she thinks your uncle's disappearance has something to do with that stupid pact between the families."

"My grandmother has very, very good intuition," Luke warned softly. "Psychic-grade intuition."

"I've heard that."

She kept her tone neutral this time because she really did not have any option. It had been annoying to get the phone call from Angela Wells, the matriarch of the clan, informing her that Luke was on his way to see her, but she knew her duty as a Harper. The pact had to be honored. Angela had made it clear she was convinced Deke's disappearance was connected to the events of the past. So yes, there had been no choice but to agree to take the job.

Now that she knew Bea was involved with Deke and might be in danger, however, she could not simply read the scene for Luke and walk away. She had to make sure Bea was safe.

"Just to be clear," she said, leaning into her most assured tones, "reading the scene is one thing. The kind of cleaning you have requested is . . . complicated."

No one in the underworld of the psychic community had any serious objections to crime scene consultations. True, there were not that many talents who could do it for real. A lot of frauds worked these gigs. But whether or not the practitioner could be trusted was the client's problem. There was nothing inherently unethical about the practice.

Cleaning up the paranormal evidence of a crime, however, while not technically illegal—after all, that kind of evidence could not be presented in a court of law—was severely frowned upon in a certain quarter of the paranormal community—namely the Agency for the Investigation of Atypical Phenomena, otherwise known as the Foundation.

The organization assumed it had the right to police the members of the psychic community. And, okay, maybe some entity had to take on the responsibility, because regular law enforcement could not be expected to deal with the bad guys who were amped up with paranormal talents—for the most part regular law enforcement didn't even believe psychic criminals existed. The Foundation had a role to play, but it was a well-known fact that its agents were inclined to be extremely judgmental.

The Harpers, like many others who made their livings with their psychic talents, preferred to keep a low profile.

Wells, Inc., on the other hand, was said to take contracts with the Foundation. No surprise. It was just like the Wells family to work both sides of the street and get away with it, Sophy thought. The clan was powerful. It had nothing to fear from the Foundation.

"Let me worry about the complications of a housekeeping job," Luke said.

"All right." She took a deep breath. "I'm ready."

She paced to the far end of the room and took off her black-and-crystal-framed glasses. She slipped them into a soft case and dropped the case into the depths of a coat pocket. Reaching into another pocket she took out the oversized mirrored sunglasses and put them on.

"Please turn off the light," she said.

She could tell from his expression that Luke had some questions about the glasses, but he was smart enough not to ask them. Instead, he went to the wall switch and flipped it. The weak bulb in the overhead fixture winked out, plunging the room into the sort of absolute darkness that can only be found in an isolated mountain cabin—a cabin like this one.

She was braced for the familiar flash of acute claustrophobia—had trained herself to breathe through it—but that didn't stop the panicky sparks that snapped across her senses. She wondered if Luke was experiencing a similar sensation. She hoped so. It would serve him right.

She reached into a third pocket and took out the small set of metal chimes and the little wooden mallet.

With the claustrophobia under control, she steeled herself and kicked up her talent. The darkness was slowly infused with an eerie gray radiance. The temperature in the already cold room seemed to drop a few more degrees.

In the gray fog, she could see Luke standing near the light switch. He did not look the least bit nervous, let alone claustrophobic, just very, very focused. That was irritating. It would have been satisfying to know that he had a shred of vulnerability. Instead, there was a hint of energy in his eyes.

She suddenly realized he was watching her intently. That answered one question. He might be a no-talent compared to the other members of his family, but he was not without a psychic vibe. He had some paranormal-grade night vision. A useful ability for an assassin.

Bruce the hellhound was watching her, too. But that was not surprising. Dogs have pretty good night vision.

She turned slowly, examining the room. There were no bloodstains, no body, and no obvious physical evidence, but the energy laid down by violent death had soaked into the well-worn wooden floorboards and permeated the walls. The currents of dark light came in a range of colors that her second sight had learned to interpret, at least to some extent.

"How does this work?" Luke asked.

"I'm going to go into a self-induced trance," she said. "I will narrate what I see. I'll do my best to observe details but don't try to ask questions or direct me in any way. You'll shatter the trance."

Before he could say anything else, she gripped the handle of the chimes in one hand and lightly tapped a metal bar with the mallet. A crystalline note echoed in the room, sharp and clear. It seemed to linger endlessly. She rode it into her other vision, across the borderlands that separated the waking state from the dreaming state. As usual, the journey was surreal and disturbing. For a heartbeat or two the panic threatened to overwhelm her. No matter how many times she went into the trance she never overcame the fear of being trapped in the in-between world.

And just like that she was inside.

The first ghost materialized near the window, a dark, shadowy figure in the luminous gray light. He was smoking a cigarette.

TWO

BRUCE ALERTED, EARS SHARPENING. SOPHY COULD HAVE SWORN THAT THERE WAS SOME serious energy in his amber eyes. He growled softly.

"*It's all right,*" she said to the dog. "*The ghosts aren't real.*"

She was in her trance voice now. She knew it sounded eerie, as if she was one of the ghosts. But the dog did not seem to care. Maybe he was accustomed to creepy voices.

He padded forward and stopped beside her. When he leaned against her right leg she realized he was shivering with battle-ready tension. She rested a hand on his head.

"*I know the feeling,*" she said. "*But it's not real. You need to think of this as an instant replay.*"

When, as a teen, she had begun encountering the shadowy figures that hovered near scenes of violence and tragedy, she had been traumatized by the possibility that she was seeing ghosts. Aunt Bea had explained that the visions were her intuition's way of making sense of the paranormal energy deposited in such places. Violence of any kind left a lot of residual radiation. The spectral shadows were just an example of metaphysics in action.

Her logical side accepted the scientific explanation for the manifestations but that did not change the fact that when she was in the zone the phantoms seemed all too real. Nor did it alter her emotional and physical responses. Those she had to suppress with raw willpower.

She studied the smoking ghost.

"*The curtains are closed but I can tell that it is night,*" she said in her otherworldly voice. "*A figure is pacing back and forth. I can't make out a face or give you a description but something about the way he moves tells me I'm watching a man. He's excited. Sweating. Smoking a cigarette. Working himself up to do something . . . intense. Thrilling. There's a vibe of madness. It's as if he can barely hang on to his control.*"

She watched the shadowy figure stalk around the small space for a moment, trying to pick up more insights, but nothing else about the apparition stood out. She resumed the narration.

"*He's got something in his right hand. A gun, I think. He hears a sound that makes him go to the window. He peeks through the curtains. Now he's even more excited but in a very sick way. I can sense the anticipation of violence in the energy he left behind. I think he hears a knock on the door because he suddenly heads back across the room. His energy field is suddenly spiking. He's hot. On fire.*"

"What do you mean by *on fire*?" Luke asked.

His question slipped into the dream in the most casual manner. For a second or two she wondered if it was her imagination. No one had ever been able to communicate with her while she was in the zone, not without breaking the trance. The awareness of just how alone she was when she employed her talent at full strength was one of the many reasons she hated doing crime scene work.

"Are you referring to his talent?" Luke continued when she did not respond.

She had not imagined it. He was communicating with her even though she was deep in the trance. For once she wasn't alone in the ghost zone. But why did Luke Wells have to be the one person who could reach her?

She took a deep breath and reminded herself that she was a professional. She concentrated on Smoking Ghost. Fierce, erratic waves of energy crackled in the air around the figure.

"*He's got a powerful talent of some kind,*" she said, aware that she was still in her trance voice. "*I think he intends to use his psychic ability to murder whoever is at the door.*" She hesitated, trying to read the energy around the ghost. "*It won't be his first time. He knows it will give him a rush.*"

"So he's the killer," Luke said on a note of cold satisfaction. "And we know he smokes. With luck he will have left some cigarette butts here in the cabin. I'll look for them later. Try to get a read on his talent."

"*Will you please shut up?*" she said in her other voice. "*I'm about to witness a murder. Do you realize how much I hate watching someone get killed knowing there's nothing I can do to stop it?*"

"The murder has already happened. You're just reconstructing the scene. This is what you do. You told Bruce it was a kind of instant replay."

"*One more word out of you, Wells, and I'll come out of the trance before the killer opens the door. If that happens you won't get any more answers.*"

Bruce whined. Apparently Luke got the message. At least he stopped talking. Sophy fought the fear and frustration that sluiced through her veins as she waited to witness a murder. She absolutely hated this part.

"*The ghost is watching the door, waiting for it to open,*" she said, so consumed with dread and so off-balance from the knowledge that Luke had invaded the trance that she did not realize she had used the word *ghost* until it was too late. *Shit.* That was not good. But at least Luke didn't question it.

A spectral shadow loomed in the doorway.

"*I see the victim. He's about to enter the cabin.*"

"Just one person?" Luke asked.

She decided to ignore the interruption because it dawned on her that his voice was like a chain or a rope—a lifeline she could use to pull herself out of the trance if her worst nightmares came true and she got trapped.

She wanted to scream a warning to the individual who was about to be murdered by Smoking Ghost but that would be pointless. She wasn't watching the unfolding horror in real time. *It's over*, she thought. *There's nothing you can do now.*

She went very still and waited, her throat tight, her breathing shallow, her pulse racing. *The ghosts aren't real. Not real.*

The victim walked into the room.

"*Smoking Ghost raises the gun*," she said. "*No, not a gun, but it's a weapon of some kind.*"

The brilliant flashes of fierce energy slammed into the victim. Her first thought was that the killer had unleashed a lethal paranormal talent. The ability to kill with psychic energy was rare but there were rumored to be a few monster talents who could do it. The fact that such individuals existed was one of the excuses the Foundation used to justify its quasi police force and Halcyon Manor, the private prison disguised as a psychiatric hospital.

The victim froze as if struck by lightning, mouth open on a silent scream. He convulsed, clutched at his chest, and crumpled to the floor.

The killer stopped firing the weapon. For a moment he seemed overcome with the thrill of the kill. And then he lurched into action.

"*The killer is dragging the dead man out of the cabin*," Sophy said. "*Now they are both gone.*" She paused. "*Does your uncle smoke?*"

"No."

"Are you sure?"

It was weird to be able to communicate like this from the trance but it gave her a newfound sense of normalcy. That was even more weird. She was not accustomed to feeling any version of normal when she was on the other side like this.

"Deke wasn't the killer, if that's what you're thinking," Luke stated with unflinching authority.

Well, of course he would protect a family member, she thought. In his place, she would have cheerfully lied through her teeth if necessary.

"How can you be certain?" she asked, curious to see if he had a logical response.

"Uncle Deke would not have gotten worked up to a sick fever pitch by the thought of murdering someone. I'm not saying he wouldn't kill in a life or death situation. But he would not have gotten off on the prospect of ending a life. And by the way, I am offended by the suggestion that my uncle is a sociopathic murderer."

"I am, of course, relieved to hear that my aunt isn't dating a sociopath."

"I'm aware that the Harpers don't think too highly of the Wellses."

"What a coincidence. I'm aware that the members of the Wells clan believe all Harpers are cat burglars, safecrackers, and low-rent con artists."

"After what I paid you for the reading tonight, I'm willing to testify that whatever else you are, you are not low-rent," Luke said. "I suggest we forget ancient history, at least for now. We don't need the distraction."

He had a point. Also, she needed to get out of the trance. She was pushing her limits. Time seemed to flow differently when she was in the waking dreamstate. It was easy to lose track. But she had learned a few things over the years and one was that the longer she remained in the trance, the faster and harder the ice fever would strike when she emerged.

"So, we've got an unidentified dead man and a deranged killer who smokes," Luke said. "Is there anything else you can tell me?"

She thought about the strange gun the killer had used. "*The weapon is very odd. It fires some kind of energy. It reminded me of a strobe light.*"

There was a brief moment of silence while Luke processed that.

"A paranormal weapon?" he asked finally.

"*Maybe, but I can't be certain. It definitely isn't a regular pistol.*" She paused. "*You don't sound surprised by the possibility that the device might be based on paranormal tech.*"

"There are a few psi-based weapons out there," he said. "They date from the days of the old Bluestone Project. The one thing they have in common is that they are extremely dangerous to use."

"*Because they fire paranormal radiation of some kind?*"

"Well, that and the fact that most people can't handle them, at least not for long. According to my great-grandfather's journal, that was the main reason the program tasked with developing psi-guns was forced to abandon the project. They were as dangerous to the shooter as they were to the target."

Her librarian's curiosity kicked in.

"*Why?*"

"Because the act of firing the weapons produced a psychic recoil that, over time, damaged the shooter's aura. Continued use resulted in insanity and death."

"*I see. Well, this killer certainly seems unstable.*"

The novelty of being able to communicate with someone while in the trance had caused her to stay too long. She could not risk another minute. She was no Cinderella and Luke was not her idea of Prince Charming, but it might as well have been midnight in the ballroom.

She prepared to strike another note on the chimes, the one she would use to ride out of the trance and back into the waking state.

A shadow in the doorway made her hesitate.

"*Oh, shit,*" she whispered in her trance voice. "*This isn't over yet.*"

"What's happening?" Luke asked.

"*There's a figure in the doorway. A man. He enters the room. There is no hesitation. He knows his way around. He stops near the sofa.*"

"Deke," Luke said. "It must be."

"*He's got something in his hand.*"

"A gun?"

"*I don't think so. I can't see the object, but whatever it is, it's important to him. Now he's returning to the door.*"

"When did this go down? Before or after the murder?"

"*Good question. The visions are not connected. I'm viewing two separate incidents. Both are very recent but there's no way to know which happened first. This one is much weaker and fainter than the murder scene. That indicates no violence is involved, thank goodness.*"

"But it's important?"

"*Very. There's a lot of tension around the man.*"

Another ghostly silhouette appeared on the threshold, evidently waiting for Deke. She could not make out the figure's face but she would know that energy field anywhere.

She struck the chimes, got a note, and rode it out of the trance and into the heavy darkness inside the cabin.

"Sorry," she said, safely back in her normal voice. "That's it. That's all I can tell you. Please turn on the light."

Luke flipped the switch and studied her with his CIA assassin eyes. She knew he didn't believe her. That was his problem.

"Can you track the energy prints outside the cabin?" he asked.

"Across the porch maybe but that's about it. The ground absorbs the paranormal currents very quickly."

She was talking fast now because she was flying on adrenaline.

The mirrored sunglasses concealed her eyes but she knew that she had stayed too long in the trance. The ice fever would strike very soon and it would be bad. She had to get back to the shop. She needed to dose herself with the tea and then she had to come up with a plan to find Bea.

Luke, however, suddenly seemed to be in no great rush to leave the cabin.

"Where would you go to hide a body around here?" he asked.

"Pick a spot, any spot." She swept out a hand to indicate the thick woods that surrounded the cabin. "We're in the middle of a forest, in case you haven't noticed. We lose a hiker or two every summer. Sometimes the bodies are never found. There's also the lake. It's very deep."

Her teeth were starting to chatter. Damn. This was not good. Bruce was watching her in an attentive, concerned way. Or maybe that was how a hellhound looked just before he went for the throat.

"I asked where *you* would hide a body," Luke said.

A jolt of anger flashed through her. "Are you implying that I had something to do with what went down in this cabin?"

"No, I'm trying to use some logic. Connect a few dots. It's what I do. If you kill someone, you have to deal with the body. We know it wasn't left here. You grew up in Mirror Lake. You know the territory. It seems reasonable to ask you where someone might dump a—" Luke broke off, frowning. "Are you all right?"

"Yes. No." She wrapped her arms around herself but she knew nothing would stop the shivering. "I always go through this after I do a reading. It doesn't usually happen so fast, that's all. I spent too much time in the trance. I'll be okay." She managed a steely smile. "I'm a professional. Don't try this at home."

"Do you need medical attention?"

"A . . . a . . . absolutely not," she bit out through clamped teeth. "A doctor would diagnose my symptoms as a panic attack."

"Is that what's going on?"

"*No.* Please take me home. I'll make myself a nice cup of tea and I'll be fine."

"You're shivering," Luke said.

"One of the side effects of my stupid talent. Don't worry about it. I'll live."

He started to strip off his jacket. "Here, put this on."

"It won't help. I'm already wearing a coat."

"What does help?"

"A cup of tea, like I said. *Take me back to the shop.*"

"Looks like you've got all the symptoms of para-hypothermia," Luke said.

She couldn't tell if he was genuinely concerned for her health or if he was alarmed because her traumatized aura meant she might not be of any more use to him. He was a Wells, so probably the latter.

"Don't worry," she said. "Just a few chills. I've been through this before."

Okay, not quite like this, but she knew what to do. She needed the tea.

"How long until you recover?" Luke asked.

"Not long." She gave him another sharp smile. "About a half hour after I get my tea."

"We can probably speed up the recovery process if I use my energy field to help stabilize your shocked wavelengths. You know the old rule—*two auras are stronger than one.*"

Bad idea, she thought. *A really, really bad idea.* Also potentially dangerous. What he was suggesting required physical contact. In her shaky state, there was no way to know how her rattled senses would react to an attempt to calm her energy field.

"It's too risky," she said, trying to sound like she knew what she was talking about.

"Don't worry, I won't hurt you."

There was no point trying to hide the truth. So what if she scared the living daylights out of him? It wasn't like they had a personal relationship. He wasn't another experiment.

"You don't understand," she said evenly. "If you attempt to manipulate my aura you're the one who most likely will be damaged." She paused for emphasis. "Seriously damaged."

"Yeah? How?"

He sounded interested, not scared. Maybe he considered her a challenge. She was getting more annoyed by the minute.

"I could pull you straight into a nightmare," she said. "I might even shatter part of your aura." She paused and then added politely, "Accidentally, of course."

"Sounds like you've had some experience."

"Yes." She was not about to go into an in-depth discussion of her list of failed experiments. Not now.

Luke moved closer. "Don't worry, you won't damage me. What's the deal with the shades? Are they for dramatic effect? No need to impress this client."

Before she realized his intention, he reached out with both hands and deftly slipped off the mirrored sunglasses.

THREE

"NO, WAIT, STOP," SHE YELPED. SHE TOOK A STEP BACK BUT CAME UP AGAINST THE OLD sofa. She was trapped. "You don't understand."

Too late. Luke went very still and gazed into her eyes as if mesmerized. She held her breath, waiting for what she knew was coming next. He would experience a flash of primal fear. He probably wouldn't panic—he was too strong—but at the very least he would be shocked. While he might not run, he would definitely want to put some distance between them. So much for his plan to calm her aura.

She straightened her shoulders. She was a Harper. She had her pride. "Don't say you weren't warned."

Luke set the sunglasses on a nearby table. "This," he said, "is going to be interesting."

That was when she realized that his own eyes were burning—but not with horror or shock or even mild alarm. The heat was intimate and intense. Part of the energy was sexual but there was something else going on, too, something she was afraid to define.

He took one of her hands in his, pulling her close. To her

amazement, nothing awful happened. She did not know what she had expected but it wasn't this incredibly thrilling warmth, this sense of rightness. He released her fingers to cradle the back of her neck with his palm. Her frazzled nerves responded instantly, seeking and luxuriating in the heat of his body. The ice fever began to recede.

It wasn't just the inviting intimacy that was tugging at all her senses. There was a sensuality about the experience that was unique. Fascinating. She had never felt anything like it.

"I don't understand," she whispered.

Luke's mouth kicked up a little at one corner. "Neither do I, but I think you can stop worrying that you'll traumatize my aura beyond repair."

She decided not to argue or offer any more warnings. Things were going too well.

She was letting herself sink deeper into his heat when the hurricane of his aura swept over her, threatening to envelope her. Her intuition shot into the red zone. Her instincts took control in a desperate attempt to repel the invasion.

The result was a clash of energy fields that sent shock waves through all of her senses. Disoriented, she lost her balance and grabbed the front of Luke's leather jacket with both hands to keep from falling. She would have collapsed if he hadn't tightened his grip to steady her.

But he, too, was swept up in the storm they had ignited.

"Too late," he said.

He did not sound alarmed. The opposite. Masculine anticipation infused the words. He should have been worried. Why wasn't he worried? *She* was worried. Their auras were locked in the most intimate kind of combat. It was unlike anything she had ever experienced. Enthralling.

What was happening?

She came out of the strange trance with a jarring jolt to her knees.

"Ouch," she muttered. "That hurt."

"Yeah, that could have been better managed," Luke said. "In my own defense, all I can tell you is that I didn't see it coming. Well, I did, but only in a vague way. No details were provided."

She realized they were both on their knees on the hard wooden floor, face-to-face, clinging together as if trying to save each other from drowning.

"What are you talking about?" she managed.

Luke did not get a chance to answer because they were collapsing together in slow motion. He ended up on his back. She found herself sprawled on top of him in an undignified tangle of arms and legs. Her mouth was very close to his.

For a moment it was as if a silent treaty had been established between their warring auras, and the currents of their energy fields settled into an exhilarating resonance and a glorious sense of discovery. *Where have you been all my life, Luke Wells?*

In the next instant the elation gave way to confusion and disbelief.

"You're okay," she said, amazed.

"I'm not sure that's the right word to describe my current condition, but I guess it works," Luke said. A wicked amusement lit his eyes. "You look shocked."

"I was expecting a different outcome."

"You were anticipating disaster, weren't you?"

"Well, yes, to be honest."

"Based on prior experience?"

"There have been a couple of failed experiments, you see. I suppose you could say I'm gun-shy about physical contact when I'm coming out of a trance."

"Can I assume the failed experiments are now exes?"

She flushed. "You could say that."

"On the plus side, I can't help but notice that you are no longer shivering."

"No. I'm not." She took a breath. "What about my eyes?"

"You have very nice eyes."

"That's not what I meant. Do they look weird?"

"Define *weird*."

"Never mind." Bewildered, she pushed herself up off his chest. That proved embarrassing because now she was sitting astride his hips and very aware of his heavy erection.

She lurched upright and grabbed the back of the sofa to steady herself. She looked down and got another jolt. The front edges of Luke's leather jacket had fallen open. For the first time she saw that he had a small case attached to his belt. It was the kind of case people with severe allergies use to carry emergency auto-injectors filled with epinephrine.

Luke sat up slowly and uncoiled to his feet. The jacket fell back into place, covering the auto-injector case. "I knew it would be hot," he said. "But not that hot."

FOUR

"WHAT JUST HAPPENED?" SOPHY SAID, TRYING TO MAKE THE QUESTION SOUND LOGICAL. Detached. Just a matter of scientific curiosity. Or something.

"Isn't it obvious?" Luke said. "Your aura is back to normal and I survived the process. Yay, me."

He appeared almost as unfazed as Bruce. The hellhound was stretched out on the sofa, having seized the opportunity for a nap.

Sophy studied Luke.

"You're not taking this seriously, are you?" she said.

"That's where you're wrong," Luke said. He began to prowl the room. "I am taking it seriously. But we don't have time for a discussion of bio-metaphysics. We've got a few loose ends to clean up here and then I need to do some thinking."

"What loose ends? I fulfilled my part of the deal."

"Not completely," Luke said. "Ah, here we go." He took a small plastic baggie out of his pocket and crouched near the window.

"What did you find?" she asked.

"A couple of cigarette butts." He bagged his find, straightened, and went to the sofa. "You said it looked like Deke left something here."

She was so rattled by what had just happened that she had forgotten about the sofa. That was not good. She had to stay focused.

Luke evicted Bruce from the sofa and then he raised each cushion in turn. He retrieved an unmarked envelope from underneath the third one. Sophy watched him tear it open. He considered the contents and took out a business card. He glanced at the front and then turned it over.

"Well, shit," he said very quietly.

Curiosity overcame her disgruntled mood. She moved closer to see what he had found.

"That's one of my aunt's business cards," she said. "I don't understand."

Without a word, Luke flipped the card so that she could read the one word scrawled on the back.

"Kaleidoscope." Sophy looked up. "Your grandmother was right. This does involve the pact."

"Looks like it." Luke took two printouts from the envelope. "It explains why you saw your aunt and my uncle together in the cabin after you read the murder scene. They're both involved in this thing."

She groaned. "You knew I saw Aunt Bea?"

"Lucky guess."

"You aren't the type to take wild guesses."

"No," he admitted. "I just connect dots. When you suddenly went quiet and popped out of the trance I knew you had seen something that you thought you needed to keep secret."

"Forget it." She frowned at the printouts he was holding. "What are those?"

"Two passes to the Fool's Gold Canyon Art Colony."

"Fool's Gold Canyon? I've never heard of it."

"The fine print says the art colony is located at a little-known vortex site in Arizona."

"So it's one of those places that attracts the woo-woo crowd."

"You and I could be classified as card-carrying members of the woo-woo crowd."

She waved that aside. "Do you know anything about the art colony?"

"No." He glanced at the printouts again. "I'm not into art." He dropped the passes back into the envelope and removed a printout. "Looks like Mr. and Ms. Ainsley have a booking for room two-twenty at the Vortex Inn, which happens to be located on the grounds of the art colony."

Sophy held out a hand. "Let me have one of those passes."

"Why?"

"Isn't it obvious? I'm going to check out that art colony."

"Not a good plan." Luke slipped the room reservation back into the envelope. "The passes and the hotel booking are the only leads I've got. Deke left them here for me to find. He knew that if he went off the grid I would be the one who looked for him."

"Why you?"

"Because I'm pretty good at connecting dots and that's how you conduct a search."

"He left *two* passes because he and my aunt knew I would be here with you when you found that envelope. That means one of those passes is for me."

"I'm not following your logic."

She gave him another steely smile. "You don't need to follow it. Just give me one of those passes."

"We can talk about this in the morning."

"We're talking about it now. You may be good with dots but

I'm the one with the talent for reading crime scenes. Face it, Wells, you're going to need me to help you find your uncle and my aunt. Besides if you don't hand over one of the passes, I'm going to head for Fool's Gold Canyon anyway."

He considered her for a long moment. "That sounds a lot like blackmail."

"Don't be ridiculous. It's not blackmail, it's a statement of fact."

Without a word he handed one of the passes to her. She tucked it securely into a pocket and took a moment to survey the room.

"Aunt Bea, what on earth have you gotten yourself involved in?" she said quietly.

"The wind is picking up," Luke said. "You need to get busy and clean up the scene so I can drive you back to the shop before the storm hits."

She hesitated. "I'm not sure it's a good idea to scrub the evidence. I know it's only paranormal evidence, not the courtroom kind, but still, we're talking about murder."

"If you don't clean the place there's a very good chance that one of two scenarios will play out. The Foundation may get tipped off about what went down here and send out some crime scene readers of their own, in which case there's a high probability they will conclude that your aunt was involved."

She grimaced. He was right. The last thing she wanted to do was bring the heavy weight of the Foundation down on a Harper.

She took the chimes and mallet out of her pocket and prepared to neutralize the dark energy that seethed in the floorboards, walls, and ceiling. It was exhausting but it was much less stressful than reading the scene and there was virtually no psychic blowback—just a few bad dreams.

She paused before striking the note that would enable her to slip into a light trance. "You said there were two possible scenarios. What's the second one?"

Luke smiled a very cold smile. "The second scenario is that the smoking ghost or someone else involved in this situation will come around looking to get rid of people who know too much."

He was right, of course. If she had been thinking clearly she would have arrived at the same conclusions.

"Okay," she said. "But for the record, I hate cleaning."

She tapped the chimes with the mallet, found the right note, and went to work.

FIVE

"DEKE AND YOUR AUNT APPARENTLY HAVE HAD A LONG-STANDING PERSONAL RELATION-ship," Luke said. He smiled a little as he put the SUV in gear and drove away from the cabin. "Wait until my grandmother finds out. She'll be pissed. She married into the family, so she's not a Wells by blood, but somewhere along the line she became more of a Wells than the rest of us, including the Boss. Family is everything to her, and that means holding on to the old feud."

"I'm still in shock myself," Sophy said. "My sister will be stunned. But Chloe is out of the country working in a collector's private library on an island in the South Pacific. It's very hard to get in touch with her. But that's a problem for another time. We need to stay focused."

"Agreed," Luke said.

Bruce was in the back seat, but he had both front paws braced on the console, his head thrust between the two humans. Luke suspected he had chosen the position because it enabled him to get closer to Sophy. From time to time, she raised a hand and ruffled the fur behind his ears. The dog practically groaned with pleasure.

I should be so lucky, Luke thought.

He tightened his grip on the wheel. She was right. Time to focus. He was good at that. As far as his family was concerned, it was his only real talent.

Sophy was all business now. She sat, square-shouldered and tense, in the passenger seat. Evidently she had decided to pretend nothing unusual had happened between them when she had emerged from the trance. He wasn't sure how to deal with that.

The aura-resonating experience had been a first for him. He was still feeling some of the afterburn—a disorienting sense of discovery and an intimate connection that went beyond the physical. *Dad and the Boss said it would be like this.*

Both men had also warned him that situations like this could go full fubar.

What if Sophy had not experienced the same exhilarating rush of bone-deep awareness? What if she had been oblivious to the moment of resonance between them? Maybe it had amounted to nothing more than a few sparks as far as she was concerned. A momentary distraction.

Talk about a depressing answer to the *Was it good for you, too?* question.

He had not been entirely blindsided tonight. On some primal level he had been anticipating fireworks from the moment Sophy opened the door of the Shop on Hidden Lane and glared at him through her black-and-crystal-framed glasses. Something deep inside had stirred.

She had been dressed in gray joggers and an oversized sweatshirt. Her autumn-brown hair had been caught up in a careless twist on top of her head and secured with a large tortoiseshell clamp. The style emphasized her strong, feminine profile. He hadn't been able to see much of her figure because of the shapeless clothes, but that hardly mattered, because he'd been transfixed by her intense hazel eyes.

"You must be Wells," she had said. "You're late. I expected you a couple of hours ago." She eyed Bruce. "That dog should be on a leash."

"Bruce doesn't like leashes."

"If he takes off after a squirrel or a deer you might never find him."

"Bruce won't get lost unless he wants to."

"I don't see a collar."

"Bruce only wears collars for formal occasions."

"Whatever. It's not my problem if he gets picked up by animal control. There's a storm coming in. We're going to have to hurry if you want to get the reading done before it hits."

The atmosphere was charged with the vibe of the oncoming gale but there was another kind of energy around Sophy. She was not what he had expected. She was also not his type. Then again, he had never met anyone like her, so how could he be sure of that?

For a beat he felt disoriented.

"You are Sophy Harper, right?" he asked, needing confirmation that he hadn't dropped into an unscheduled dream.

"Yep, I'm afraid you're stuck with me, Mr. Wells." She smiled a smile that was too bright and too polished. "You are Luke Wells, right?"

"Pretty sure."

"Your grandmother called me this afternoon to tell me you were on the way."

"You're a reader and a housekeeper?"

"Those are side gigs. Mostly I'm a librarian. You were obviously expecting someone more exciting. I get that a lot. Don't worry, I'm good at what I do. Come on in and have some coffee while I change into my work clothes."

Her working gear had consisted of a puffy jacket that had enveloped her from neck to ankle. She wore it over the sweats. With the cat-eye glasses attached to a sparkly little chain around her neck, it was as if she was trying very hard to avoid looking sexy. It wasn't working.

He had been intrigued by her outfit because it was sartorial overkill. Sure, it was chilly in the mountains at night, but it was late spring, not midwinter. Judging by her clothes you'd have thought there were five feet of snow outside.

Now he understood why she had bundled up. She had dressed for the aftermath she knew would follow the reading. There was always a dark side to every strong talent.

He knew he had to take some of the blame for the tension that shivered in the atmosphere in the front of the SUV. But he refused to take all of it. The Harpers and the Wellses had a murky history that stretched back four generations. He felt free to hold ancestors on both sides responsible.

When he needed a crime scene reader he usually went with one of the in-house talents from Wells, Inc. But this was not just another security job. This was a family matter. You didn't use employees when it came to an investigation that touched on the past. You went with a talent who could be trusted to keep her mouth shut—a Harper.

Sophy folded her arms. "How did you do it?"

He took a deep breath, fortifying himself. She finally wanted to talk about what had happened when their auras had clashed and then resonated. This was going to be tricky. It wasn't the dreaded morning-after conversation, but it was the closest thing to it. It was the *We could be really, really great in bed together* conversation.

But in this case that probably would be followed by the *We hardly know each other* discussion, and then Sophy would point out that she was a Harper and he was a Wells. He would be forced to defend his family's legacy and she would be obliged to defend her family and that wouldn't go well.

"Do what?" he asked, stalling for time as he turned onto Lake Road.

"How did you talk to me while I was reading the scene without shattering the trance?"

He had not seen that coming. But then, it was no secret that he wasn't much of a psychic. So much for the post-resonance-experience conversation. He should probably be relieved.

"Is that what's been bothering you since we left the cabin?" he asked. "Why didn't you say something sooner?"

"A lot of things have been bothering me tonight." She did not take her attention off the narrow strip of pavement that bordered the lake. "That question just happens to be at the top of my list right now."

"I don't know," he admitted. "I just knew that it was possible to talk to you without breaking your trance."

"I'm not buying that. What kind of talent are you, Luke Wells?"

"I have some serious night vision, but that's it as far as psychic talents go. I'm sure you know they call me No-Talent Wells."

"Uh-huh."

"Do I at least get some credit for shutting down the ice fever?"

"Yes. Thank you." She continued to stare at the road through the windshield. "You saw my eyes."

"Yep. And, as I told you, they are very nice eyes. My turn. What were you afraid I would see?"

She switched her gaze to the black mirror of the lake. "It's not a good idea to look at my eyes, let alone make physical contact, when I am in a trance or when I'm coming out of one."

"Why not?"

"I don't know." She turned back to the view of the road. "I've run a few experiments. The problem is that none of my test subjects have stuck around long enough to give me a detailed analysis. I scare them. No, I terrify them. They act like they've seen a ghost or . . . something worse."

"What's worse than a ghost?"

She hesitated. "A demon, maybe."

He thought about that while he turned onto the side road that dead-ended at the Shop on Hidden Lane.

"Sounds like when you're in your zone you give off some hallucinatory vibes that can affect people who are in close proximity," he said. "Something to do with the energy it takes to will yourself in and out of a trance, probably."

"That's what Aunt Bea says." Sophy looked at him. "So why didn't you freak out tonight?"

He brought the SUV to a halt in front of the two-story house. "Maybe I've got a form of immunity because of my night vision." He shut down the engine. "What's this about running experiments?"

She paused and then cleared her throat. "Occasionally I conduct what you might call a test. Sometimes, like tonight, the experiment is accidental."

"I'm an accidental experiment?"

"Not exactly. Well, yes, in a way." She unclipped her seat belt and prepared to get out of the vehicle. "Look, this is hard to explain and it's got nothing to do with our problem."

She cracked open the door.

"Wait," he said. "I need to know what usually happens when you run your experiments."

She jumped down to the ground, turned, and looked at him. Her eyes sparked with a little heat.

"My last experiment screamed, called me a succubus, and took off running," she said. "That's the kind of thing that happens when I run one of my experiments. Satisfied? It's late. The storm will hit soon and I need some sleep. I'm going to leave for that art colony first thing in the morning, assuming the road is clear."

"A succubus?" He whistled softly. "A female demon who visits men in their dreams to have sex with them. I've always wanted to date one of those."

"You forgot the part where the succubus sucks out the victim's vital bodily juices so that he grows weaker and weaker and finally croaks."

"What's life without a little risk?"

"I'm glad you find the idea of a succubus entertaining. The man who called me one did not." She winced. "I terrified him."

"Sounds like he was a real loser."

"No, actually, he's a police sketch artist. He definitely has some talent, both the artistic kind and the psychic sort." She paused. "He said I was his Muse. He wanted to watch me work. He thought it would inspire him."

"Have you heard from him since he ran off into the night?"

"Not exactly."

"What the hell does that mean?"

"It's complicated and not important."

She shut the door with a very firm *kerchunk* and headed for the front steps of the shop.

He knew that was all he was going to get out of her tonight. He opened his own door and extracted himself from the driver's seat. Bruce bounded across the console and vaulted to the ground.

They both hurried to catch up with Sophy.

The Shop on Hidden Lane had a Victorian vibe. Luke had seen enough earlier to realize that it served as both a home and a business. Sophy had left the downstairs lights on. The windows glowed with an inviting warmth.

"Where are you staying tonight?" she asked as she went toward the front steps.

"Deke's cabin," he said.

She stopped abruptly. "You can't sleep there."

"Why not?"

She swept out her hands. "Because someone got killed there."

"Not in the bedroom."

"That's not the point."

"What is the point?"

"That cabin is stained with a lot of bad energy. It will affect your senses. Your dreams."

"You cleaned it, remember? Are you telling me you didn't do a good job?"

"I did an excellent job." She hesitated. "But no housekeeper can scrub out every last bit of the kind of stain left by the energy of extreme violence. I muddied the waters, so to speak. There's no useful evidence left but there will be a vibe. I don't like the idea of you sleeping in that house."

"I just told you, I don't have much of a talent. I doubt if I'll pick up on any residual energy."

"Everyone has some intuitive awareness of that sort of thing. We've all experienced that cold feeling you get when you walk into a structure where something terrible has happened. Do you know how many requests I get to do housekeeping work in a space where someone died? Listen up, Wells, sleeping in that cabin would be a dumbass thing for anyone to do."

"The alternative is sleeping in my vehicle, which, while certainly doable, would be inconvenient and uncomfortable. I'll risk some bad dreams in exchange for access to convenient indoor plumbing."

"Bad idea."

"Okay," he said. He held up both hands, palms out. "I'll see if I can get a room at the B and B."

"Forget the B and B. It's closed. The owner sold it last month and the new owners haven't reopened. There's no help for it. You'll have to stay here. You can sleep on the sofa."

"I appreciate your gracious offer of hospitality, but aren't you afraid having my vehicle parked in front of the shop all night will cause gossip?"

"Got news for you: it's too late to worry about my reputation. By noon tomorrow everyone in town will know your car was seen outside my aunt's shop tonight, long after closing time. They already know that Bea is gone and that I am the only one in residence."

"Is that going to be a problem for you?"

"Don't worry about it. Nothing I can't handle." She paused, remembering the case attached to his belt. "I don't mean to pry, but I noticed your auto-injector. What are you allergic to? Anything I should know about?"

He glanced at the house. "No. My allergy is to a rare kind of pollen. Nothing that's in bloom around here."

"Okay." Reassured, she took out the small wooden mallet and chimes and played a short series of notes.

"Why are you doing that now?" he asked. "Are you going into a trance?"

"No. Listen. Do you hear that?"

He stopped talking. The wind chimes on the front porch clashed angrily in the night. The music was discordant. Disturbing. It raised the hair on the back of his neck and sent a stiff shot of adrenaline through him.

Bruce growled softly, ears pricked, his gaze intent on the front door of the shop. That was not a reassuring sign, Luke thought.

"The storm is rattling the chimes," he said. "That's all I hear. What am I missing?"

"That's Aunt Bea's alarm system," Sophy said quietly. "We've got a situation."

"What kind of situation?"

"The chimes indicate that an intruder entered the shop while we were out."

SIX

"STAY HERE WITH BRUCE," LUKE SAID. "I'LL GO INSIDE AND TAKE A LOOK."

"I'm not sure that's a good idea," Sophy began. Her senses were still sparking in response to the warning of the chimes.

"I assume there's a back door?"

She wasn't going to talk him out of taking the risk, she realized. Credit where credit was due. He was a Wells. He might not have any impressive talent but he had grown up in the security business and he was slated to become CEO of the firm. He probably knew a lot more than she did about handling a situation like this. She could almost hear Aunt Bea whispering in her ear. *Let the man do his job.*

"Yes." She hesitated and then decided that under the circumstances there was no need to protect *all* of the Harper family secrets. One or two could be sacrificed. Luke was risking his neck for her. "There's also a concealed door in the storage shed attached to the side of the house. Electronic lock. The code is zero, zero, zero."

"Seriously?"

"Aunt Bea believes in keeping things simple."

"No offense, but that is beyond simple. The word *amateurish* comes to mind."

"You're kind of a hard-ass, aren't you?"

"I'm in the security business, remember?" Luke looked at Bruce. "Guard."

The hellhound immediately took up a position next to her. Once again, battle-ready tension shivered in the atmosphere around him.

She watched Luke melt into the night. He wasn't even using the flashlight on his phone to navigate the darkness.

She waited with Bruce, aware of her tight breathing, until the front door opened and Luke appeared on the porch. He had a gun in his hand. She was very certain he had not had one on him when he went into the house.

"The chimes sent the right message," he said. "There is someone inside but currently he's not a threat."

"Where did you get the gun?"

"Took it off your visitor."

"He had a gun?" Shocked all over again, she hurried up the steps. Bruce bounded up beside her, no longer in guard mode. "What's going on?"

"Damned if I know. Come in and take a look."

Luke led the way across the main sales floor of the shop. Crystals of various shapes and colors, chimes, incense sticks, and boxes of Bea's specially blended herbal teas were artfully arranged on the sparkling glass display shelves. Jewelry made with polished stones and small amulets glittered in a locked cabinet. Many of the pieces had been crafted by local artisans. Bea had used her talent to infuse them with faint currents of positive energy that most people could pick up intuitively, if unconsciously.

On one side of the room there was a floor-to-ceiling bookcase crammed with books and magazines focused on trendy metaphysical themes—dreams, meditation, astral travel.

Sophy knew the layout of the shop and its wares by heart. She and Chloe had grown up in it. They had taken turns behind the counter and they knew how to slip into the smooth patter Bea used to close a sale.

Luke had been right. Most of the objects on display in this room were aimed at the tourist crowd and curiosity seekers who showed up at the lake from May through late September. There was another pop of business in the week before Halloween. But winter and early spring were quiet. There were no ski resorts to attract visitors during that time of year, and the lake was too cold for swimming.

There was, however, another sales floor down in the basement, one that provided an excellent year-round income stream. Bea referred to it simply as "the office." She called herself a psychic forensic consultant and she worked by referral only. She possessed a sensitivity to certain kinds of energy that had been infused into objects. She used crystals to help focus her talent.

Clients searching for missing persons brought jewelry or other personal possessions to her for analysis. Others wanted her to advise them on issues of inheritance, money, or trust. *Is he lying to me?* was a common question.

Bea's clients arrived in every season and at all hours, sometimes in the middle of the night. Most paid her without any hesitation. But not everyone could afford her, so she did a fair amount of pro bono work. She always stressed the importance of using one's talents to help others.

Luke went behind the sales counter. Bruce trotted after him. They both stopped and looked down.

"He's not dead," Luke said. "But he seems to have fallen sound asleep in the middle of searching the shop. His ID says he's a homicide detective from Elk Cove."

"What in the world?" Sophy leaned over the counter and looked at the handsome man sprawled on the floor. "Damn. Just when I thought this night could not get any more complicated."

Luke held up a leather badge holder. "You know him?"

"Oh, yeah." She grimaced. "His name is Mack Rivington. I've worked a few cases with him this past year."

"And?"

"And we dated for a while," she said. "Not that it's any of your business."

"Things did not end well?"

She gave him a sharp, cold smile. "Whatever gave you that idea?"

Luke nodded. "Got it. One of your failed experiments. Any idea what he's doing here in your aunt's shop in the middle of the night?"

"I'm sure Mack came here for the same reason you did. He wants something from me. Probably my help on a case."

Irritation flashed in Luke's amber eyes. She got the impression he didn't like having his motives for contacting her compared to Mack's.

"Would you happen to know why he fell asleep on the floor?" he asked coldly.

"Smell that faint whiff of herbs?"

"Yes."

"He tripped one of Aunt Bea's aromatherapy traps. They are part of her security system. I set them tonight before we left for the read at the cabin."

"Why isn't it affecting us?" Luke glanced at Bruce. "Or him? His sense of smell is a hell of a lot better than a human's."

"Aunt Bea's traps are designed to have a very limited range. Once released, the drug dissipates quickly in the atmosphere."

"How long will Rivington be out?" Luke asked.

"Hard to say because we don't know when he got hit or how much he inhaled. Best guess is several hours. The more important question is, what am I going to do with him tonight?"

"I'll put him in his own cuffs. When he wakes up I'll have a chat with him."

The cold edge on the words was alarming.

"What do you mean?" she said. "I'm not Mack's biggest fan, but he's a good cop. I'm sure he's not involved in whatever went down at Deke's cabin."

"If he's such an honest cop, where's his vehicle? It isn't parked out in the driveway."

"It's probably at the back of the house. Mack doesn't come here very often but when he does, he is always careful to park out of sight."

"Why does Rivington want to sneak around?"

For some obscure reason she felt obliged to defend the sleeping man. Mack was in no position to speak for himself.

"He doesn't sneak around," she said. "Not exactly."

"Okay then, why does he go out of his way to avoid being seen here at Bea's shop?"

"Why don't you try connecting a few obvious dots?"

Luke nodded. "He's afraid that if rumors he consults a psychic get back to his boss it would not look good on his record."

She sighed. "You know how it is. The police don't like to admit they occasionally use psychics. Often they do it only because the family of the victim insists. And it rarely goes well when they do bring one in."

"Because they end up hiring a fraud who tries to fake it with some vague line like '*I see the body near water.*'" Luke glanced down at Mack and then looked at her, eyes tightening a little. "You, however, are the real deal, and Rivington knows that, doesn't he?"

"I think so, but he tells himself that I'm just a very keen observer and that I have excellent intuition. Cops do believe in intuition. Everyone does."

Luke got a knowing look. "Did he keep his dates with you a secret, too?"

She elevated her chin. "We liked our privacy."

"Thought so. He didn't want any of his cop pals to see the two of you together, did he?"

"It wasn't like that. Not exactly. My apartment is in San Francisco, so there was no reason for us to eat at restaurants here in Mirror Lake or Elk Cove." She made a face. "Okay, it was a lot like that."

"Don't you think it's a striking coincidence that he broke into your aunt's shop on the very night that I arrived to hire you to read a scene linked to the disappearance of Deke and Bea? For all we know, Rivington is investigating that murder at the cabin. If so, maybe he considers your aunt a suspect. Maybe he came here to search the place."

A jolt of panic snapped across her nerves. "I hadn't thought of that. I just assumed he came here because he knew I was in town and wanted me to work for him again. You're right. We need answers."

"Which is why he will be sleeping in cuffs."

"You are not going to question him on your own. I want to hear what he has to say. Besides, he's more likely to talk to me than he is to you."

"Because the two of you had a relationship?"

"We're still friends," she said evenly. "I think."

The freight train rumble of thunder interrupted her. Lightning slashed the darkness outside. It was followed by a gust of wind that rattled the windows. Bruce tensed.

"Take it easy," Luke said quietly. He rested a hand on the dog's head. "Just a storm."

The lights blinked.

Bruce whined. He moved out from under Luke's hand and began to prowl the shop.

"That settles it," Sophy said. "No one is going anywhere until this storm ends. You and Mack and Bruce are staying here tonight."

"Thank you," Luke said. "That's an excellent idea."

She folded her arms on the counter. "Why do you suddenly sound so enthusiastic about it?"

"You've already had one of your exes—correction, one of your failed experiments—break in tonight for unknown reasons. In addition, we have agreed that Deke and your aunt are in trouble. You should not be on your own here."

"I don't need a bodyguard, if that's what you're implying."

"Why don't you think of me as an old friend of the family?"

"Is that intended to be a joke?"

"I thought it sounded better than 'a potential failed experiment.'"

"Don't worry." She unfolded her arms and straightened. "Failed experiments are an entirely different category. You and Mack and the hellhound can sleep in the living room. Follow me."

She stalked behind the sales counter and opened the door to the private quarters.

"There's a bathroom down that hallway," she said.

Luke surveyed the cozy living room with its large hearth, reading chairs, thickly cushioned sofa, braided rug, and wooden coffee table. An old-fashioned desk stood in the corner, its top cluttered with papers and books.

"This will do," he announced, looking pleased.

"I can't tell you how thrilled I am to hear that. I'll let you haul Mack in here, unless you plan to leave him out there on the shop floor."

"No, I want to keep an eye on him, and I can't do that from here."

"I'll get some blankets and a couple of pillows."

She went up the stairs, switched on a wall sconce, and turned to go down the hall to the linen cupboard. The click of dog nails on the steps made her pause and turn around. Bruce was following her.

When he reached the top of the stairs she touched his head. "It's okay. Just a storm. You'll be fine. Don't worry, I won't tell the other hellhounds that thunder makes you anxious."

Bruce seemed to accept the reassurance, but he followed her to the linen cupboard, waited while she gathered up an armful of quilts and pillows, and then followed her back downstairs.

Luke was waiting for her. "What are you doing to my dog?"

"Nothing. He's a little nervous because of the storm. I told him it was going to be okay. We'll probably lose the power soon. There's a generator but it's just big enough to keep the refrigerator, hot water heater, and stove going."

"All the necessities."

She looked at Mack, who was snoring softly on the braided rug. "I take it he's the one who will be sleeping on the floor?"

"We flipped a coin for the sofa. He lost."

"Maybe because he's asleep?"

"You snooze, you lose."

“Good night, Luke. And whatever you do, do not attempt to intimidate Mack when he wakes up. This is my house, at least it is while Aunt Bea is gone, so my rules. One more thing—remove the handcuffs.”

“And you called me a hard-ass.”

SEVEN

THE SOFA WAS NOT AS UNCOMFORTABLE AS HE HAD FEARED. OR MAYBE, LUKE THOUGHT, he was more exhausted than he had realized, because he fell into the wrong dream . . .

. . . The next curve comes up in the headlights. He automatically reduces the speed of the SUV. It's late. The fog is getting heavier. The night feels endless. So does the road. He can't remember why he needs to keep driving. He only knows he's looking for something important. He can't stop until he finds it.

He drives out of the curve, accelerating gently because he does not know what lies in wait on the other side. He is surprised to see a straight stretch of pavement ahead of him. Good. He can increase his speed.

But he can't accelerate, because there is a dog in the middle of the road, wolflike eyes gleaming a hellish gold in the deep night. It's a medium-sized animal, not a large one, but there is nothing fluffy about him—nothing to disguise the predator under the surface.

The creature does not move. Just stands there, waiting. Panting.

He brings the SUV to a halt a few yards away. Still the dog does not move off into the forest. In the glare of the headlights, it's obvious there is something wrong with the animal's shoulder. The fur is wet. Matted.

The dog is bleeding. In shock.

He climbs out of the SUV and walks cautiously forward. An injured animal is a dangerous creature. But the dog does not snarl a warning; he just stands there, waiting.

Luke stops and holds out a hand. The dog swipes his tongue across Luke's fingers.

"Can you make it to the car?" Luke asks.

The dog starts toward the SUV as if he understands the words. But he doesn't get far. He's too weak. Luke lifts him and carries him to the rear of the SUV, loads the animal into the cargo bay, and wraps an emergency blanket around him.

That is when he realizes the creature is not wearing a collar.

"Maybe you've been chipped," he says.

He closes the cargo bay door, gets behind the wheel, and does a tight three-point turn to reverse course.

He takes the dog to a twenty-four-hour emergency veterinary clinic.

"An interesting hybrid," the vet says as she closes the wound on the dog's shoulder. "But without a DNA test I couldn't tell you what the breed mix is. He hasn't been chipped and there's no collar. I don't know of anyone who is looking for a lost dog that fits this description."

"What will happen to him?" he asks.

"I can't keep him here," the vet says. "You'll have to take him to a shelter. They'll make sure he gets follow-up care. By the way, this dog was not hit by a car. He was shot."

She uses a medical instrument to hold up the smashed bullet she has just removed from the dog's shoulder. It is surprisingly shiny, almost as if it was made of silver.

Just a trick of the light, he thinks. No one uses silver bullets, not in the real world.

EIGHT

A GROAN EMANATING FROM THE VICINITY OF THE FLOOR BROUGHT HIM OUT OF A LIGHT sleep. Luke opened his eyes and took stock of his surroundings. The first thing he noticed was that Bruce was not draped across his legs or curled up next to the sofa. That was not normal. Ever since Bruce had appeared in his life three months earlier, the dog had rarely left his side.

His next observation was that the storm was over. His internal sense of time told him it was morning and his watch confirmed it was still early, but there was only a thin hint of light outside. Sunrise came late in the mountains regardless of the season.

As Sophy had predicted, the power had gone off during the night. He could hear the faint, muffled sound of a generator.

On the floor, Rivington fumbled his way out of the quilt, braced himself on his elbows, and stared at Luke with blurry, bewildered eyes.

"Who the fuck are you?" he asked.

"Not your new best friend." Luke pushed the blankets aside,

swung his feet to the floor, and sat up on the sofa. "My name is Wells. Luke Wells. I'm just another overnight guest here at Bea Harper's shop. I checked your ID, so I know you're Mack Rivington, a failed experiment."

"Huh?" Mack pushed himself to a sitting position. "What are you talking about?"

Luke leaned forward, picked up the badge holder on the coffee table, and tossed it to Rivington, who caught it automatically.

"I've been given strict instructions not to intimidate you," Luke said. "But I do have a few questions for you."

"Yeah?" Mack scrambled to his feet. His hand went to the empty holster under his crumpled jacket. When he realized his weapon was missing, his jaw clenched a couple of times. "I've got some for you."

"Sure. By the way, your weapon is in a cupboard in the kitchen." Luke reached for his shirt, wincing. He had slept in his trousers and T-shirt, the same clothes he'd been wearing since he had gotten the call from his grandparents more than twenty-four hours earlier. He needed a shower and a shave. "You're probably curious to know how you wound up sleeping on the floor. We agreed to a coin toss."

"Evidently I lost."

"It was a tough call."

"Where's Sophy?"

"Right here," Sophy said from the top of the stairs. She had a flashlight in one hand. "And before this conversation gets any more exciting, I'm going to make a large pot of coffee."

"Good plan," Luke said.

He got the stirring sensation again—as if he had been standing on an empty mountain road at night in the fog, waiting for her.

He watched her descend the stairs. Bruce padded enthusiastically after her.

That answered one burning question, Luke thought. He now knew where the dog had spent the night.

When she reached the bottom of the staircase, Sophy switched off the flashlight. In the weak glow of dawn he saw that she was wearing jeans, a rust-brown pullover, and sneakers. Her hair was once again in a casual knot on top of her head, secured with a clip. The black-and-crystal glasses were perched on her nose.

Mack shoved his fingers through his hair and looked at Sophy. "I could use some coffee. What the hell happened to me last night?"

"You tripped one of Aunt Bea's aromatherapy alarms when you broke in," Sophy said. "I warned you that they really do work."

Mack groaned. "I didn't break in. I entered because I was concerned about you. Your car was in the drive but you didn't answer the door. Naturally I was worried."

"Thank you for your concern. As you can see, I'm fine. Luke, will you please get a fire going?" She crossed through the living room and went into the kitchen. "Thank heavens for the generator."

Mack watched her with a speculative expression, evidently strategizing his next move. Then he sauntered down the hall to the bathroom with the easy familiarity of a man who is making it clear that he knows his way around the house.

Bruce trotted across the living room to greet Luke.

"You spent the night on her bed, didn't you?" Luke rubbed the dog's side. "While I had to make do with a couch and a roommate who snores."

Bruce rested his head briefly on Luke's thigh as if offering sympathy and then trotted off toward the kitchen.

"One of these days we should probably talk about the concept of loyalty," Luke called after him.

Bruce vanished into the kitchen. A door opened and closed. Sophy had let him out.

Luke pulled on his boots. There were fresh clothes and shaving gear in the duffel stashed in the SUV but he had been given orders to build a fire.

He crouched in front of the hearth and went to work arranging the kindling. Through the kitchen doorway he caught glimpses of Sophy as she spooned ground coffee into the machine. Her words echoed in his head. *I'm sure Mack came here for the same reason you did. He wants something. Probably my help on a case.*

He crumpled some old newspapers and tossed them into the fireplace. Yes, he was in Mirror Lake because he wanted something, specifically her help on a case. But he had paid for the reading. That made him a client, not a potential failed experiment. The latter implied a romantic relationship that had gone bad. He and Sophy were nowhere near that territory. Yet.

He thought fleetingly about how intensely arousing it had been to have her sprawled on top of him at the cabin, her brilliant eyes on fire. Hell, he was getting hard just thinking about it.

He needed to focus.

He stood, took a long match out of the box on the mantel, struck it, and lit the crumpled newspapers. He brooded on the flames for a moment, waiting to make sure they took hold. When they did, he turned, intending to go outside and retrieve the duffel and the sack of dog food from the SUV. He was halfway across the room when he noticed the books on the desk. He got a ping of curiosity and changed course.

There was, he quickly concluded, a theme to the subject matter. *The Woman in His Nightmares: A History of the Fear of*

Female Empowerment. Sirens and Succubi: Monstrous Women in Art. She Haunts His Dreams: A Psychological Analysis of the Succubus Legend.

"Who's afraid of you, Sophy Harper?" he said very softly. "Or are you afraid of yourself?"

NINE

HE EMERGED FROM THE BATH, SHOWERED, SHAVED, AND WEARING A CLEAN SET OF clothes. He was as ready as he would ever be to hold his own with Failed Experiment in the kitchen, so he followed the aroma of freshly brewed coffee down the hall.

He was halfway to his destination when he came to what looked like a closet door. But something about the sturdiness of the door was off. It was too stout for an interior door. Too solid-looking. It was more formidable than the front door of the house.

When you were in the security business you noticed things like reinforced doors.

This particular door looked like it had been designed to camouflage the entrance to a vault or a safe room. Experimentally, he tried the old-fashioned knob—and got a small but painful jolt of electricity. He yanked his hand away, shook his fingers a couple of times, and smiled. He had just discovered the entrance to Bea Harper's office.

He continued down the hall and went into the living room. Sophy's voice came from the kitchen.

"I'm afraid I can't help you, Mack. I'm working another case at the moment."

"Is it more important than catching a killer?"

"Don't try to guilt-trip me. It's your job to hunt down the bad guys, not mine. You're the homicide detective. I'm the scary, delusional psychic who thinks she sees ghosts, goes into trances, and talks in a creepy voice."

"I've told you a hundred times that I'm sorry you overheard that conversation with Jennifer. I've explained that I'd had a couple of drinks and I was celebrating. We had just closed the Harding case."

"Thanks to me. If I hadn't given you the lead that took you to the well where the body was dumped, you would still be chasing Harding."

"You said you didn't want me to tell anyone that you had been involved in that case. You said you wanted to keep a low profile."

"You didn't tell your cop pal that I had helped you find the body," Sophy said. "You told her that a so-called psychic had insisted on interfering in the case and afterward had tried to seduce you."

"You've got to admit that you were in a very strange mood after you read that crime scene for me."

"Maybe, but I didn't try to seduce you. You're the one who grabbed me and kissed me, remember? It's not my fault my sunglasses fell off. I warned you."

"I overreacted," Mack said. "I'll be prepared next time."

"Forget it. There isn't going to be a next time."

He'd heard enough, Luke thought. He walked into the kitchen. Sophy was at the counter, cheeks flushed, arms crossed as she faced Rivington.

The cop was sitting in one of the chairs at the old oak breakfast table. He looked frustrated but determined. His pistol was back in the holster.

"Don't let me interrupt the conversation." Luke held up a hand. "I'm just here for the coffee."

"It's ready." Sophy swung around, grabbed the glass pot off the warming plate, and poured three cups. She picked up one and then waved at the other two mugs. "Help yourself. This is a self-service restaurant."

"Thanks." Luke went forward and selected a mug. He held up the sack of dog food. "Got a bowl Bruce can use?"

"Certainly."

"Sure," he muttered. "Anything for Bruce."

Sophy glanced at him, frowning, as she opened a cupboard. "What?"

"Nothing."

She took down a bowl. He poured kibble into it and set it on the floor. When he straightened he noticed there was a pot of oatmeal bubbling on the stove. It had been a long time since he'd had oatmeal for breakfast. It sounded good.

Without a word, Mack got to his feet, crossed the kitchen, and picked up the last mug of coffee. He returned to the table.

A scratching sound made everyone glance at the door.

"That will be Bruce," Sophy said. "His feet will be muddy. I'll get a towel."

She put down her mug, opened a cupboard, and took out a couple of well-worn towels. She spread them on the floor and opened the door.

Bruce trotted over the threshold, saw Luke, and started forward.

"Stop right there," Sophy ordered.

Luke watched, intrigued, as Bruce abruptly halted and gave Sophy an inquiring look.

"Good dog." She crouched and wiped all four paws, fluffed his fur a few times, and then stood. "You're free to go."

Bruce licked her hand and hurried toward Luke. They exchanged their customary greeting and then Bruce went directly to the bowl of kibble.

Mack eyed Luke. "I assume you're the reason Sophy isn't available to consult for me. Who are you? Cop? The Feds?"

"Neither," Luke said. "Private."

Sophy took a carton of cream out of the refrigerator and shut the door. When she turned around Luke saw the amused look in her eyes, but she did not say anything.

"What kind of case are you working?" Mack asked, not bothering to hide his dismissive attitude.

"Missing persons. I heard you say something about chasing a killer?"

Mack grunted. "That's my take on it but I can't convince the captain. The ME says it looks like a heart attack or stroke. The victim is male. Early forties. Dressed in running gear. On the surface it looks like the guy went out for a jog and dropped dead. But there was no ID on the body. No phone. No keys. Nothing. They're running fingerprints now."

"What makes you think the victim was murdered?" Sophy asked. "There must be something that made you uneasy."

Mack hesitated. "The lack of ID and a key bothered me. But it was the running gear that clinched it. All the clothing was dark and there was no reflective tape. Also, the shoes weren't right. They were sneakers, but not the kind specifically designed for running."

Luke lounged against the kitchen counter and automatically began connecting dots. Bad habit, he thought, but hard to break. "A thief casing the neighborhood?"

"Maybe," Mack said.

"Who found the body?"

"Got a call from Mayor Madeline yesterday afternoon. She said someone here in Mirror Lake had seen the body on the side of the road. She checked. Didn't recognize the victim as a local so she contacted Elk Cove. The captain sent me out to take a look."

Sophy went still. Luke paused his mug of coffee in midair and waited for the other shoe to drop.

"Mayor Madeline called you?" Sophy asked carefully.

"That's right," Mack said.

Luke glanced at Sophy. "What am I missing?"

"Madeline Stockton is the mayor of Mirror Lake," she said evenly. She focused on Mack. "Are you saying the body was found here? Not Elk Cove?"

"Yes," Mack said. "But the mayor didn't recognize him, so the victim isn't someone from the area."

"Why do you want Sophy to take a look at the scene?" Luke asked, giving himself a beat to decide how to handle the new development.

Mack scowled. "She's got a good eye for detail."

"I know what you mean." Luke drank some coffee and lowered the cup. "It's amazing, isn't it? You would think she has a genuine psychic talent for reading crime scenes."

Sophy shot him a repressive look. He ignored it.

Mack's eyes hardened. "Look, I don't know who you think you are—"

"I'm an old friend of the family. The Harpers and the Wellses go back a long way."

"Sophy's never mentioned you."

Luke shrugged. "She's never talked about you, either."

Sophy was starting to look exasperated. That was probably not good. He assured himself he was not lying. Until last night, Sophy had not told him about Rivington. The fact that he and Sophy had not met until last night did not alter the truth of the claim.

"Let's get one thing clear," Mack growled. "This does not involve you. This is between Sophy and me."

"Stop it, both of you," Sophy snapped. She turned to Mack. "Where was the body found?"

"About a mile or so from here. Just off Hudson Road."

The location was not far from Deke's cabin.

"If this is murder, is there any reason to think the killer might be local?" Luke asked.

"Who knows?" Mack said. He rubbed the back of his neck. "At this point I can't even be sure I've got a case. All I can tell you is that there's something wrong and I could really use Sophy's opinion."

Luke met her eyes and knew they were both recalling the tense conversation at the cabin. He had asked her where she would dump a body because he had assumed the killer would have wanted to conceal it. Why go to the trouble of removing it from the scene if that wasn't the case?

But Sophy had said the killer appeared unstable. Hyped-up. Nervous. What if he had intended to conceal the body but changed his mind and dumped it by the side of the road instead? Maybe he had wanted it to be found. He would not be the first murderer to get a thrill out of displaying his handiwork. Murder by paranormal means was a damn near perfect crime.

Sophy inclined her head once in silent agreement and looked at Mack.

"All right," she said. "I'll take a look this morning."

"Thanks." Mack was clearly relieved. "I appreciate it."

She picked up a ladle and started to serve the oatmeal.

The sound of a vehicle pulling into the driveway caught everyone's attention. Bruce looked up from his breakfast.

Sophy set the ladle back in the pot and disappeared into the living room. Luke went to the entrance of the kitchen and watched her open the door that separated the shop from the rest of the house.

"It's Mayor Madeline," she called over her shoulder. "I'll let her in."

Bruce padded after her. Luke heard the chimes above the front door clash lightly.

"Come in," Sophy said. "I've just made coffee. You probably need a cup."

"I'd appreciate one." The mayor's voice was robust, energetic, and good-humored. "Thanks. I'm making the rounds, checking each house to make sure everyone's okay. Tree fell on Darrell Rushton's place over on Gill Road, but he's okay."

"Thank goodness."

"Everyone told him he should have cut that damn tree down last year, but you know Darrell. Doesn't listen to anyone. I see you have a visitor and a dog."

"Three visitors, actually. Two humans and Bruce."

"Bruce being the dog, I assume. Fine-looking animal. Does he bite?"

"Probably. He's a dog. But I don't think he'll bite you. I'll introduce you to the person who goes with him."

The middle-aged woman who followed Sophy into the kitchen fit the voice: tall, solidly built, and infused with the charisma of someone who intuitively knows how to take charge.

"Madeline, you already know Detective Rivington," Sophy said.

Madeline gave him a friendly nod. "Mack. Thanks for taking care of the dead runner. Any ID yet?"

"Not yet," Mack said.

Madeline cocked a brow. "Surprised to see you here this morning."

"I got caught by the storm last night," Mack said smoothly. "Sophy was kind enough to let me spend the night."

"And this is Luke Wells," Sophy said quickly. She handed Madeline a mug of coffee. "He's a customer. He was trapped by the storm, too."

"Uh-huh." Madeline peered at Luke. "Any relation to Deke Wells, that wildlife photographer renting the cabin on Hudson Road?"

"Is that what he's calling himself these days?" Luke smiled. "Yeah, I'm a nephew."

Sophy glared at Madeline. "Do you know Deke Wells?"

"Bea introduced us. Something about him being an old friend of the family." Madeline winked at Sophy. "Everyone here in Mirror Lake knows they're an item."

Sophy's mouth tightened into a grim line. "I didn't know that."

Madeline shrugged. "They keep to themselves when he's in town." She turned back to Luke. "So you showed up here in the middle of the night to shop for crystals?"

"Something like that," Luke said. "I was planning to stay with Deke. I didn't realize he was out of town."

"And you got caught by the storm like Mack," Madeline concluded.

"That's pretty much how it went down," Luke said.

"That's right," Mack said.

"And now here you are, all three of you, eating breakfast together." Madeline snorted and gave Sophy an approving smile. "Nice work. We don't see a lot of ménage à trois arrangements here in Mirror Lake. I do believe this is a first. It will make for some interesting conversation down at the post office."

TEN

"WHAT THE HELL HAPPENED WHEN RIVINGTON TRIED TO KISS YOU THE LAST TIME YOU read a scene for him?" Luke asked.

Sophy focused on the view of the road through the windshield of the SUV. Bruce was riding in the back seat, front paws braced on the console. He was clearly thrilled with the outing. Mack was ahead of them, leading the way to the site in his vehicle.

She was too warm because she was dressed for the read in her usual gear—long down coat and boots—but it was morning, not the middle of the night. The sun streaming through the windows of the SUV was heating the interior. The conversation was making things worse because it was awkward. Embarrassing. She could feel herself turning pink. Or a blotchy red. Probably blotchy red.

"So you did overhear that conversation in the kitchen," she said.

"Hard not to. The house isn't that big."

"If they are standing too close, some men and some women sometimes get . . . excited . . . when I come out of a trance."

"Sexually."

She cleared her throat. "Well, yes. There's a lot of energy in my aura in those first few minutes. It can send mixed signals."

"Rivington took advantage of the mixed signals?"

She wasn't sure how to respond to that. Did she even want to respond?

"We'd had a few dates by then," she said. "But they had all ended before we got to the bedroom stage. I made it clear I was in no rush. I wanted to take things slowly because I thought our relationship had real potential. I didn't want us to get distracted by sex, not if things weren't doomed. He seemed fine with that."

"Define *potential*."

"You know what I mean. We enjoyed each other's company. He seemed to respect my crime scene reading ability, even though he couldn't bring himself to admit that I might have a sixth sense for the work."

"He prefers to think that you just have a keen eye for details."

"I'm pretty sure Mack has a little talent himself, but he writes it off as intuition. At any rate, we seemed to be moving toward a serious relationship. I decided to risk a stress test under controlled conditions."

"You were planning to take off the sunglasses."

"Yes, but I intended to do so slowly. Carefully. I wanted to try to explain what was happening and that it was just a matter of adrenaline and paranormal biophysics. But he grabbed me and things went horribly wrong."

"How wrong?"

"My sunglasses flew off. I didn't have time to explain anything. Mack saw my eyes. He looked like he'd seen a monster. He leaped back, stumbled, and fell. I scrambled around trying to find my glasses. But they had skidded under a table. I finally got them on but by then it was too late."

"He ran screaming into the night?"

She winced. "No. He's a homicide detective. Worked in San Francisco. He's seen some scary stuff. He didn't scream, but he was badly shaken. I knew the relationship was over."

"A failed experiment that didn't even get off the ground."

"That's a very cynical way of looking at it," she said, annoyed. "It makes me wonder, again, why you didn't have a problem with my eyes last night."

"I told you, I apparently have some immunity."

"I'm not sure I'm buying that. I know you've been labeled No-Talent Wells."

He groaned. "Some nicknames really stick."

"Trust me, I'm aware of that. They call me the Housekeeper, remember? But here's the thing. Aunt Bea has advised Chloe and me not to believe everything we heard about the Wells family." Sophy paused deliberately. "Something to do with their reputation for secrecy, I believe."

"This isn't a good time to go into the feud."

"True," she admitted. She reached over to rub Bruce's ears. "You mentioned your psychic-grade vision. Is there anything else I should know about your paranormal profile?"

"Nope. I'm just good at connecting dots," he said. "It's not a talent—more like a character flaw."

"Why do you say that?"

He hesitated so long she wondered if she would get an answer.

"Sometimes," he said finally, "I'm afraid that one of these days I will start seeing connections that aren't real."

"Ah, got it," she said. "I wouldn't worry about that, if I were you."

He shot her a wary look. "Why not?"

"If you ever get concerned, you can hire me or Chloe or Aunt Bea to tell you if you're in danger of falling down a conspiracy rabbit hole."

"What makes you three experts?"

"We're librarians. We are duty-bound to establish the credibility of sources. We know how to do research. We can help you confirm or dismiss your theories."

He concentrated on his driving for a moment. Then his mouth twitched a little in a small smile. "At triple the usual rates?"

"Of course. I told you, special prices for members of the Wells family."

"I'll keep that in mind," Luke said. In the blink of an eye, he was all business again. "Here we go. Rivington is turning onto Hudson Road. Whatever happens, remember our number one priority."

"Protect the families."

"This isn't only about protecting Deke and Bea. We'll be doing Rivington a very big favor, because he'll be in way over his head if it turns out the runner was murdered by paranormal means."

"I know," she said.

They followed Mack onto Hudson Road. Luke stopped the SUV behind the other vehicle. He rested his hands on the wheel for a moment and studied the scene. "If this was a murder, whoever dumped the body didn't even try to hide it."

"No," she said.

Luke climbed out. Bruce bounded across the console and onto the ground.

Sophy took off her regular glasses and let them dangle on the rhinestone chain. She replaced them with the oversized sunglasses. The visions were never as strong in daylight as they were after dark, and neither was the fever. But she knew from past experience that she would still get the scary eyes.

She got out of the passenger seat and joined Luke and Bruce. They all walked toward Mack, who was waiting beside his vehicle.

"Why the Hollywood shades?" Luke asked quietly. "You said Rivington has seen your trance eyes."

"I'd rather not go through that embarrassing scene again. Oddly enough, it's hard on my ego when people lock eyes with me and then proceed to panic. Go figure."

"Your eyes didn't bother me last night."

"Yes, well, evidently you're different."

"As in, not normal?"

"I didn't say that."

"I know what Mack saw when he got a good look at your trance eyes," Luke said, "because I'm pretty sure I saw the same thing."

She stopped in mid-step. Shocked. "How bad was it?"

"It wasn't bad at all."

"What did you see?"

Luke smiled an edgy smile that sent a little flash of lightning across her senses. "I saw power," he said, "a lot of it. And it was sexy as hell."

ELEVEN

SHE CAME OUT OF THE TRANCE ON AN ADRENALINE TIDE AND HASTILY RAISED ONE HAND to make sure her sunglasses were securely in place. The daytime readings were accompanied by less psychic blowback—something to do with the natural ebb and flow of energy currents, according to Bea—but they were not a walk in the park.

She realized Bruce was pressed against her right leg. He watched her, ears sharp, amber eyes intent.

She patted the top of his head and glanced at Luke. He, too, was watching her, his expression unreadable.

She turned to Mack, who was leaning against the fender of his car, arms folded. Like her, he was wearing dark glasses. Cop glasses. She sensed his wariness but also his determination.

"That's all I can tell you," she said, dropping back into her normal voice. "You're right. This was murder. In my vision, the killer appears quite suddenly on the side of the road, so he probably brought the body here in the trunk of a car. He dragged it into the ditch and left it."

"You're sure the killer was a man and that he was alone?" Mack asked.

"I'm certain that the person who left the body here was a man. I can't be absolutely positive that he was alone. All I can tell you is that no one else appeared in the vision. It's possible there was another person in the car, but I doubt it."

"Why?" Luke asked before Mack could.

"I'm not sure," she admitted. "It's just a feeling. The killer seemed to be working alone and in a great hurry. Excited. He didn't interact with anyone else. No one helped him get the body out of the vehicle."

She pulled up the collar of the down coat. The adrenaline would wear off soon and the chills would follow. "I realize that's not very helpful, Mack."

"You've confirmed that this was murder, that the killer dumped the body here, and that he was in a hurry," Mack said. "That's enough for now." He hesitated, studying her intently through his own dark glasses. "Unless there was anything to suggest that the killer or the victim might have been local?"

He really was a good cop, she thought. His intuition was telling him that she knew more than she had let on. She stuck to a narrow version of the truth.

"I'm as certain as I can be that the killer was not local," she said. "It feels like the site of the body dump was chosen at random."

"Or maybe because it was sure to be found," Luke suggested quietly.

Mack nodded. "Yeah." He unfolded his arms and straightened away from the vehicle. "I need an ID on the victim. There's usually a connection with the killer."

"Yes," Luke said.

Sophy nodded in agreement, but she didn't try to speak,

because she was feeling a little shaky. She realized Luke was moving closer to her. Alarmed, she tried to step back. This was no time to risk unleashing the storm winds of their auras. Not in front of an audience.

Luke draped an arm casually around her shoulders. For a heartbeat she hovered on the knife edge that separated panic from thrilling anticipation. She braced herself for the heat and fire of the connection. Maybe it would not be as strong in the daylight. Paranormal energy was always more powerful after dark.

But this time Luke did not overwhelm her aura. Instead, his energy field whispered to hers. Intimate. Comforting. Warm. The shaky feeling subsided.

Mack watched them for a moment, then he opened the car door. "That does it for now. I'll be on my way. You can get back to your missing persons case." He paused before he got into the driver's seat and looked at Luke. "About those missing persons. Have they been reported to the police?"

"No," Luke said. "It's a private matter. The families don't want the authorities involved. They think it's a runaway lovers situation."

Mack nodded, evidently satisfied. "Got it. Couple of kids decided to hit the road together. The families want to avoid the publicity."

"Yes," Luke said.

Mack looked at Sophy. "Thanks for taking a look at the scene."

"You're welcome," she said.

Mack smiled a humorless smile. "Almost like old times."

She let that slide.

"Good luck convincing your boss you've got a case," Luke said.

Mack grimaced. "Thanks. Sophy, give me a call if you think of anything else that might be helpful."

"Okay," she said.

Luke waited until Mack had driven away before he spoke.

"Are you all right?" he asked.

"Yes." She took a beat to process that simple fact. "Yes, I'm fine. Thanks. Your ability to resonate with my aura is handy." She took a breath. "But it felt different this time. Not so overwhelming."

"Last night you took me by surprise." He took his arm off her shoulders. "And that's an understatement. You weren't the only one who got swept up in that wild thunderstorm. But this morning I had a better idea of what to expect. You can ditch the sunglasses now."

She hesitated and then slowly reached up with both hands to slip off the dark glasses. Luke's eyes heated in a way that sent a seductive thrill across her nerves. She didn't need the physical contact now—the chills had receded—but she missed the warm weight of his arm. She could get used to his touch. That was probably not good news.

"Sadly, this isn't the time or place," he said. "We need to focus."

She decided it would be a very dumb idea to explore that cryptic statement. She dropped the mirrored shades into the pocket of her coat and picked up the cat-eye glasses dangling on the chain around her neck.

"I told Mack the truth," she said, positioning the frames firmly on her nose. "But not all of it."

"I know. What else have you got?"

"I'm pretty sure the victim was the man who was murdered in Deke's cabin. The killer was the smoking ghost." She winced. "I mean, the killer was the man who smoked in the cabin."

Luke surveyed the landscape with a thoughtful expression. "Was the smoking ghost the one who dumped the body?"

"He wasn't a real ghost," she said coldly.

"I know," he said, unconcerned.

She sighed and adjusted her glasses. "Yes, Smoking Ghost left the body here. I think he threw away a cigarette after he dragged the victim across the pavement."

"Let's see if Bruce can find it."

Luke took the small baggie of cigarette butts out of the pocket of his jacket, unzipped it, and held it out to Bruce.

"Search, pal," Luke said.

Bruce tensed with excitement and immediately began sniffing the brush at the side of the road.

"Is he a search and rescue dog?" Sophy asked, intrigued.

"I don't know," Luke said. "I think he's had some kind of high-end military or security training, but it's not like any I've ever come across. It's almost as if he can read my mind at times."

"All animals have a psychic vibe. Everyone knows that."

Luke smiled. "They do?"

She frowned. "You don't know anything about his past?"

"No. I found him on a mountain road about three months ago."

"Abandoned?"

"I don't know. He wasn't chipped. Hard to believe anyone would dump a smart dog like Bruce. But people are strange." Luke paused. "He'd been shot."

"No." She was horrified.

"A farmer probably caught him stealing chickens. The vet who removed the bullet suggested I take him to a shelter, but that didn't seem like a good idea to Bruce or to me. So here we are, three months later."

They watched Bruce stop abruptly and sit down, golden eyes intent on Luke. The dog grinned a canine grin that revealed his impressive fangs.

"Looks like he found something," Sophy said.

Luke went forward, crouched, and pointed to a half-smoked cigarette. He rubbed Bruce's neck. "Nice work. Thanks, pal."

Sophy could have sworn Bruce looked smug. She could imagine him thinking the canine equivalent of *You think finding that was hard? I could have done it with my eyes closed.* Which, given that he was a dog and therefore relied heavily on his nose, was probably true.

Luke used a fallen leaf to scoop up what was left of the cigarette and transfer it to the baggie. He stood up.

"Same brand as the ones in the cabin," he said.

"A stranger is murdered by another stranger in Deke's cabin and Deke and Bea are apparently on the run. I still can't get past the idea that those two were—are—having an affair. It feels so . . . so un-Aunt-Bea-like."

Luke snorted. "And here my grandmother was convinced that Deke would never be able to overcome the loss of his wife."

"Your uncle's wife died a few years ago, didn't she?"

"She was murdered."

"I see. I hadn't realized. Was the killer caught?"

"He died of natural causes before an arrest could be made."

"Natural causes?"

"That's what the authorities put down on the death certificate."

So maybe the causes had not been entirely natural, she thought. Deke was a Wells, after all. There was probably more than one CIA assassin in the family. She cleared her throat. "Whatever. The situation must have been very traumatic for your uncle."

"It was."

She narrowed her eyes. "Maybe he's using my aunt as a convenient distraction. If he's taking advantage of Bea in an attempt to help him forget his wife's death—"

"What if your aunt is the one who's using my uncle?"

"No."

"Hell, maybe they're using each other." Luke gestured toward the woods and the lake in the distance. "It's not as if a single person has a lot of options in a town this small."

"Now just one damn minute. My aunt has lived here for years. She seemed perfectly happy as a single woman. When she wasn't busy with her consulting work, she took trips to visit interesting private libraries around the world. She collected books for her own library. She cruised the Mediterranean and the South Pacific. Now, out of the clear blue sky, your uncle shows up and seduces her. The question is, why?"

"Are you always this suspicious?" Luke held up a hand. "Don't answer that. Of course you're suspicious of a Wells. You're a Harper."

"Are you going to tell me the feeling is not mutual?"

"This discussion is getting us nowhere. I'll give my grandparents a call when we're on the road. Maybe they'll have some idea of what's going on here."

"The road to where?"

"Down off this mountain to the airport in Santa Rosa, where the company jet will be waiting." Luke raised his brows. "I assume you're still planning to head for that art colony in Fool's Gold Canyon?"

"Absolutely."

"Might as well go together."

"Translated, that means you're afraid that I'll screw up your investigation if I try to find Aunt Bea on my own."

"Now that you mention it, yes," Luke said. "But here's another excellent reason for sticking together. We're walking into a potentially dangerous situation. We won't be able to trust anyone except each other."

"Which we recently concluded is not a natural state of affairs for a Wells and a Harper."

"We don't have any choice this time."

"Because of the pact."

"And because your aunt and my uncle might be in serious danger."

He was right. They needed to stop arguing and get to work.

"We have to go back to the shop so that I can pack," she said. "Also, I want to pick up a few books from the library."

"I assume you're not suggesting that we stop by the local public library to pick up some vacation reading."

"No, I'm talking about Aunt Bea's private library in the basement of the Shop on Hidden Lane."

TWELVE

"OKAY, I'M OFFICIALLY IMPRESSED," LUKE SAID. HE STOPPED JUST INSIDE THE DOORWAY and surveyed the interior of the large basement beneath the house on Hidden Lane. "Not sure what I expected, but this isn't it."

Sophy sniffed. "You thought my aunt worked with Ouija boards, crystal balls, and astrology charts, didn't you? Admit it."

"Let's just say I wasn't expecting a serious library."

She was so accustomed to Bea's library—she and Chloe had spent many hours in it—that she sometimes forgot how it might look to others. The rows of floor-to-ceiling shelves were crammed with leather-bound tomes, manuscripts, books both very old and very new, long runs of arcane journals, handwritten memoirs, government documents, and reports and papers from various academic institutions and research centers. All of it was devoted to the paranormal.

"I thought you knew that Bea is a librarian and a rare books specialist," she said. "The psychic consulting is a sideline. She feels a strong obligation to use her talents to help people find answers."

Luke moved to the nearest shelf and studied the spines of

the books. "You said your sister is on some island in the South Pacific?"

"A reclusive collector invited her to check out his collection. He said he wants to give her some of his most important items if she will promise to personally escort them back to the U.S. and house them in Bea's library."

Luke raised his brows. "He wants to *give* them to your aunt?"

"He told my sister that he's afraid of some of the materials in his collection. That happens. Collectors can be very eccentric and superstitious. He claims to have some documents linked to the old Bluestone Project."

"Why didn't he contact the Foundation? They'll take any Bluestone documents or artifacts with a solid provenance and they'll pay top dollar."

"This may come as a shock to you, Mr. Wells, but a lot of us in the paranormal community prefer to avoid dealing with the Foundation."

He shrugged. "Wells, Inc. has a good working relationship with the organization."

"How lovely for you. Perhaps it hasn't occurred to you that most of us in the community lack the muscle and the cash it takes to make sure the Foundation treats us with the same respect that it shows your family. It seems to think it has a right to police those of us who are just trying to make a living with our talents and be productive members of society."

"Let's skip this argument and stay focused. What are we doing here in your aunt's library?"

He had a point. They were on a mission. They had to move forward.

She went to the old-fashioned card catalog and pulled open the drawer marked *V–Z*. She started thumbing through the subject headings.

"*Vanishing Islands*, *Visions* . . . here we go, *Vortex Sites, U.S.*" She closed the drawer and headed into the stacks.

Luke followed. So did Bruce.

She turned a corner, went down another aisle, and stopped in front of a large section labeled *Vortices, Ley Lines, and Natural Power Sites.*

"There's a ton of literature written about vortex sites," she said. "But surprisingly little about the Fool's Gold Canyon location."

"Maybe because it's not a true vortex site," Luke said. "There are a lot of small towns and communities and resorts all over the world that promote themselves as natural power sites in order to attract tourists."

"True. Still, it seems odd." She plucked a thin volume off the shelf. "This is what I was looking for, *An Investigation into the Fool's Gold Canyon Vortex*. Self-published. Now, there's just one more book I want to take with us. It's in the vault."

"You've got a vault in here? This whole basement feels like a vault."

"Don't tell me the Wells family doesn't have a very special vault."

"Well, sure, but that's because we have some old secrets to protect."

"So do the Harpers."

She stopped in front of a bookcase that looked exactly like all the other bookcases. She removed a volume, pressed the button behind it, and then channeled a little energy into the crystal that secured the Harper family vault.

She felt Luke's stunned surprise before he spoke.

"Is that what I think it is?" he asked, moving closer to join her. "A psi-lock?"

"Crystal-based tech," Sophy said proudly. "Only Bea, Chloe, or I can unlock this vault."

Luke flashed a brief, amused smile. "As every Wells knows, the Harpers are very, very good with locks."

She raised her chin. "Yes, we are."

The entire bookcase slid aside, revealing a chamber lined with steel plates. Steel and glass shelves were arranged floor to ceiling. They were crammed with the most important—and the most dangerous—books, crystals, Bluestone artifacts, and memorabilia that the Harper family had acquired over four generations.

Currents of paranormal energy flowed out through the entrance. Sophy felt her hair stir as if in response to static electricity. Luke's dark hair looked as if it had been ruffled by a slight breeze. Bruce hovered at the entrance and whined softly.

Luke whistled and moved inside. "Hotter than hell. The Foundation would kill for some of these items."

"It's the 'kill' part that worries us," Sophy said.

"I was speaking metaphorically."

"Uh-huh. Hang on, I'll get the logbook."

She went down a narrow aisle to the back of the vault, found what she was looking for, and headed toward the door.

Luke eyed the black, leather-bound volume with deep interest. "What is it?"

"One of Great-grandfather Tobias Harper's personal journals. It covers the time period during which the decision to establish the pact was made."

"Forget the Foundation—Wells, Inc. would pay a fortune for that volume. Just name your price."

"You can't afford it." She tightened her grip on the logbook, momentarily afraid he might try to yank it out of her hand. "It's a family heirloom. Priceless."

"It would be safer in the Wells family vault."

"Harpers can take care of their own heirlooms, thank you very much."

He gave her a cool smile. "We can discuss it some other time. Right now we need to get on the road."

"When it comes to this logbook, there is nothing more to discuss. But you're right, we should be on our way. It will only take me a moment to grab my stuff."

"Out of curiosity, I have to ask if you're planning to take the puffy coat to Arizona?"

"Of course not. I have another coat I use for warm climates."

She locked the vault and led the way toward the door of the library.

"You know," Luke said, "I dated a librarian for a while."

"Really?" Sophy said. "And how did that go for you?"

"It did not end well."

"She has my sympathies, whoever she is. I've had a few bad endings myself."

THIRTEEN

"DEKE HAS ALWAYS BEEN THE IMPULSIVE TYPE," ANGELA WELLS SAID. PHONE IN HAND, she got up from the leather chair and moved to stand in front of the desk. She stabbed the speaker button on the heavily encrypted phone and set the device down on the polished surface. "It's that talent of his. It makes him overconfident. Reckless."

On the other side of the study Harry looked up from his laptop, gray brows quirking. She had been married to him for decades, long enough to know that he didn't agree with her assessment. Unfortunately, she didn't agree with it, either. Yes, their eldest son had a history of chasing adrenaline thrills, but in the immediate aftermath of his wife's death he had plunged into a very dark place. He had taken the most dangerous assignments from the Agency. For over a year she had been terrified that he would not return to the surface.

She had been so grateful when he had appeared to pull back from some awful brink. In the past three or four years he had seemed more settled. Happier. More content. He had begun to concentrate more and more on his photography hobby.

But now she was afraid that the dark had reclaimed him.

"You were right," Luke said on the other end of the connection. "Deke is in trouble."

Angela sighed. "I was afraid of that. I thought that after he retired from the Agency he would finally settle down."

"Hold on right there," Sophy said. "Are you saying Deke Wells worked for an intelligence agency? Which one? CIA? FBI? NSA? DHS? Or is it some shady, off-the-books Foundation outfit?"

Angela winced. She was talking to a Harper. She had to watch every word. When Luke had called from the road a short time ago he had warned her that Sophy Harper was in the car and that the phone was on speaker, but Sophy had not said a word. Until now.

"Never mind," Angela said smoothly. "This is Wells family business."

"Which seems to have become Harper family business," Sophy shot back. "Trust me, I'm not thrilled to be involved in this, but we both know that under the circumstances I don't have any choice. It looks like your son has dragged my aunt into serious trouble."

Angela took a grip on her temper. "Have you considered the possibility that Beatrice Harper might be the one responsible for whatever happened?" she said in her iciest tones. "It's difficult to believe, but from what Luke says, Deke and your aunt apparently have some sort of relationship. Bea Harper probably seduced him. He's been very vulnerable since he was widowed."

"Deke's wife died five years ago. There's no way you can blame my aunt for this unfortunate situation. But I agree with you on one point: it's hard to think of those two as a couple. I can't imagine what she could possibly see in an *overconfident*, *reckless* Wells, especially one who evidently worked for a clandestine government *agency*. A Wells who apparently has no visible means of support, since he is now retired. Really, who can make a living with photography, especially at his age? I doubt if he's the social media type."

"How dare you?"

"Maybe Deke Wells is still working for that supersecret Agency. The photography night be a cover. I wouldn't be surprised to learn that he dragged Aunt Bea into a dangerous case and now they're both in trouble."

"You," Angela said through clenched teeth, "have a very active imagination. You should try sticking to the facts. It will get you much farther."

"Here's a fact," Sophy said coldly. "There's a high probability that Deke and Bea are in trouble because of something that involves the pact between the families. Luke and I have no option but to work together to find them."

"I doubt very much that Luke needs your assistance. He's quite capable of conducting this investigation on his own."

"I'm not about to let him handle this by himself, not while Aunt Bea is in danger."

"This sort of thing is hardly in your wheelhouse. You're just a crime scene reader and a housekeeper. You did what you were paid to do. Your services are no longer required. I'm sure Luke would be delighted if you stayed out of the way. Let him handle this."

Luke cleared his throat. "Uh, Grandma, I don't think you understand the situation. Sophy is committed to this project. She's worried about her aunt and she is determined to go to Fool's Gold Canyon. It makes sense for us to work together."

"No, it does not," Angela snapped. "This is a job for a trained security analyst. The Harpers have never had any abilities that would be useful in a situation like this."

"I realize that the Wells clan thinks it's superior to the Harpers because it controls a business empire," Sophy said, "but we both know that empire was founded on my great-grandfather's inventions."

"Xavier Wells and Tobias Harper were partners. They developed those first security devices together. It's not our fault that your great-grandfather did not have a head for business."

"It's a fact that Xavier Wells forced Tobias out of the company," Sophy shot back.

"Xavier bought out Tobias. Your great-grandfather was not forced out. He wanted to pursue his own research and he needed money to do it. Xavier gave him the cash, a lot of it. Your great-grandfather blew it on weird inventions that never found a market."

"He was a concept guy," Sophy muttered. "A visionary."

But now she was on the defensive. Angela moved in fast.

"Regardless of what happened in the past, both men agreed that the secrets of the Kaleidoscope weapons should not be allowed out into the world," she said. "They made a sacred pact between the families and we are all bound to honor it."

"Exactly," Sophy said, very cool again. "That means Luke and I work together. Right now we need information—specifically everything your husband knows about Kaleidoscope."

"Harry does not take orders from a Harper," Angela snapped. "Luke, do something about her."

"Are you kidding?" Luke said. "I might not be the smartest man in the world, but I'm not dumb enough to try to break up a cage match fight between two women."

"Very wise," Harry announced from the other side of the study. He closed the computer, got to his feet, and strolled toward the desk. "Maybe we should all try to focus here."

"The Boss has a point," Luke said.

Angela pulled herself together. "Yes, he does."

"Sophy is right," Luke said. "We do need information about Kaleidoscope. For our generation it's ancient history. We know bits and pieces of the story, but neither of us has a complete picture."

"It wasn't contemporary history for me, either," Harry said. "I was born after the pact was made and after Dad and Tobias Harper ended their partnership. My father never talked much about Kaleidoscope or Pandora's box. He just emphasized that both were extremely dangerous."

"Hold on," Luke said. "Pandora's box disappeared in the Fogg Lake explosion. What does it have to do with Kaleidoscope?"

"There were issues with the Kaleidoscope weapons," Harry said.

"Right, the psychic recoil problem."

"The crystals in Pandora's box were developed to deal with the recoil. But in the end Dad and Tobias Harper concluded the crystals were even more dangerous than the weapons. To the end of his days Dad hoped the stones had been buried under tons of rock in the Fogg Lake explosion, but he always wondered if someone might have smuggled them out."

Sophy sniffed. "Someone named Tobias Harper, for instance?"

"Of course not," Harry said. "When it came to Kaleidoscope and Pandora's box, Xavier and Tobias trusted each other. They had no choice."

"The good news is that this doesn't involve the crystals in Pandora's box," Angela put in quickly. "If that were the case, Deke would have written something else on those passes. Evidently he was just worried about Kaleidoscope."

"She's right," Harry said. "Look, I need to do some research in the vault. I'm going to pull the old Kaleidoscope files and see if there is anything useful in them. I'll call you as soon as I have something."

"Thanks," Luke said. "We're on our way to Santa Rosa. I ordered the company jet to meet us there. Let me know what you find out in the vault."

"Will do," Harry said.

He ended the call.

Angela retrieved her phone and glared at him. He was the love of her life, but she had never met a more stubborn man. *Typical Wells*, she thought affectionately.

He had vowed to retire that year and she had been thrilled. They were booked on a long cruise. Plans had been made. Until six months ago, the management transition at the top of Wells, Inc. had been going far more smoothly than most people, including most industry watchers, had anticipated. It was a given in the business world that succession arrangements within tightly held family firms were invariably messy. But there had not been so much as a ripple of resentment when Harry had announced he was stepping down and would be handing the reins to Luke.

Their oldest grandson was the obvious choice, and not just because he lacked any of the psychic-grade engineering and scientific talents that ran in the bloodline. It had been clear from the cradle that Luke's father, Matthew, would always prefer his engineering lab to running the company, and Deke's restless nature, which had become even more pronounced after the death of his wife, meant he would never be able to concentrate on running Wells, Inc.

Luke, on the other hand, could focus on the arcane intricacies of business the way others in the family did on research and development. Until the disaster six months ago, he had been not only content with his future role as the head of Wells, Inc., but enthusiastic about it, too. *Driven* was not too strong a word. Like all the Wells men, once he set a goal or took on a responsibility, he was mission-oriented.

He had been obsessed with the challenge of taking the company into the future—right up until the wrong woman had walked into his life. Victoria Ellsworth hadn't just broken his heart—that would have been bad enough—she had shattered his confidence in himself. That was the damage that Angela could not forgive.

Harry was convinced that the problem was temporary, that Luke simply needed time to accept that he had made a mistake. Yes, it was a serious mistake, but catastrophe had been averted. He had learned from his error in judgment. He would soon be ready to move forward.

Angela had told herself the same thing—at first. Lately, however, she had become increasingly concerned. Luke was not bouncing back the way they all had hoped.

But right now, she, too, needed to focus.

"Sophy Harper is going to be a problem," she announced.

"Whatever gave you that idea?" Harry said. His mouth twitched at the corner. "Judging by what I overheard, it sounds like the two of you have a few things in common."

"That is not funny."

"You can worry about Sophy Harper some other time. Right now we've got a bigger problem."

"I know," Angela said. "Kaleidoscope."

Harry headed for the door. "We need to go down to the vault."

FOURTEEN

"YOUR GRANDMOTHER IS A FORMIDABLE WOMAN," SOPHY SAID.

Luke almost laughed. "You noticed that, did you? All I can say is that you handled her brilliantly. I am in awe."

They were out of the mountains now, driving through the rolling hills of the northern California wine country, heading for the Santa Rosa airport. A corporate jet was waiting to fly them to a small regional airport in Arizona. After landing they would drive the rest of the way into the state's dramatic red rock region. If all went well they would arrive at the art colony in the evening.

"I've been thinking," Sophy said. "Maybe we're wrong about Deke and Bea's relationship. It's possible they could have been thrown together by circumstances." She paused to scratch Bruce's ears. "Like you and me."

"We don't know how or when Deke and Bea got together, but it's clear that what they have is more than a casual relationship. The scene in the bedroom of that cabin looked damned cozy."

She groaned. He was right.

"It's amazing that they've been able to keep their affair a secret from all of us," she said. "Wait until I tell Chloe. But that's a problem for another time." A thought struck her. "Did your parents ever discuss the history of the pact and the breakup of the partnership?"

"Not in detail. I don't think they knew that much about it. Or cared. My dad is an engineer with his own Wells lab. Mom is a doctor. They've always been focused on the future, not the past. What about your family? Did they talk about it?"

Sophy absently rubbed Bruce's ears. He grinned, showing his fangs in what was probably intended as a friendly gesture.

"Chloe and I lost our parents and our grandparents in a car crash when we were very young," she said. "They were driving to a convention together. A drunk driver hit their vehicle and sent it over a cliff. Aunt Bea took on the responsibility of raising us."

"Raising two orphaned girls is a huge responsibility for a young woman."

"Bea was in her early twenties, just starting out in life. She was my father's sister. Chloe and I have a few other relatives but none of them stepped forward. Bea took us into her heart. Money was tight but she managed to hold things together until her business got up and running. Chloe and I are very aware that we are extremely fortunate. We would do anything for Bea."

"I assume everything you know about the feud came from her?"

"Yes. She's always been very keen on the history of the families, but it's possible she was a tad biased in favor of the Harpers."

Luke smiled his fleeting smile. "The way my grandmother is when it comes to the Wellses. It might be interesting to compare the version of the history of the pact you and your sister got with the one my brother and I received. I doubt if they are identical."

"That's the thing about history, isn't it?" she said. "No two people tell it quite the same way."

"No two families do, either. What version did you get?"

She contemplated the vast fields of grapevines that lined both sides of the road. "Aunt Bea told us that my great-grandfather and yours were recruited for the Bluestone Project. They were assigned to the Fogg Lake lab. Their small department was tasked with designing the perfect spy weapon—a gun that used paranormal light to take down a target without leaving any evidence."

"The way Smoking Ghost killed his victim," Luke said, a grim edge on the words.

She shuddered. "Yes. The code name for the project was Kaleidoscope because the design involved mirrors and crystals."

"Tobias Harper and Xavier Wells succeeded in building two prototypes, but ultimately the project was shelved."

"Literally," she said, slanting him a sideways look. "In your family's private vault."

"True," Luke said. "Harper and Wells made the decision to shut down development for several reasons. One was the recoil problem, but another issue was range. Even in the hands of a strong psychic the guns were effective only within a very short distance. Ten or twelve feet at most. Human-generated psychic energy has a very limited reach."

"The guns were only as powerful as the person pulling the trigger?"

"Exactly," Luke said. "It was clear that the weapons were not going to be cost-effective for military or intelligence use."

"No kidding." Bruce nudged her hand. She looked at him and saw that he was gazing down at the console with a rapt expression.

"I store the treats inside the console," Luke said.

"I get the message."

She opened the console and fished a couple of snacks out of the bag of dog treats. Bruce accepted them with gracious enthusiasm and rewarded her with an adoring look.

"You are a manipulative little hellhound, aren't you?" she said.

"Hellhound?" Luke asked.

"Never mind." She closed the console and sat back.

"Before abandoning the Kaleidoscope problem, Tobias and Xavier decided to take one more stab at it," Luke continued. "The theory was that they could make the guns more user-friendly and scale up the size and power of the weapons if they figured out how to fire them remotely."

"If the person pulling the trigger did not have direct contact with the weapon, the psychic recoil issue would no longer be a problem."

"That was the plan," Luke said, "but they ran into one of the most fundamental roadblocks in paranormal engineering—the battery problem. They needed to come up with a material that could be used to store large amounts of paranormal energy and release it on demand. The third engineer in the lab, Maxwell Coburn, was a materials expert. He worked on that end of the project."

"Even if you found a way to store serious quantities of energy, you'd have to figure out how to channel it, not only to charge the batteries, but to focus it so that it fired the weapons. You would need crystals. Very powerful crystals."

"You may have missed your calling," Luke said. "You would have made a good para-engineer."

"Nope. I don't do math of any kind. I am a Harper, however, so I know something about crystals."

"Tobias and Xavier developed six lab-grown stones they believed could handle strong energy—assuming Coburn's batteries worked. That's when they started having second thoughts. They worried that the crystals might fall into the wrong hands. As a precaution Tobias Harper tuned each one so that only someone with a special psychic talent could unlock the stones."

"A talent that is strong in the Harper family bloodline," Sophy said, not bothering to conceal her pride.

"Apparently your great-grandfather did not make that small fact entirely clear at the time," Luke said.

She shot him a warning look. "Don't go there. It wasn't Tobias Harper's fault that your great-grandfather lacked the talent required to unlock the crystals."

"Xavier didn't like the idea that only Tobias or someone with his talent could unlock the crystals, but there was no other option. They stashed the crystals in a glass box and stored the box in a safe in the lab. They were the only ones who knew the code to open the safe."

"What about the other engineer? The one working on the battery problem?"

"Shortly before the Fogg Lake disaster Harper and Wells became suspicious of Coburn," Luke said. "They thought he might be a Communist spy. In those days everyone was looking for Communists under the bed. Xavier and Tobias did not give him the code to the safe. Then the explosion occurred."

"I know this part," Sophy said. "In the chaos that followed the disaster, our great-grandfathers grabbed the two prototype Kaleidoscope weapons and some of the classified documents associated with their project. But when they unlocked the safe they discovered that the six crystals were gone."

"They assumed Coburn had managed to open the safe and steal the crystals, but there was no time to search for him. They had to run for their lives like everyone else. Later they were told that Coburn had died in the explosion. But who knows? After Fogg Lake, whoever was in charge of the Bluestone Project couldn't move fast enough to shut down all the labs and destroy the records."

"Tobias and Xavier agreed to hide the weapons and documents in the Wells family vault," Sophy said. "They told themselves that even if Coburn had faked his death and managed to steal the crystals, he wouldn't be able to do anything with them because he couldn't unlock them."

"And then they made the truly disastrous mistake of going into business together," Luke concluded. "Within a year they were at each other's throats."

"Xavier bought out Tobias's share of the company, got married, and went on to build an empire. My great-grandfather got married and went on to become a failed inventor. End of story."

"Except for the part where your great-grandfather claimed it was one of his designs that Xavier used to launch the business into the big time," Luke said.

"And the part where your great-grandfather said that they had agreed on a deal back at the start and refused to renegotiate after the company went big. And thus, a half-baked feud was born between the Wells and Harper families. Ridiculous."

"Probably the defining attribute of a feud," Luke said.

FIFTEEN

"SHIT," HARRY SAID. HE STUDIED THE EMPTY SHELF INSIDE THE VAULT, MORE SHAKEN than he wanted to admit. "This is not good."

"No." Angela folded her arms. "It's not. When was the last time you checked on the weapons?"

"It's been a while," Harry admitted.

The large vault had been built into the basement of the big house. He had supervised the construction himself. It had been designed to store the artifacts and memorabilia that the family had collected over the decades, and it was crammed.

A lot of the objects on the shelves—from vintage government-issue coffee mugs, typewriters, and pencil holders to clunky-looking office equipment and furniture—had been collected over the years in the wake of the shutdown of Bluestone. All of it had absorbed a paranormal vibe, the result of having spent time in one of the long-forgotten labs.

"A year ago when Luke said he was ready to start taking control of the company I brought him down here and showed him the weapons," Harry said. "I also reminded him of the story of Pandora's box and the importance of the old pact."

"I remember," Angela said. "You said he took it all very seriously."

Harry rubbed his jaw, thinking. "Dad and Tobias Harper never really believed the crystals were destroyed in the Fogg Lake explosion. They were both convinced that in the chaos afterward someone grabbed the box and vanished with it."

"There are no accurate records of who made it out of the lab alive that day and who died, at least none that we know about. The government did everything it could to bury the Bluestone Project." Angela turned and walked briskly out of the vault. "We must call Luke and the Harper woman. They need to know that this thing has taken another nasty turn."

Harry followed her. "The Harper woman's name is Sophy."

"I'm aware of that."

"Thought so."

Once outside of the vault Harry reset the security system and then shook his head. "Hard to believe someone got past this lock. It's the latest tech out of the Wells, Inc. lab."

"I understand the Harpers are good with locks," Angela said coldly.

Harry grunted. "I know."

SIXTEEN

"THE KALEIDOSCOPE DOCUMENTS AND THE PROTOTYPES ARE MISSING?" LUKE PUT THE phone on speaker and raised his voice a little to be heard above the muffled roar of the jet's engines. "Stolen? That's hard to believe. Are you sure they weren't misplaced? Maybe they fell off the back of the shelf. There's a lot of junk stored in that vault."

The sharp edge on his words sent a whisper of alarm across Sophy's senses. She had just selected a slice of aged cheddar from the lavish tray of munchies that had been waiting for them when they boarded the sleek private jet. She paused before popping it into her mouth.

She wasn't the only one who reacted to Luke's tone. Bruce, secured in a safety harness in the passenger seat directly across the aisle, caught the vibe. He looked up from the fake bone he had been gnawing.

"No mistake," Harry said. "The guns and the documents are gone."

"Any idea when or how?" Luke asked.

"The most likely time was while Angela and I were in Europe

a few months ago. As for the how, that's the more interesting question."

"Yes," Luke said, "it is."

"It's also an embarrassing question," Sophy said. She took a bite of cheese. "So much for the reputation of Wells, Inc."

"I heard that," Angela snapped on the other end of the connection.

Harry cleared his throat. "Ms. Harper has a point. This doesn't make the brand look good."

"No," Luke said. "It doesn't."

"No one," Harry said, "absolutely *no one*, outside this family"—

"And mine," Sophy inserted.

—"and the Harpers," Harry continued, "will be informed about this situation. Is that clear?"

"Very clear," Sophy said. "But you're forgetting that someone outside the families already knows that your vault is vulnerable. The thief."

An acute silence followed that observation. It took her a beat to register what had been left unsaid. Anger set fire to her senses.

"If any one of you dares to so much as hint that a member of my family broke into your stupid vault, I swear I will spend the rest of my life taking revenge," she vowed. "The current feud between the Harpers and the Wellses will look like a picnic in the park compared to what will come afterward."

Luke took charge with a speed that she could not help but admire.

"Obviously, we're dealing with a thief who had access to some very sophisticated lockpicking equipment," he said. "Possibly someone in-house. It wouldn't be the first time the employee background checks failed to catch a rogue."

There was another short, tense silence. Sophy's intuition pinged. This time the part left unsaid was not aimed at her or her family. She was pretty sure Luke was blaming himself for whatever had happened when a background check had failed.

"No need to get paranoid," she said briskly. "There are a lot of people around who are good with locks. What we all should keep in mind is that whoever broke into the Wells family vault knew about Kaleidoscope and where to find the weapons. We're talking about someone deep in the paranormal community, possibly someone with a long-standing connection to Bluestone. That should narrow the suspect list."

Angela sighed. "She's right."

"Thank you, Angela," Sophy said.

Harry cleared his throat before Angela could respond. "There are other questions," he said. "For instance, where do Deke and Bea Harper fit into this? And why was that man murdered in Deke's cabin?"

"Good questions," Sophy said. She opened her phone and pulled up the app she had been using to make notes. "I've been researching the Fool's Gold Canyon Art Colony. One of my sources, a little book titled *An Investigation into the Fool's Gold Canyon Vortex,* has a couple of interesting facts. We already knew that the first art colony was abandoned a few years after it was established. But what we didn't know was that the man who founded it is said to have been driven mad by the strong vortex forces in the area. He died there. Over the years a number of conspiracy theories about the site have circulated, most of which involve extraterrestrials and alien abductions."

Harry grunted. "Anything else?"

"Not much." Sophy looked up from her notes. "I checked out the bio of the author. He died a few months after he self-published the book, so we can't contact him."

"Probably abducted by aliens," Angela muttered.

Sophy ignored her. "Newer sources note that the site was

abandoned for decades. Then, about eighteen months ago, the current art colony was founded by a tech bro named Trent Hatch. He's got an advanced degree in physics. His area of expertise is photonics."

"The science of light," Harry mused. "That's pretty sophisticated stuff."

"Hatch is a billionaire who made his fortune with an invention that proved to be a game changer in the field of medical imagery," she continued. "The device allows doctors to see deeper into the brain. It's used as both a diagnostic and treatment tool. He holds the patent, so he's going to remain very rich for a long time."

"I've heard of him," Luke said. "But that's all I can say. After developing the imaging tool he disappeared from the tech scene."

Sophy scrolled through her notes. "That's because he announced that he was going to retire at thirty and turn his attention to what he calls 'the art of light.' He rebuilt the Fool's Gold Canyon Art Colony and now invites artists who are exploring the use of light in their work to apply for a one-month residency at the colony. A maximum of eight artists are in residence at any time. There is a small inn on the grounds."

"Can anyone stay at the inn?" Harry asked.

"No," Sophy said. "It operates like a private club. Invitation only."

"And Deke had a booking for two people?" Angela asked, her voice rising.

"Not under his own name," Luke said. "The booking is for a Mr. and Ms. Ainsley."

"A cover, probably," Harry offered.

"That sounds likely," Luke said.

"I knew it—he's a spy," Sophy said.

The others ignored her.

"Are you and Ms. Harper planning to check in under those

names?" Angela said. She did not attempt to conceal her disapproval.

"Don't worry, Angela," Sophy said. "Separate beds. It will be like camping out. Luke's virtue is safe with me."

Luke spoke up quickly. "We're getting off topic here. Sophy and I are going to play this by ear. We have no idea what we're heading into. We'll take it one step at a time. This trip to Fool's Gold Canyon could be a dead end, but it's the best lead we've got."

"I know," Harry said. He paused before adding, "Don't forget the water."

"Already ordered," Luke said. "A twenty-four-bottle case. It will be in the vehicle."

"Good," Harry said. "You two be careful. Don't hesitate to call in backup if you need it."

"We won't," Luke said.

He disconnected.

Sophy looked at him, brows raised. "What was that about water?"

"We're going into the desert," Luke said.

"Please don't tell me you're thinking we might have to camp out. I'm not really the camping type."

"I'll keep that in mind."

SEVENTEEN

"WELCOME TO FOOL'S GOLD CANYON ART COLONY, MR. AND MS. AINSLEY," THE SECURITY guard said. He appeared to be in his sixties. He examined the passes and handed them back to Luke through the open window of the SUV. "The inn is the first right after you go through the gates. Park in the garage. You won't need your vehicle again until you leave. No cars are allowed on the grounds beyond the inn. Feel free to use any of the golf carts that you come across. There's a bunch of them scattered around for the guests."

"Thanks," Luke said.

"There's no cell service here in the vortex canyons, so you might as well forget using your phones."

"Understood," Luke said.

Sophy studied the massive steel gates in front of the SUV, aware of a chill in spite of the balmy evening air. The unsettling sensation had gotten steadily stronger during the long drive through miles of empty desert as night took control.

She knew that the desert was not truly empty. It came alive after dark as a varied population of creatures—snakes, bats, owls, insects, spiders, small rodents, and more—took the night shift. Nevertheless, there had been times during the past couple of hours when it felt as if she and Luke and Bruce were the only living beings on the planet. There were no streetlights on the old highway. No truck stops. No motels. No fast-food restaurants.

The first reassuring signs of life had appeared when they stopped for gas in the tiny community of Fool's Gold about ten miles back.

Now they had arrived at a small valley nestled deep in the red rock canyons.

As if he sensed her unease, Bruce leaned around the edge of the seat and nuzzled her. She reached up and ruffled his fur.

"Good-looking dog," the guard said.

Bruce grinned, flashing his fangs.

The guard frowned. "Does he bite?"

"Of course not," Sophy said. "He's really quite friendly."

Bruce went into what he evidently considered his adorable mode. Unfortunately, that look gave the guard another glimpse of fang.

"I don't recognize the breed," the guard said, wary now.

"Neither does anyone else," Luke said.

"You'll need to make sure he's on a leash while you're here." The guard stepped back. "I'll open the gates. You picked a good time to arrive. The colony is amazing after dark."

He went back into the guardhouse. The small space was crammed with a lot of exotic high-tech equipment. It looked like the flight deck of a fighter jet.

"They take security very seriously around here," Sophy said.

Luke glanced into the guardhouse. "Not seriously enough."

"Why do you say that?"

"They are not using Wells, Inc. products."

She almost smiled. "Does it worry you that the guard is armed? I mean, this is supposed to be an art colony, not a secret military base."

"We're in Arizona," Luke said. "You can assume everyone is armed."

"Including you?" she asked before she could stop herself.

"I don't like guns," he said. "They are loud, heavy, and dangerous. Also, I'm not a good shot."

She processed that while she watched the big gates slide open.

"Huh," she said.

"What?"

"I guess I just assumed that, what with you being in the security business and all, you probably carried a gun."

Luke drove through the gates. "You may be under a misconception about my career path. I'm what you might call a data analyst."

"A data analyst who is set to take control of one of the most powerful private security companies in the country."

"Maybe."

Startled, she turned to look at him. He certainly did not sound thrilled with the prospect of becoming the CEO of Wells, Inc. Interesting. Maybe he preferred his career as an assassin and wasn't looking forward to a desk job.

She did not ask any more questions, because she was riveted by the glowing, sparkling fairy-tale wonderland inside the compound.

"This is incredible," she said.

"Looks like a cross between the Las Vegas Strip and a theme park."

"Maybe," she agreed. "A bit."

The art colony was a small, picture-perfect community constructed around a large sculpture garden. The individual pieces of artwork in the garden glowed, glittered, dazzled, and blazed in the night. Much of it was abstract in style. All of it was illuminated with dramatic lighting effects.

Several casitas bordered the garden. There was a large house behind them. All of the structures were done in the contemporary Southwestern architectural style known as adobe revival. It was an elegantly rustic look that combined stucco walls with a lot of glass, wood trim, and courtyards.

At the far end of the compound an architectural anomaly loomed. It was a sprawling, single-story structure that looked much older than the other buildings in the compound. The style reminded Sophy of a Frank Lloyd Wright design, but it lacked Wright's sense of balance and proportion. Light from outside fixtures sparked on darkened windows, giving the impression that the interior was filled with night.

"That house at the other end of the garden looks more like a prison than a home," Sophy said. "All it needs is a barbed wire fence."

"Interesting." Luke turned right on the narrow lane and drove toward the brightly lit inn. "Must be a holdover from the days of the first art colony."

The Vortex Inn was an attractive, two-story affair in the same contemporary adobe style as most of the other buildings. Balconies marked the rooms on the upper floor. Small patios fronted the ground-floor rooms.

Luke stopped at the entrance. A smiling attendant who looked about eighteen greeted them.

"Welcome to Vortex Inn," he said. "I'll take care of the luggage and park your car in the garage while you check in at the front desk. Hey, you've got a dog. That's great. Let me know if you need someone to walk him while you're here. I love dogs."

Sophy could have sworn that Bruce understood. He practically smiled at the attendant and did a canine version of fluffing up. His fangs glinted in the light.

The attendant blinked. "Does he bite?"

"No," Sophy said very firmly. "He's a very friendly dog."

"Looks sort of like one of those dogs the military uses," the attendant said.

"Yes, he does," Luke said. "I'll put the vehicle in the garage myself. You can take my wife's suitcase."

Sophy automatically opened her mouth to correct him—she was not his wife—but belatedly remembered their cover. She closed her mouth and smiled at the attendant.

"No problem," the attendant said, oblivious. He hurried around to the other side of the SUV and opened Sophy's door.

"Thanks," she said.

She reached into the rear seat, grabbed her trench coat and tote, and climbed out. Bruce followed.

"I'm afraid the dog will have to be on a leash, Ms. Ainsley," the attendant said.

Sophy looked back at Luke. "Uh, do you—?"

"Here you go," Luke said from behind the wheel. He reached into the console and retrieved a pink, rhinestone-studded collar and a dainty matching leash. "You'll need these."

She caught the leash and collar, looked at Bruce, who was sniffing around the base of a nearby fountain, and then turned back to Luke.

"Where in the world did you get this stuff?" she hissed. "It's ridiculous for a dog like Bruce."

"Talk to Bruce. He's the one who picked it out in the pet supply store."

"I thought you said Bruce didn't like being on a leash."

"Tell him it's a formal occasion. I'll park the car and meet you in the lobby."

He put the SUV in gear and drove past the entrance before she could respond.

Sophy winced. "Uh, Bruce, this is a formal occasion. Do you mind?"

She had no idea what she would do if Bruce ignored her, but he didn't. He left the fountain and trotted back to where she stood. He waited patiently while she attached the glittery pink collar and dainty leash.

"Good dog," she whispered. "Thanks for not being difficult about this."

Bruce did not actually shrug but he somehow managed to send the message that he was okay with doing her a favor.

The attendant grabbed her suitcase and headed toward the lobby door. She clutched the end of the leash and started after him. Bruce fell into step beside her. They were walking past the fountain when she felt the hair on the back of her neck lift. The icy little frisson of awareness sparked across her nerves.

She stopped and glanced around, trying to see what had pinged her senses. Bruce halted and looked up with an inquiring expression.

When she saw nothing that appeared menacing or unsettling, she started to walk forward again.

Another ping sent a shiver of awareness through her. And not in a good way.

The chill of wrongness was coming from the fountain.

The focal point of the feature was an abstract sculpture that sent sprays of water cascading into the pool. A constantly shifting aurora of different-colored lights transformed the miniature falls into liquid jewels—emeralds, sapphires, amethysts.

Pretty, she thought. But that was not what intrigued her. She took a couple of steps closer—and got the ping again. Sharper this time. She was picking up a whisper of focused energy. It gave her a little buzz, but there was a dark side to what should have been an effervescent flutter.

This is way off. You should not be feeling this way.

"Ms. Ainsley?" the attendant said. "Is something wrong?"

"No," she said. "I just want to take a closer look at the fountain. It's a very interesting piece of art. I'll meet you inside."

"Okay."

He disappeared through the glass doors with her suitcase.

She was examining the fountain, trying to find the source of the vibe, when Luke came around the corner of the inn and walked toward her. He had his duffel in one hand and a six-pack of bottled water in the other.

She knew the six-pack was from the twenty-four-bottle case that had been stowed in the cargo bay of the SUV when they picked up the vehicle at the airport. There had been other items inside, too, including a carton of protein bars. She had tried not to think about the possibility of having to camp out in the desert.

"What's going on?" Luke said when he reached her. "Why aren't you inside?" He frowned. "What the hell?"

"Interesting, isn't it?" she said quietly.

"Feels like the first sip of a good whiskey. But without the whiskey."

"I was thinking champagne. It's not the first time I've gotten a hit off a work of art. It happens. Artists infuse energy into their creations, consciously or unconsciously. But the vibe is usually more complex. Nuanced. That's why no two people react the same way to the object."

"This is like standing in front of what passes for modern art while an expert tells you that it's not really a cartoon. There's a disconnect."

"You're not a fan of modern art, are you?"

"No, but that's not the problem here," Luke said. "Someone

managed to embed a hypnotic suggestion into this fountain. You can almost hear a soothing voice telling you that you are in your happy place. Nothing to worry about. Nothing to see here. That should be damn near impossible. Looks like Deke sent us to the right address. Time for Mr. and Ms. Ainsley to check in."

EIGHTEEN

"THE HONEYMOON SUITE?" SOPHY ASKED, HER VOICE RISING IN DISBELIEF. "IT JUST happens to be the only room left? Seriously?"

Luke glanced at her and saw that she had unclipped Bruce's leash and was now staring at the enormous bed that dominated the room. Four posts secured a canopy hung with gossamer curtains. White satin pillows were stacked all the way up the headboard. The white quilt and the satin sheets were partially folded back in an inviting manner.

"Not my fault," he said, annoyed with himself for feeling defensive. "You heard what the clerk at the front desk said. This is the room the Ainsleys booked and there's no way to switch because the inn is full."

He set the duffel on a luggage stand and put the six-pack of water on the table, giving himself a moment to get a handle on Sophy's reaction to the suite.

Her shock was real but he told himself it was over-the-top. Okay, the frilly room with its white-on-white decor and bath equipped with a whirlpool tub and two-person shower was a bit much but it wasn't a catastrophe. Was it?

"I know we're stuck with it," Sophy grumbled. "But this is—"

"What?"

"I don't know." She waved one hand. "Awkward. Or something."

"We're adults," he said. "I think we can deal with this situation. That bed is the size of a small island. If you're worried that I'll be driven mad with lust we can use some of the pillows to form a barrier between us."

"You don't understand."

He turned to confront her. "Is it because I'm a Wells? Are you afraid I'll assault you? Does your distrust of my family run that deep?"

Her expression tightened with resolve. She angled her chin. "No, of course not. I'm overreacting. I'm not afraid of you. You're right. A line of pillows down the middle of the bed will work just fine." She checked the time. "We need to get dressed. The reception starts in an hour. After that comes the gallery tour. Everyone will probably be wearing black. Lucky for you, your entire wardrobe seems to be black."

Luke watched her hang the long, many-pocketed trench coat in the closet.

"Sophy—" he said. And stopped because he did not know how to move forward.

When she turned around there was a steely sheen in her eyes. "No, I'm not afraid of you. But maybe you should be afraid of me."

He blinked a couple of times and then smiled. "Are you worried that you'll be tempted to ravish me?"

"I'm not joking, Wells. It's best if I sleep alone. Aunt Bea warned me early on that people with my talent don't usually do well sharing a bed. My psychic ability is directly linked to my dreamlight. When I'm awake it's under control. But when I go into a trance or fall asleep and dream, I can't predict the effects of my aura on others. You seem to have some immunity from my talent but we don't know if that extends to sleeping in close quarters."

Relief splashed through him. "So that's what all the fuss over the bed is about. You think I'll panic if you have a bad dream. Don't worry, I can handle your aura even in my sleep."

"What makes you so sure of that?"

"I've been thinking about the immunity theory," he said. "I don't have any—not to your talent. Just the opposite. I can resonate with it. That's a very different situation."

She looked doubtful. "Are you sure?"

"I'm not a para-engineer but I come from a long line of engineers who work with hot psi. I know the basic para-physics."

Her eyes brightened with something akin to hope. "So, I'm not dangerous?"

"Not to me."

The spark of hope faded. "Oh."

"I'll try not to take that personally."

She reddened and concentrated on lifting a slinky-looking black dress out of the suitcase. "You know what I mean."

"No," he said, "I don't."

"It's not as if you were one of my experiments," she said quickly. Too quickly. "I mean, if you were someone I happened to be dating, your immunity or whatever would be a very hopeful sign."

"Damn right," he said through his teeth. "I am not an experiment."

She narrowed her eyes. "You're the one who made it clear at the start that you were not interested in having any kind of relationship with me."

She was right. He had said something along those lines.

He gave up trying to analyze the new twist in their non-relationship relationship and reached into the duffel to pick up his shaving kit. He paused when Bruce whined softly. The dog was probably bored with the sniping.

But Bruce didn't look bored. He was sniffing around a waist-high, transparent acrylic pedestal that held an abstract sculpture made of highly polished metal. The artwork was about two feet tall, round, with a large hole in the middle.

"Do you think he's going to pee on that pedestal?" Sophy asked. "Housekeeping won't be thrilled, that's for sure."

"Bruce knows better than to mark his territory indoors," Luke said.

But Bruce was paying a lot of attention to the pedestal.

Luke set the shaving kit on a nearby table and walked to stand in front of the sculpture. He touched Bruce's head.

"What is it, pal?" he asked softly.

Bruce sat down, ears sharp, and watched Luke with an expectant expression.

"He's alerting, isn't he?" Sophy asked, intrigued.

"I think of it as his *do something, dummy* mode," Luke said.

He reached out and cautiously brushed his fingers against the side of the circular sculpture. It was cool to the touch.

Sophy watched him. "It looks like a big silver doughnut."

"I was thinking the same thing," he said. "But I admit I don't have an eye for modern art."

She gave a small cough. "Maybe it's supposed to have some romantic symbolism to suit the theme of the room."

"Sometimes a silver doughnut is just a silver doughnut." He kept one hand on the sculpture and walked slowly around the pedestal, examining it closely. He stopped when he was once again in front of the artwork and moved his hand inside the opening, feeling for seams in the metal.

Sophy set the black dress on the bed and crossed the room. She halted beside Bruce. "You're thinking about the fountain out in front of the inn, aren't you?"

"Yes."

"I'm not picking up any focused energy from this sculpture."

"Neither am I. That's a good thing, because I don't like the idea of sleeping in a room with an object that's giving off a strong vibe, even if it is a cheery one."

"This is the honeymoon suite," Sophy reminded him in ominous tones. "Who knows what kind of vibe the artist might have infused into it? Cheery might be the least problematic."

"If you suddenly start talking dirty to me I will conclude that this thing got switched on and sent out a hypnotic suggestion."

Sophy flushed. "Not likely, and that's enough with the sexual innuendos."

"Technically speaking, it wasn't an innuendo. More like a statement of fact."

"What I meant was, it's not likely that a psychically infused hypnotic suggestion could be switched on and off." She paused, brows crinkling above the black-and-crystal frame of her glasses. "Is it? You're the tech expert here."

"I don't know of a mechanical way to do it. Close contact is needed to infuse a strong vibe of any kind into an object, and one as precise and focused as a hypnotic suggestion would require considerable talent." He paused, thinking. "It would also fade quite rapidly, much faster than regular hypnotic suggestions do."

"A hypnotist can renew a suggestion," Sophy reminded him.

"Yes, but not remotely. Maybe I should say, I've never heard of it being possible. When it comes to psi-tech, never say never. We know so little about para-physics. The Boss says—"

He stopped because his fingers had brushed against an almost invisible seam in the polished metal.

"Find something?" Sophy asked.

"Maybe. Turn out the lights."

Sophy went to the master light panel at the entrance of the room and pressed the *All Off* button.

The room went dark but the glow from the multitude of lights outside poured through the windows.

"Close the curtains," he said.

Without a word Sophy pressed the button that closed the blackout shades, plunging the suite into cave-like night.

He heightened his senses and studied the small, mirror-finish panel set into the base of the sculpture. It gave off a faint but discernible radiance.

"See anything?" Sophy asked. Excitement hummed in the question.

"Yes," he said. "A small, mirrored tile. There's a little residual energy in it but it's not emitting a focused signal. I need to get some tools and pry it out of the sculpture. I want to see what's underneath."

"Luke," Sophy gasped. "I think they were here. Right here in this room."

"Who?" he asked.

"Deke and Bea."

An electric spark of knowing zapped across his senses.

"Are you sure?" he asked.

"No. The energy isn't very strong, but there's something here. I need to do a reading. Now."

In the eerie light of his other vision he watched her take the chimes and the mallet out of her suitcase. She tapped one of the metal rods. The clear note sounded, hanging in the atmosphere for a time before fading.

He heard Sophy take a sharp breath.

"Are you seeing ghosts?" he asked.

"*Yes,*" she said in her trance voice.

It dawned on him that she didn't correct his use of the word *ghosts*. A dark current of despair surged through him. *I screwed up again. I was too slow. Too late. This time somebody died.*

He steeled himself.

"Are Deke and Bea dead?" he asked.

"*There's no sign that anyone died here.*"

Cautious relief crackled through him. There was still hope.

"*No signs of violence,*" Sophy continued. "*The shadows are very faint but something isn't right. There's a lot of tension. I think Bea may have used her talent.*"

"You said she's good with crystals."

"*Yes. I think something happened over there by the sculpture. There's a lot of residual energy.*" She paused. "*Deke may have used some talent, too. What kind of ability does he have?*"

"Deke is good with cameras."

"*That doesn't make much sense.*"

"With Deke you never know."

"*I don't think they ever slept in that bed, Luke. I think they left this room and never returned.*"

NINETEEN

SHE CAME OUT OF THE TRANCE ON A WAVE OF ENERGY, AWARE THAT THE ROOM LIGHTS were on. Luke was standing directly in front of her.

Casually he closed one hand over her shoulder. She remembered she was wearing her regular black-and-crystal frames, not the mirrored sunglasses. But Luke seemed oblivious to whatever he saw in her eyes. He was very focused now, but not on her.

She took a clarifying breath and forced herself to concentrate. It wasn't easy, but the exhilarating rush was already fading.

He took his attention off the sculpture long enough to give her a quick, searching glance. "Are you okay?"

"Yes." She felt the heat rising in her cheeks. Luke was the only person outside Bea and Chloe who knew just how rattled she was when she came out of a trance. It made for a certain awkwardness. She did not like the idea that she might look weak—especially not in front of a Wells. "Yes, I'm fine." She raised her chin. "Thank you."

"No problem." He took his hand off her shoulder. "The fact that we're in the same room that Deke and Bea checked in to can't be a coincidence."

"I agree, but I didn't see any evidence of violence in this room, so if something happened to them it must have happened elsewhere. Maybe someone grabbed them. I'll bet the front-desk clerk was in on the plot."

"I doubt it. The kid behind the desk is about eighteen. This is a part-time job. He's a small-town boy who can't wait to get to the big city. Trust me, he is not a member of a criminal conspiracy. No one would be dumb enough to invite him into a criminal conspiracy, because the first thing he would do is announce it on social media."

She narrowed her eyes in an assessing look. "What makes you so sure?"

"His high school ring told me he's a graduating senior. He kept checking his cell phone even though there's no service here because it's a habit. He had a set of earbuds stashed behind the counter and I overheard him telling the attendant who met us at the entrance that he knows someone in Phoenix whose folks will be out of town for the weekend. Evidently there's going to be a party."

"You noticed all that while we were checking in?"

"I told you, I'm good at connecting dots."

"Impressive. Well, here we are in the same room that Deke and Bea checked in to. As you say, that can't be a coincidence." Adrenaline splashed through her. Not the ice fever shivers—this was the rush that came with knowing they were making progress. "Someone knows who we are. They want to keep an eye on us."

"Probably."

She frowned. "Are you always this indecisive?"

"When I don't have enough information, yes."

"We can't just hang out here and wait for someone to drug us and haul us away in a couple of laundry carts."

Luke raised his brows. "You came up with that scenario just now? Including the bit with the laundry carts?"

"Isn't that how the bad guys who arrived with room service get rid of dead bodies in the movies?"

"You have a very interesting imagination. But your theory has some plausibility, so, just to be on the safe side, we won't order room service."

"The inn doesn't offer room service."

"Problem solved. We need data, so for now we're going to stick to the schedule."

"Seriously?"

"Seriously."

She raised both hands in surrender. "You're the one who's gotten us this far, so I guess you know what you're doing."

"Thank you for that vote of confidence."

She shot him a severe look, crossed to the bed, and picked up the printed program they had been given when they checked in.

"First up is dinner," she said. "The only restaurant is the one here in the hotel." She glanced at Luke. "Are we going to risk it?"

"Yes. I'm hungry. It's either the restaurant or a couple of protein bars and some of Bruce's kibble. I don't know how he'll feel about that."

"You're not worried that someone will try to poison us in the restaurant?"

"No. Too complicated, too much chance of something going wrong. If anyone tries to drug us it will be here in the suite."

She winced. "So we don't eat any chocolates we might find on the pillow tonight."

"There won't be any chocolates," Luke said. "It's a small inn with minimal staff. No turndown service. And no one else will pop in uninvited while we're gone, because Bruce will be here."

"Good point." She turned back to the program. "The welcome reception starts at eight. It will be followed by the grand opening of the Maze, 'a gallery dedicated to the Art of Light.' Evening attire is requested." She looked up. "I don't suppose you have a black blazer in that duffel bag?"

"Of course I have a black jacket in there. CIA assassins never leave home without one. There's a dress code for the profession."

"How did you know—?"

"That you think I might be an assassin? Deke mentioned that the Harpers were in the habit of making certain assumptions about his career path and mine. Now I know where he got that inside info."

She groaned. "From my aunt."

"Evidently."

She switched her attention to the sculpture. "What about that mirrored tile you found in the doughnut?"

"It may be nothing. We need to eat. It's been a long day. After dinner comes the reception and the gallery tour. I'll deal with the doughnut tonight."

TWENTY

"WELCOME TO THE FOOL'S GOLD CANYON ART COLONY. AS MOST OF YOU ALREADY KNOW, I'm Trent Hatch, founder of a little start-up that created a new way of looking deep into the brain. Between you and me, my goal back at the start was to invent a new game, make a fortune, sell the company, retire at thirty, buy some fast cars and a yacht, and date beautiful women. Simple dreams, I know, but in my own defense I would like to remind you that I was a very young man at the time."

A ripple of laughter swept across the small crowd gathered inside the reception hall. Sophy stood at the back with Luke. Like everyone else in the room, they each held a glass of champagne. The booze was being handed out freely.

She estimated there were about thirty people present, all guests at the inn. Almost everyone was wearing black. She and Luke fit right in, she thought.

Trent Hatch was in his early thirties. In the photos and videos taken during his days in the tech world, he'd had a pleasant if unremarkable face that looked like it would soften quickly with age, a body that went with the face, and limp brown hair that had been in desperate need of a stylist.

The man onstage tonight was Hatch 2.0. His sculpted profile was a work of art that could only have been created by a skilled cosmetic surgeon. His hair was cut quite short. He, too, wore black—black T-shirt, slouchy black jacket, black jeans, and white running shoes. The outfit paired back to his tech wizard origin story and coordinated equally well with his new role as a patron of the arts.

". . . I sold the company and got ready to live the dream," Hatch continued. "I went shopping for a Lamborghini and called a couple of yacht dealers. But fate intervened. I discovered that I no longer cared so much about expensive toys. I was drawn to the relationship between light and art . . ."

Sophy studied the two striking Valkyries standing on either side of the stage. They appeared to be identical twins and they had gone to extreme lengths to make the point. Each had to be nearly six feet tall. Each had her hair done up in a severe chignon. They looked fit and toned in a way that indicated they took their gym workouts a lot more seriously than she did hers. Their tuxedos had an Armani edge.

Beneath the cover of another round of laughter and applause, Sophy leaned close to Luke and whispered into his ear. "Hatch may have ditched the fast cars and the yachts, but it looks like he was able to fulfill his dream of dating beautiful women. I'm guessing he goes for the dominatrix type. Got to admit those two blondes make the outfits look good. I wonder if they carry little whips."

When she straightened, Luke leaned in and whispered back. "The blondes are carrying guns under those tux jackets, not whips. You're looking at Hatch's personal security team."

Startled, she took another look at the two women. "Are you sure?"

"I'm in the security business, remember? I can recognize other people in the same line."

Onstage, Hatch concluded his welcome speech.

". . . Rather than stand here for another hour and lecture you on the astonishing works that our artists in residence have created, I invite you to immerse yourself in the Art of Light Experience. The Maze Gallery is now open for your viewing pleasure."

Another, shorter round of applause punctuated the announcement.

"A word of warning," Hatch continued. "For your own safety, please stay on the illuminated path inside the gallery. Decades ago, the eccentric art collector who built the house transformed it into an elaborate maze. He is said to have died there. Got lost in his own private puzzle. History repeated itself a couple of years ago when the last owner died inside. So stick to the path or I guarantee you will spend a long night wandering into dead-end corridors."

That generated nervous laughter from the audience.

Hatch smiled. "We would, of course, find you eventually, but it would take a while. Enjoy the exhibition, and remember, most of the pieces will be presented at the auction that will be held three days from now. All proceeds will go to charity."

There was another round of applause.

"Let's go," Luke said quietly.

"Fine by me."

They made their way out into the brightly illuminated night and followed a glowing path toward the sprawling house that served as the gallery. The evening was cool. Sophy pulled her light silk wrap more snugly around her shoulders and took a couple of peeks at Luke in his black jacket. He looked good in it, she decided. Not better than he looked in the leather bomber—just a little different. The garment took him from standard-issue CIA assassin to James Bond status.

"You don't look anything like Hatch's security team," she said.

Luke's mouth twitched. "One sentence into this conversation and I'm already lost. Care to explain?"

"The Valkyries looked like they were wearing costumes."

"Valkyries? Never mind. Those tuxes aren't costumes. They're uniforms."

"Whatever. My point is, you make that black outfit look good."

"Thanks. I told you, there's a dress code for assassins."

"You will note that I am not amused."

"Noted. By the way, you make that slinky black slip look terrific."

"Thank you. It's not a slip. No one wears slips these days. It's a dress. Thanks for the compliment. There's a dress code for professional con artists, psychic grifters, and cat burglars."

"Good to know," Luke said. "We're even now, right?"

"Sort of. Sheesh. This is creepy, isn't it?"

"Trash-talking each other's career paths?"

"No, the gallery. It looks like a haunted house," she said.

Luke snorted. "Have you ever actually seen a haunted house?"

"Yes," she said. "I see them a lot in my work as a crime scene reader and housekeeper. I'm not saying I believe in ghosts and spirits, but the energy of death and violence is very real. It makes a place feel haunted."

"Okay, I won't argue with that." He studied the house. "According to Hatch, at least two of the previous owners died inside the gallery, so there may be some bad vibes in there."

"At least the energy will have faded somewhat."

Earlier, viewed from a distance, the house had appeared to be filled with darkness. Now that they were approaching it, she decided nothing had changed. It certainly wasn't getting brighter or more welcoming. The exterior gardens and outdoor sculptures were artistically lit, but there was no hint of a glow from inside.

"You're right," Luke said. "It is creepy."

They were among the first to be ushered through the doors by two gray-haired attendants, who, like the guard at the front gate, appeared to be retirement age. To Sophy's great relief, the room that served as a lobby was glamorously if dimly illuminated. She glanced around, wondering why there had been no light showing through the windows. Then she saw the heavy drapes.

"Blackout curtains," she whispered. "That explains why the place appears so dark from the outside."

Before Luke could respond, a stocky, gray-haired attendant opened a door into a heavily shadowed room.

"Welcome to the Art of Light Experience," he said, sounding like the jovial greeter at a big-box store.

Sophy started to move forward but paused when Luke touched her arm.

"I want to check out one of the windows before we go inside," he said quietly.

He steered her toward the nearest set of heavy drapes and positioned her so that she was standing in front of him. She heard the curtains shift ever so slightly and knew he had tweaked one aside.

"Thought so," he said. There was cool satisfaction in the words. "All right, we can go in now."

Together they moved toward the entrance, joining others who were streaming into the exhibition area.

"What did you find?" she whispered.

"Behind the curtains the windows are covered in some kind of black glass. Old glass. It probably dates from when the house was constructed."

"You heard Hatch tonight. The man who built this place and established the first art colony was notoriously eccentric. Maybe he was paranoid about people spying on him."

"The glass in the windows is hot, Sophy."

"I take it you don't mean from sitting in the desert sun all day."

"No, it's the kind of residual heat glass and other materials pick up when they are exposed to paranormal energy over long periods of time."

She took a long breath. "Interesting."

"Very."

"There is a certain buzz in the atmosphere," she said. "The other guests are probably unaware of it. Or maybe they chalk it up to the effects of the free champagne."

They followed a small group into an antechamber. When the attendant closed the lobby door they were plunged into dense darkness. There was some uneasy laughter.

"What's going on?" someone said, sounding annoyed.

"Hatch is all about the drama," a woman answered.

"Well, it is an art gallery," a third person said. "You've got to expect drama."

"Yes," the first person said, "but this is like the start of a dark ride at a theme park."

Sophy stilled as the first shiver of claustrophobia kicked in. She felt Luke's hand close around her upper arm. Instinctively she heightened her talent a little. The chamber was now illuminated in a familiar gray light. She felt energy shift in Luke's aura and knew he had gone into his excellent night vision.

"*Do not be concerned,*" a disembodied female voice intoned in warm, reassuring accents. "*The darkness will last for only sixty seconds. It will give your eyes time to adjust to the gallery lighting so that you can truly appreciate the art.*"

The small group muttered, not entirely satisfied.

Anticipation sparked through Sophy. It took her a couple of heartbeats to realize that it was not coming from her own senses.

She turned her head, searching for the source.

"Look up," Luke said quietly.

She raised her gaze to the low ceiling and saw a small, oblong mirrored panel about the size and shape of a subway tile. It glowed faintly with paranormal energy. The hit of excitement and anticipation was coming at her in small waves. Like all emotional reactions, it was contagious.

The effect on the other guests was immediate and dramatic. The nervous muttering was replaced with a bubbly, slightly intoxicated vibe.

"Way to warm up the crowd," Luke said into Sophy's ear.

"*Remember to follow the illuminated path through the gallery,*" the disembodied voice said. "*It is the only route to the exit. For your own safety, please be aware that the velvet ropes that block the entrances to the dead-end corridors are there for your protection. Gallery attendants have been positioned along the path. Please feel free to speak with one if you have questions or are in need of assistance. Enjoy the Art of Light Experience.*"

Another set of doors slid open, revealing a deeply shadowed corridor punctuated by two brilliantly lit installations. Another rush of artificially induced anticipation bubbled through the small crowd. People streamed out of the antechamber and began exclaiming over the art.

She and Luke trailed after the others and joined a group gathered in front of the first installation, a glass sculpture in the shape of a large vase. It glowed dramatically thanks to some strategically placed fixtures.

"Spectacular," someone announced. "Incredible color saturation."

"I love what the artist did with the design," another guest offered. "Extraordinarily sensual."

"Amazing," a third person said.

They moved on to the next installation. Sophy stepped closer to the glass vase.

"It's certainly attractive," she said to Luke. "But I've seen a lot of glass art that looks very similar. There's nothing unique about it."

"Eye of the beholder and all that," he reminded her, deadpan.

"True."

She leaned in to read the small card on the wall. It was inscribed with the title—*Sunset*—and the name of the artist. In addition to the information, she got something else—a small shock of lust. It felt wrong in every way.

Instinctively she retreated a couple of steps and came up against an immovable object. Luke. He put a hand on her shoulder to steady her. She got another little sensual thrill. This time it was real.

She caught her breath, regained her balance, and put some distance between them.

"Do you feel that?" she asked.

"Oh, yeah." There was some heat in his eyes, the kind of energy that enhanced the twist of desire that she had experienced when he touched her a moment ago.

"This is not good," she said in low tones.

"Not to mention unnecessary, at least as far as I'm concerned."

She frowned. "What are you talking about?"

"Never mind. The heat is coming from a tile at the base of the pedestal. Take a look."

She glanced down and saw the dimly lit oblong panel. The faint current of lust was emanating from it.

"What is going on here?" she said.

"Someone has found a very interesting way of manipulating the reactions of the viewers."

"To drive up prices at the auction?"

"Maybe."

The thoughtful note in the one word made her glance at him, but he did not elaborate.

They moved on to the next installation, a miniature model of the art colony and the imposing red rock canyon walls that surrounded it. The scene was about three feet square, and as far as she could tell, it was accurate. She recognized the inn, the sculpture garden, the casitas, and the workshop. The old house that now served as the Maze Gallery was also in the scene. An ominous, pulsing aurora emanated from deep within the landscape.

Sophy watched the small group of people gathered around the model. They looked fascinated.

"It's interesting," she whispered, "but I'm not sure it qualifies as art. It looks more like one of those small-scale models developers use to illustrate their plans for a shopping center."

"Move a little closer," Luke said.

Gingerly she went forward—and got an annoying pulse of artificial lust. This time she was braced for it. She stepped back.

"This is actually getting scary," she said. "We're dealing with a psychic hypnotist who can manipulate the response of the viewers. A porno vibe is one thing, but what if it were some other emotion? Despair could push a vulnerable person over the edge. Panic could generate a stampede. Mob violence is a thing."

"I know," Luke said. "But the wavelengths are very short, much less than the average range for human-generated paranormal energy. I estimate the reach is only about three feet, max. Notice how rapidly the power levels fall off when you move away from the installation?"

Experimentally she took a couple of steps back. The pulse of focused energy became extremely weak and then disappeared entirely.

"Yes," she said.

"It's impressive that any talent could embed a hypnotic suggestion into a mirror or any other material and have it activate remotely. Whoever is behind this has made a significant engineering advance, but it is obviously still in the development stage."

"This is seriously dangerous technology," she said. "It's one thing to have to listen to 'Jingle Bells' for two months during the holiday shopping season. I don't want to even think about what would happen if the currents of music were carrying a hypnotic suggestion to buy more stuff."

"That would be the least of the potential damage this tech could do . . . Huh."

She shot him a quick, searching look. "What?"

"Someone has found a way to record a static message in the tiles, but based on everything I know about human-generated psi, the hypnotic suggestion has to be renewed frequently—by a human with a talent for the work."

She studied him, intrigued. "You really do know a lot about the physics of paranormal energy."

"For a CIA assassin, you mean?"

She was suddenly grateful for the darkness, because she could feel herself turning red. "I never actually said you were an assassin."

"You didn't have to say it."

"Are we going to refight the old feud here?" she shot back. "In public?"

"Nope. I think we've insulted each other enough for one day. I suggest we focus on our problem."

"Good plan," she muttered.

"The interesting thing about this conversation is that it's given me an idea."

She realized that they were alone in front of the installation. The other guests had disappeared down another glowing hallway.

"I'm listening," she said.

"The development of this tech would have required more than one talent. Yes, a hypnotist is involved. But someone else probably invented the mirror tiles. We're talking about two very different kinds of psychic ability. Then there's the money angle. It took a fortune to reopen the art colony and another fortune to keep it running."

"All that just to sell mediocre art?"

"I think it's more likely the art marketing is a cover for what is really going on here."

"Which is?"

"A series of experiments. If you're developing a new technology you need to run a lot of tests. What better way to do that than keep an inn full of carefully selected test subjects on-site?"

"Oh, shit."

"Yeah." He urged her forward with one hand. "We can talk about it later. We need to keep moving."

"Thanks for the *we*," she grumbled. "I feel so honored to know you consider me a member of the team."

"I sense sarcasm."

"Actually, I'm pissed off. I don't like the idea of being a test subject in an experiment no one told me about. There was no informed consent here."

"Like one of your dates?"

"That's ridiculous. All dates are, by definition, experiments. Everyone knows a date has the potential to end badly."

"Interesting logic. Never mind. At this point my theory is just a theory. I'm still gathering data. Connecting dots."

They followed the illuminated path to an intersection. Two of the three branching corridors were barred with velvet ropes. On the other side of the ropes, the hallways were drenched in darkness. An attendant politely raised a hand to indicate the one glowing corridor.

Sophy peered down an unlit path as they went past the entrance. "Why would anyone turn an entire house into a maze? The man who built it must have been beyond eccentric."

"Or full-on paranoid."

"Do you think he built the maze to trap intruders?"

"You know what they say—just because he was paranoid doesn't mean he didn't have enemies."

"Maybe he hid an extremely valuable painting in here somewhere and wanted to protect it."

The trail led to another installation that was surrounded by a small group of admirers. Sophy stopped a few steps away from the piece and considered the twisted sculpture on the pedestal. It appeared to be made of transparent plastic molded into bulbous shapes and lit with cleverly arranged lights.

"It looks like a balloon animal," she whispered to Luke.

"Yes," he said. "It does."

He took a few steps closer, paused a moment, as though examining the ballon animal, and then came back to join her.

"Another example of mirror tile hypnosis at work?" she asked.

"Definitely," he said.

She went forward, curious, and stopped abruptly when she picked up the vibe of one of the men who was standing nearby. There was no mistaking the currents that charged the atmosphere. He was sexually aroused. When he noticed her he turned, his eyes glittering. Sweat beaded his brow.

"Are you alone?" he asked.

"No," Luke said before she could respond. He came up behind her and took her arm in a way that was clearly proprietary. "She's not alone. She's with me."

For a beat Sophy thought the stranger would argue the point, but when he got a close look at Luke, he evidently changed his mind. He grunted and returned his attention to the sculpture.

"That was a tad unnerving," she murmured as Luke led her away.

"Only a tad?"

"I could have handled him," she said quickly.

"I don't doubt that for a moment."

She made a face. "But thanks anyway."

"You're welcome. I assume you would do the same for me if the situation was reversed."

"Rescue you from a sex-maddened connoisseur of balloon art? Absolutely. That's what allies do."

"Good to know."

He released her arm. She realized immediately that she missed his touch. *Don't get accustomed to it.*

A thought occurred to her. "I wonder how long the effects of the suggestion last?"

"Good question. Probably not long, considering how weak the currents are."

The next installation was titled *Into the Woods*. They walked through a small forest composed of columns of light projected downward from concealed fixtures.

"I have to admit that I like this artwork," she said. "Maybe because it's interactive." She caught the faint pulses of energy from a nearby tile and knew she was supposed to be sexually aroused. "Forget it. The hypno-tile ruined it for me."

She turned the corner . . .

. . . and froze at the sight of the life-sized sculpture at the end of the short passageway. Her pulse slammed into fight-or-flight mode. Icy perspiration trickled down her sides. She shivered as adrenaline-fueled panic threatened to overwhelm her.

Luke came up behind her. "What's wrong?"

She could not speak.

"I see," he said, his voice dangerously soft.

It was impossible to tell what the sculpture was made of—molded, high-tech plastic, perhaps, Sophy thought. There were two figures, a male and a female. The woman appeared to float in midair. The folds of a dark purple cape whipped around her. In the shadow of a hood, her eyes blazed, wildfire hot. Her gleaming red nails were sharpened into claws. The crimson lips were parted in predatory sexual hunger, revealing the pointed tips of white teeth. She held a set of gleaming metal chimes in one hand.

A partially nude male was sprawled beneath her. Asleep, perhaps. Or dead.

The white card on the wall did not give the name of the artist, just the title of the installation. *Succubus.*

TWENTY-ONE

"WANT TO TELL ME WHAT'S GOING ON HERE?" LUKE ASKED QUIETLY.

He did not take his eyes off the installation labeled *Succubus*. It required raw willpower to suppress the fury heating his blood. He wanted to smash the artwork and then destroy the artist who had created the monstrous sculpture. Unfortunately, at that moment neither option was available. But sooner or later . . .

"He's here." Sophy sounded as if she could barely breathe. "Somewhere. He's *here*."

A man and a woman entered the display space. They were both giggling in the odd, artificial way that indicated they were still partially under the influence of the previous installation.

"What the fuck?" the man rasped.

The woman gave a small, stifled yelp.

"Forget it," she said. "Let's get out of here."

"No problem." The man pivoted and headed toward the intersecting hallway. "I didn't come here to see a fucking horror show."

Luke focused on the one thing of which he was certain: Sophy knew the artist.

"Sophy?" he prompted softly.

She did not respond. She stood in front of *Succubus*, staring at it as if she, too, was an immobile work of art. The energy in the atmosphere around her was charged with a toxic mix of rage and panic and disbelief.

He did the only thing he could think of—he tightened his grip on her shoulder and tried to soothe the wildly sparking currents of her aura with some of his own energy. Seeking resonance.

"Stop trying to make me calm down," she said, her voice shivering a little. "I'm not a startled horse. I've got every right to be pissed."

He took his hand off her shoulder. "Yes, you do."

He wasn't hurt by the rejection, he told himself. He was . . . surprised, maybe. Yes, that was it. Surprised. Here he had been telling himself that they were getting along well, assuming you didn't count the occasional sniping. Now he wondered if he had been misreading her.

Or maybe deceiving himself. It wouldn't be the first time. He had a history.

She turned away from *Succubus*. "I'm sorry. I'm the one who should apologize. I shouldn't have snapped at you. Let's get out of here."

"Fine by me."

Cautiously he took her arm, not in an attempt to ease her tension this time, but to steer her toward the intersecting hallway. She did not resist his touch.

A small man loomed at the entrance. His shaved head gleamed. Behind the lenses of his wire-framed glasses his pale eyes were bright and intense. At the sight of *Succubus* he snorted.

"Utter trash," he said. "Derivative, cartoonish, uninspired."

"We agree," Luke said. "Do you happen to know the name of the artist?"

"No, but I can safely predict he won't go far, not with that sort of amateurish work. No gallery will display that shit."

"This one did," Sophy said.

"That tells you a lot about the quality of the rest of these installations. Third-rate."

"You seem very sure of your verdict," Luke said. "Are you an artist?"

"I'm an art *critic*. Professional, I might add. The name is Marlon Whitley. And you are?"

"Larry and Susan Ainsley," Luke said before Sophy could fumble the introduction.

She shot him a sidelong look that made it clear she was aware he hadn't trusted her to keep the cover story straight, but she did not say anything.

Whitley's birdy eyes tightened with speculation. "Correct me if I'm wrong, but didn't I see the two of you coming out of the honeymoon suite earlier this evening?"

"That's right," Sophy said.

"Thought so. I'm on the same floor. Are you collectors?"

"We're just starting out," Luke said. "We're both interested in light art but we're discovering there's a lot to learn."

"That's an understatement." Marlon grunted. "I usually charge a minimum of five figures to provide a consultation but I'll make an exception for a pair of honeymooners. Pro tip: none of the pieces in this gallery is worth buying at the auction. Take this installation, for example." He gestured toward *Succubus*. "Nothing but special effects with lights. Might as well be CGI. It's certainly not art. Now, if you'll excuse me, I'm going back to the inn. I need a real drink. The champagne isn't doing it for me."

TWENTY-TWO

BY THE TIME THEY REACHED THE LOBBY OF THE GALLERY, SOPHY HAD REGAINED CONTROL of her badly rattled nerves. Luke was impressed by her fast recovery. She had grit, as the Boss would have said.

They made their way outside into the brightly lit sculpture garden and walked along the glowing path that would take them back to the inn. There was a buzz in the atmosphere, he thought, and not all of it was coming from the unusual paranormal energy in the canyon. Some of it—the good stuff, the vibe that hit his senses like an exhilarating tonic—was generated entirely by Sophy.

"I realize you have a lot of questions," she said.

"Oh, yeah."

"So do I. Unfortunately I don't have many answers. Remember that police sketch artist I told you about?"

"The jerk who called you a succubus and took off running when he saw you without your sunglasses?"

"That jerk. Yes."

"You think he did that installation?"

"I'm absolutely certain of it."

"He told me his name was Vincent Grant." Sophy clutched her wrap in one tight fist, crushing the delicate fabric. "He said I was his Muse. That was before he called me a succubus, of course."

"You were okay with being a jerk's Muse?"

Sophy slanted him a warning look. "At the time I was dating him I didn't know he was a jerk. I was flattered."

"Just asking a question. How did you meet him?"

"Vincent said he contacted me because he heard a detective talk about my ability to read a crime scene. He said he was curious because he wondered if I might have some psychic talent. He had some, too. He pointed out that we both did freelance work for the police so we probably had a few things in common. We agreed to meet for coffee. When we did, we recognized each other in the way that people with strong abilities do. You know how that is. It makes for a connection of sorts."

"Not necessarily."

She cleared her throat. "He had a few other things going for him, as well."

"Let me guess. He was good-looking, dark, and brooding in a tortured, starving-artist way."

"He wasn't starving. He drove a nice car and he was expensively dressed. But yes, he was quite attractive. However, his real appeal was that he was one of those men who is very good at making conversation with women."

"Conversation."

"Vincent was intense, but when he talked to me, he focused on *me*, if you know what I mean."

Luke ran the words through his dot-connecting algorithms a couple of times and gave up. He tried to ignore the cloud of impending doom that seemed to have taken up a position over his head.

"No," he said. "If he was talking to you, who else would he focus on?"

"Himself. Never mind. The point is, Vincent didn't try to convince me that he was a brilliant artist or that he had money. He was eager to hear what I had to say about crime scene work, about art, about food. Anything and everything. He said he valued my insights because my talent allowed me to see things that were hidden from him."

Luke tried to remember if he had ever asked her for her thoughts on her police work or art or food. He couldn't remember having done so.

"You and I spend a lot of time talking," he said, aware that he sounded defensive. "We've talked a lot since I landed on your doorstep in Mirror Lake. Pretty much nonstop."

"That's different," she said in a flat tone that made it clear the statement was not open to argument. "Our association is a matter of necessity. We have no choice but to communicate."

The term *association* was not promising, but *communicate* struck him as downright cold. "What does a Muse do?"

"I'm not sure," she admitted. "Vincent said my aura had an inspiring effect on his creativity."

"As pickup lines go, that doesn't sound very original. I'll bet artists have been using it for years. Make that centuries."

"Before you offer any more of your own opinions, I would like to point out that being an artist's Muse seemed like a nice change. More fun than working with people who think I'm weird and scary but want to use me anyway."

The cloud of doom over his head was growing more ominous.

"For the record, I have never thought you were weird or scary," he said.

"Fair point. Whatever else I can say about you, I admit that you don't seem to be afraid of me."

"You don't have to sound disappointed."

She gave him a fierce look.

"I assume you did a background check on Grant?" he continued.

"Of course," she said, indignant. Then she sighed. "Well, sort of. I checked him out online. He had a website where he displayed his work. It looked legit."

"He *had* a website? Past tense?"

"It's gone now. After the pictures started popping up on my phone I tried to find him online again, but it was as if he never existed."

"What pictures?"

"They are all variations on the same theme as that *Succubus* we just saw. A scary woman holding a set of chimes." She paused. "The body of the man beneath her feet was new, however."

"When did the pictures start arriving on your phone?" he asked.

"Three days after our last date."

"Did you go to a restaurant or the theater? There might be some way to trace him."

"No. We went to an alley where a murder had occurred a few years earlier."

"An alley."

"At midnight."

"A murder scene in an alley at midnight. Your idea?"

"Well, yes."

"You're a real romantic, aren't you?"

She raised her chin. "I decided it was time to run the test. It's easier to read a scene in darkness, and for the record, I'm not interested in your views on my social life or lack thereof."

"Can I just say that a date in a dark alley where a murder occurred sounds a little unusual?"

"You get used to it," she said.

"I'll take your word for it. Looks like we have a new problem."

She frowned. "What?"

"We still don't know how Deke and Bea got caught up in this thing, but now it looks like you might be a target."

"Me?" She gave that a second to settle. "Okay, the *Succubus* sculpture turning up in the gallery tonight can't be a total coincidence. But what about you? Maybe you're a target. You and Deke both."

"Or maybe we just happened to get in the way because of the old pact between the Wellses and the Harpers."

"Another coincidence?"

"No," he said. "A major miscalculation by whoever is running this op."

TWENTY-THREE

"THE EXHIBITION WAS A SUCCESS." TRENT HATCH POURED TWO GLASSES OF SCOTCH AND handed one to his half brother. "The mood tiles were quite effective. The Alchemist will be pleased. By the way, congratulations on your *Succubus*. It caused quite a stir."

The thing you had to remember about artists was that they craved positive feedback.

Vincent stopped pacing the room long enough to snatch the glass out of Trent's fingers. He took a long swallow and resumed pacing. He was energized. On fire.

He was also, Trent thought, increasingly unstable. The streak of borderline insanity came from Vincent's father's side, along with his head-turning good looks and ability to charm women. Their mother's second marriage had not ended well. Her husband, Conrad Grant, had spent his final days in a psychiatric hospital.

"The bitch saw *Succubus*, Trent." Vincent gulped some more whiskey. "She recognized herself. She was terrified. She finally understands that not only do I know the truth about her, I can and will control her."

There was a feverish excitement about Vincent that was growing stronger and more worrisome by the day. Trent watched him stalk back and forth across the study. He was not the only one keeping an uneasy eye on his half brother. He knew the security team was, too. That was not good news. Monica and Moira—he had never figured out which was which—were well aware that his brother was becoming increasingly erratic. The only thing protecting Vincent for now was the fact that the Alchemist needed him. That state of affairs would not last much longer.

Trent had tried to explain that Vincent's mood swings were a natural aspect of the artistic temperament, but he knew Monica and Moira were not buying that story. Vincent was clearly deteriorating, and the psychedelics he was using to *open the inner path to the wellspring of his creative powers* were not helping.

Trent drank some whiskey. As usual, he had made sure the scrambler was running when he and Vincent walked into the room a short time ago. The faint pulse of paranormal radiation was almost undetectable, but it was enough to make any conversation sound like it was coming from deep underwater.

He was reasonably certain that the Scary Blondes could not eavesdrop, but he no longer took anything for granted when it came to the project. The sense that a doomsday clock was ticking beneath their feet had been growing stronger for weeks now. The paranormal radiation levels had risen so much recently that even those without any measurable talent were picking up the vibe. The turnover in artists and staff would soon be unsustainable. Even some of the test subjects at the inn had started to notice the disturbing energy.

"The Harper woman needs to be afraid," Vincent said. "She must learn that I am the master of my Muse. She can no longer control me."

"I know you blame her for your inability to fuck, but—"

"*It's her fault*," Vincent shouted. He abruptly stiffened, his eyes widening in panic. He stared at the door of the living room, evidently remembering the security team on the other side.

"Vincent, listen to me—"

Vincent took a shaky breath and managed to lower his voice. "She's responsible for what's happening to me. She's a *succubus*, I tell you. The real thing. She came to me in my dreams and stole my energy. My essence. My artistic vision. The only way for me to recover is to possess her. If I can't control her I will have to destroy her. There is no other option. This is life or death for me. You have to help me."

Trent swirled the whiskey in his glass. "She's here. She has seen your art. I promise that you will have your time with her, but meanwhile, we have an agreement with the Alchemist."

"Yeah, yeah, I know." Vincent gulped down some more of his drink.

"Speaking of which, the gallery mirrors were drained tonight. The fountain is very low, too."

"I'll take care of them." Vincent folded his right hand into the shape of a pistol and aimed his forefinger at Trent. "Just remember, when the project is finished the succubus is mine."

"I won't forget."

Vincent downed the last of the whiskey, yanked open the study door, and slammed it behind him.

Trent waited a moment, letting the silence settle before he went to the window to look out at the empire he had created. The lights of the colony sparkled and dazzled in the night. The windows of the inn glowed, deceptively warm and welcoming. It was late. Most of the employees had driven back to their homes in the small community of Fool's Gold, leaving only a skeleton staff. The gates were locked. The cutting-edge security systems and cameras were being monitored by the Scary Blondes.

The compound was a fortress. It was also a prison. He ought to know. He hadn't left it in months. That, too, was part of the deal with the Alchemist.

He was heartily sick of pretending to care about art. He longed to escape and mingle with his own kind—the rich, brilliant, hard-charging, self-made entrepreneurs of tech who were changing the world.

He reminded himself that when the project was concluded he would not only take his rightful place among the tech bro kings, he would be free to focus on his new invention.

He just had to hold things together for a few more days. It would all be worth it.

Back at the start, he had struggled. There had been failure after failure. He possessed a psychic-grade talent for photonics, and he was convinced that certain light waves from the paranormal end of the spectrum could be used to slow the aging process of cells in the human body. But he had been unable to secure funding. Venture capitalists had laughed at the idea of wasting money on what they slammed as *the woo-woo thing*.

Reluctantly he had turned his attention and his talent to the medical imaging device that had made him rich. It was based on cutting-edge photonics but did not involve light from the paranormal ends of the spectrum.

He had been successful, but instead of enjoying the money and the status, he had succumbed to boredom and a slow, creeping depression. It turned out fast cars terrified him and he got seasick on yachts. The women had been fun for a while but none of them had been interested in his passion for photonics, let alone his theories about paranormal light waves. He had needed more—his work.

Just as he had begun to despair he had been contacted online by a reclusive inventor who had identified himself only as the

Alchemist. The deal had been struck over a highly secure messaging app and it had seemed too good to be true.

Now he woke up every morning remembering the old advice about the risk of dining with the devil. But there was no turning back.

He crossed the room and opened the door. The Scary Blondes were sitting in chairs positioned in front of a massive array of computer and camera monitors. They immediately stood. They did not actually salute but they might as well have.

Trent stifled a sigh. In the old days he had been obsessed with tall, gorgeous blondes. He had dreamed of having a couple of them draped on his arms. He supposed this was a classic case of *be careful what you wish for.*

He had been assured that the twins were skilled in various forms of martial arts and that they were expert with firearms of all types.

The pair had been sent by the Alchemist, who had insisted they be hired. Trent had to admit the women were impressive. He certainly felt safe knowing they were on guard. But Moira and Monica towered over him. He told himself he shouldn't let them make him nervous, but he couldn't shake the uneasy feeling he got when he was around them.

"Sir," Monica said.

Or maybe she was Moira.

"Sir," the other one said.

"I'm going into my sauna for a while." He tightened his grip on the doorknob, eager to escape. "Please make sure that I am not disturbed."

"Yes, sir."

"Yes, sir."

He closed and locked the door and turned to make his way down a hall to his private spa. The white-tiled room gleamed. He stripped off his clothes, grabbed a fluffy towel, and entered the chamber.

With its wooden walls, low, soothing light, and heated rocks, the interior of the small space looked like a traditional sauna. It could function as one, as well. But as with everything else in the art colony, there was a secret under the surface.

He sat down on a wooden bench and tapped in a code on the control panel. When he was finished he slipped on a pair of heavily tinted goggles and sat back.

The energy level in the room rose slowly but steadily. Through the darkened lenses of the goggles he watched the light come up and shift from the visible end of the spectrum to the nameless colors at the far end. It was light that only some insects, birds, and humans with a certain psychic sensitivity could perceive.

The little sparks of electricity across his senses told him the treatment was working, stimulating his body at the cellular level, repairing the damage done by the aging process.

He had begun the treatments as soon as the radiation chamber had been completed two months earlier, but he was certain he was already experiencing the effects of the light therapy. He felt more vigorous. He was sure his psychic senses were becoming sharper.

The Alchemist had come up with the answer to the old question *What do you offer the man who has everything?*

The answer, Trent thought, was a uniquely equipped lab, one that allowed him to tap into energy generated by the beating heart of nature. The Alchemist had made it possible for him to test his theories concerning the possibility of harnessing paranormal light to cure disease and lengthen the lifespan.

He was the first test subject.

TWENTY-FOUR

"THE USEFUL THING ABOUT HAVING A DOG AS A PARTNER IN AN INVESTIGATION IS THAT it gives you an excuse to take extended strolls at odd times of the day or night," Luke said.

Sophy looked down at Bruce, who was ambling along the footpath next to Luke. The dog had been happy to greet them when they returned to the room and eager to go for a walk, even if it meant having to tolerate a leash. The three of them were now exploring the glowing paths that wound through the colony. There was a definite shiver of energy in the atmosphere—paranormal radiation was always strongest at night.

They were not the only guests strolling through the brightly lit garden. Most of the others were sipping cocktails or glasses of wine. The alcohol was being served free of charge at an outdoor bar set up in front of the inn.

She couldn't stand the suspense any longer. "You haven't told me if you were able to connect any dots after I showed you those succubus images on my phone."

"Aside from the fact that Grant is a lousy artist, I can tell you he's escalating. But after seeing his installation tonight we knew that. He's obsessed with you, Sophy, and the obsession is getting worse."

She took a breath. "Obviously. But how could Vincent be involved with what is going on here at the art colony?"

"Just another dot waiting to be connected. Tonight we're doing recon. Getting a feel for the layout of the compound."

"What, exactly, are we looking for?" she asked.

"I don't know."

"But you'll know it when you see it?"

"That's the plan."

She studied the brightly lit casitas. There were eight of them, but only six showed signs of being inhabited. "I wonder if any of the artists are involved in whatever is going on here."

"According to the brochure in the suite, the resident artists stay for only a month. When they leave, other artists take their place. The people we're looking for are those who are here on a permanent basis."

"That includes Trent Hatch and his security team and the employees."

"I had a chat with the clerk at the front desk. He said that most of the employees live off-site in that little town we passed on the way here."

"Fool's Gold."

"Right. He told me that the workers always go home after their shifts. He also said that employee turnover was fairly stable until a few months ago but lately several people have quit and many of the positions are vacant."

She heightened her talent a little and opened herself to the currents of the night. "Maybe this canyon really is a natural vortex of some kind."

The fit-looking woman walking toward them overheard the comment. She stopped, smiled, and swept out both arms.

"It's a genuine vortex," she said. "That's why the original art colony was established here."

Sophy stopped. So did Luke and Bruce.

"Sounds like you know something about the history of the colony," Sophy said.

"A little. My name is Diane Buxton, by the way."

"Susan Ainsley," Sophy said.

Luke nodded. "Larry Ainsley. And this is Bruce."

"Does he bite?" Diane asked.

"No," Luke said. "He prefers to be adored."

Diane leaned down to give Bruce a couple of pats. "Cute collar. You've got excellent taste, Bruce."

Bruce grinned.

Diane glimpsed the fangs and straightened quickly. "You're the couple in the honeymoon suite, aren't you? I saw you checking in earlier this evening."

"That's right," Luke said.

"Congratulations."

"Thank you," Luke said.

There was a short pause. Sophy suddenly realized she was supposed to acknowledge the congratulations.

"Thanks," she said.

Okay, that sounded a trifle brusque. She did not dare look at Luke, who was probably doing an eye roll.

"There was another couple in that suite, but they didn't stay long," Diane said.

Sophy stilled. "Did you speak to the other couple?"

"No, I never got an opportunity. They checked in when I did but they were gone the next morning. I remember thinking they were a little old to be honeymooners. Probably a second or third marriage. You never know these days."

"Did you see them leave?" Sophy asked.

"No. But it must have been very early, because they were not around for breakfast. What did you think of the gallery show this evening? Weren't the installations amazing? Most of them, anyway. So much intense emotion. Very visceral. Light art is usually cool and abstract."

"They were certainly interesting," Sophy said. "Do you really think Fool's Gold Canyon is a vortex?"

"Oh, yes. Years ago my grandparents retired to the little town about ten miles from here. They used to tell stories to us kids when we visited."

"What kind of stories?" Luke asked.

"Ghost stories, mostly." Diane lowered her voice to an amusingly ominous tone. "This valley has always had a reputation for being haunted. People who live in the town will tell you that it is the energy in the area that caused the original colony to be abandoned. It's one thing to visit a vortex for a short period of time. It's another thing altogether to live in the vicinity of one."

"Makes sense," Sophy said.

"And now Trent Hatch has established a new version of the original art colony," Luke said. "Interesting."

"Yes." Diane looked around, surveying the sparkling fairyland garden. "We'll see how long it lasts this time."

She started to give Bruce a goodbye pat. He made the mistake of grinning, showing off his fangs. Diane changed her mind. Bruce looked disappointed.

"It's getting late, so I'm going back to the inn for a nightcap and bed," Diane said. "It was a pleasure to meet you both, and Bruce, too, of course. I'm sure I'll see you around the inn."

"Do you plan to attend the auction?" Luke asked.

"Definitely. I've got my eye on that gorgeous vase. Wish me luck."

"What about the sculpture titled *Succubus*?" Sophy said, trying to sound casual.

"What a monstrosity." Diane shuddered. "That was the one installation I thought was an utter failure. Someone said the artist was probably attempting to convey female power, but it looked like a Halloween costume or the villain in a low-rent horror film. All that sculpture needs is a bloody knife. I doubt if anyone will be bidding on it at the auction. Enjoy the honeymoon suite."

Sophy watched the woman walk away along one of the illuminated paths. "She saw Bea and Deke. I was right. They *were* in the suite."

"Did you doubt your reading?"

"Sometimes I wonder if I'm conjuring the visions," she admitted. "I'm always relieved when the police find hard evidence at the scene of the crime that verifies my read."

"Believe me, I understand the need for confirmation," Luke said.

The grim intensity of the words made her look at him. But he went on before she could ask any questions.

"We know for sure that Deke and Bea were in the suite and we know they disappeared sometime during their first night at the inn."

"Now what?"

"They're still here," Luke said, very certain.

She stared at him, stunned. "What makes you sure of that?"

"Simple psychology. No psychic talent needed. This place is a fortress. As far as anyone knows, Hatch never leaves the compound. This is where he feels secure. Where he hides his secrets.

We know Deke and Bea were here. If they left under their own power they would have contacted us. That did not happen, so we have to assume they never got out of the compound."

Sophy stared at him, unable to breathe. "Oh, my God, are you saying they are dead?"

"I think it's more likely they are in hiding around here."

"What makes you think that?" She was grasping at straws but she needed reassurance.

"If they were dead, whoever was responsible would have arranged for the bodies to be found. There would also have been a good cover story to explain why the son of the CEO of one of the most successful security firms in the country died under mysterious circumstances. Trust me, no one wants the Wells family breathing down their necks."

"I see what you mean. If Bea was murdered, only Chloe and I would care. But a missing or dead Wells would draw a lot of attention."

"You're wrong, Sophy."

The edge on the words startled her. She looked at him and saw that his amber eyes looked a lot more feral than usual.

"What do you mean?" she said.

"If anything happened to you or Bea or your sister, the Wells family would come looking for answers."

A shivery chill whispered through her. "Because of the pact."

"The pact is what connected the families back at the start, but now it's personal."

She wasn't sure how to interpret that statement. Maybe she was afraid to read too much into it. Regardless, they were in this together.

She looked around, taking in the brightly lit scene. "How do we even begin to search this place? It's not like we're the police or the FBI. We can't get search warrants and go door-to-door."

"We don't need search warrants. Let's go back to the inn. I want to take a closer look at that silver doughnut."

"I thought we were supposed to be doing recon."

"We've done enough for now."

"All right."

They turned and walked toward the warmly lit windows of the inn.

"I've been thinking about that installation in the gallery tonight," she said after a moment. "Maybe it wasn't the *Mona Lisa* or Botticelli's *The Birth of Venus*, but was it that bad?"

"What are we talking about? I need a hint."

"*Succubus.* Do I look like a creature from a horror movie when I come out of a trance?"

"Vincent Grant is an unstable, obsessive psychopath. Why are you taking his work personally?"

"Because it is a very personal work of art. It was *me*, Luke. Right down to my chimes and . . . and my eyes. Don't try to deny it."

"I can't believe we're arguing about this."

"Neither can I."

"You want an opinion on that damn sculpture? How's this? By invoking the ancient myth of the succubus, the artist attempted to convey a sense of female power, mystery, and sexuality while also acknowledging the ancient tensions between the sexes. The use of the chimes is of particular significance. It brings ambivalence to the scene, implying the potential for harmony as well as discord."

She stared at him for a moment and then she could no longer contain the laughter. It bubbled up and spilled into the night. Aware that two people passing by on the path were looking at her, she clapped a hand over her mouth until she regained control.

"I am impressed with your insightful analysis," she said.

"Thanks."

"No wonder your family wants you to be the next CEO of Wells, Inc. You're pretty good when it comes to thinking on your feet."

TWENTY-FIVE

SOPHY SAT ON THE WHITE VELVET HASSOCK, BRUCE AT HER FEET. TOGETHER THEY watched Luke use the flat tip of a tiny screwdriver to pry the mirror-finish tile from the inside of the silver doughnut.

"Got it," he said.

He handed the screwdriver back to her. She slipped it into the miniature tool kit that he had produced from his duffel bag.

Of course he carried a miniature tool kit, she thought, amused. Whatever else you could say about the Wells family—and there was a *lot* that could be said, according to Bea—a talent for engineering was in their DNA.

"Well?" she prompted. "What is it? Some kind of paranormal recording device?"

Luke held the small tile in both hands, examining it intently. "I don't know. I've never seen anything like it."

He set the tile down on top of the pedestal and leaned into the doughnut hole to take another look. "Here we go. This is much more familiar."

He reached into the sculpture and removed a small object.

When he turned around she saw the palm-sized crystal in his hand. The stone was a dark sapphire blue and shaped like a pyramid.

"There's energy in this crystal," he said. "Even I can sense it."

Sophy remembered the ghostly shadows of Bea and Deke moving around the pedestal. Somewhere out on the psychic plane she heard the pure, clean notes of invisible chimes.

She held out her hand. "Let me see that."

Without a word, Luke gave her the pyramid. He watched as she closed her fingers around it and opened her senses.

She flinched in surprise when she caught the intense vibe.

"You're right," she said, "there's energy inside. But it's locked."

"That's interesting. The question is, why would someone lock it?"

Sophy smiled, feeling rather smug, in spite of the gravity of the situation. "It wasn't locked by the bad guys. This is Aunt Bea's signature."

Luke's eyes sharpened. "What are you talking about?"

"My aunt is very good with crystals. She can tune them and lock the energy inside—at least until someone like me comes along."

"Are you telling me you can unlock that crystal?"

"I can neutralize the currents of the lock, which amounts to the same thing. Just a little light housekeeping."

Luke's eyes tightened at the corners. "Got to admit, I'm impressed."

"I'm delighted, of course, but I would appreciate it if you didn't mention that *extremely confidential, private, and personal information* to the Foundation people. They would probably jump to some awkward conclusions."

"I'm hurt that you think I would even consider conveying gossip to the Foundation. Would you please unlock that damn crystal?"

"Yep."

She focused on the currents that locked the crystal, intuitively searching for the anchor.

"Got it," she said. "Bea didn't try for complicated. She must have wanted the stone unlocked as soon as it was discovered. That implies she knew, or maybe she hoped, that I would be around when it was found."

"Yes it does," Luke said. "And she was right."

The currents that had been locked in stasis inside the pyramid began to oscillate. The crystal glowed faintly in her palm.

"Uh-oh," she said. "I'm not sure where this is going."

The life-sized figure of a rugged-looking man in his late forties or early fifties sprang up in the middle of the room. Sophy gave a shriek of surprise and bolted to her feet.

The figure bounced around the space as if it was the beam of a flashlight.

Bruce yipped, scrambled out of the way, and gave Sophy a reproachful look.

"Sorry," she said. She patted him gently. "Didn't mean to step on your toes." She held the crystal steady. The figure stopped moving. "What in the world?"

"It's a paranormal hologram," Luke said. He shook his head in admiration. "I knew Deke was working with some old cameras that he was sure were Bluestone tech. Looks like he figured out how to take a photograph and lock it in that crystal. When you unlocked the crystal it was like flipping a switch."

"That person who is now hovering a foot off the floor is your uncle?"

"Meet Deke Wells."

"Hmm."

The man in the holographic image was about Bea's age. He was lean and fit. His dark hair, streaked with silver, was swept back from a peak on his forehead and fell to the collar of his khaki shirt. Faded jeans and low boots completed the outfit. Something about his eyes reminded her of Luke.

In the hologram he held up a sheet of yellow notebook paper in one hand. There was a message written in ink. Luke moved closer to read it aloud.

Luke, if you're reading this, I fucked up. Not sure what Hatch is doing here in this so-called art colony but I think it involves those old Kaleidoscope weapons. Hatch has a talent for photonics and I remember Granddad saying the guns were designed to fire lethal light waves. Got to be a connection.

The more immediate problem is that the para-rad levels here in the compound are climbing. The high-tech lighting scattered around the grounds is masking most of the heat, but Bea says not for much longer. She thinks the place is a tinderbox. I agree.

A lot of the energy is natural—this canyon is a true vortex—but there's more to it. The epicenter is the gallery. Bea and I are going to take a look inside later tonight. If you're here because we disappeared, don't waste time looking for us. The priority is to find the source of the instability, get the hell out of the canyon, and call in the Foundation. It's the only outfit that can handle this mess.

One more thing—after you fix this problem, stop blaming yourself for what happened six months ago. You made a mistake. You handled the fallout. Now get over it and get to work. The family needs you. So does the company. There are a lot of people depending on you.

TWENTY-SIX

SOPHY DID SOMETHING TO THE CRYSTAL. THE HOLOGRAM WINKED OUT.

Luke contemplated the empty space where the ghostly image of Deke had been a few seconds earlier, silently running the new data points. After a couple of minutes he realized that Sophy had not spoken. He looked at her. She was sitting on the hassock, stroking Bruce, who had his head on her knee. Her eyes glistened with unshed tears.

"What is it?" he said, unsure how to handle the situation. "Are you okay?" Stupid question. She was not okay.

"They're both gone, aren't they?" she said, sounding numb. "Hatch and his gang murdered them. We're too late."

He tried to think of a way to soften the obvious conclusion, but inspiration did not strike. "It's possible."

She closed her eyes. Tears slid down her cheeks. Some of them landed on Bruce's head. He pushed more heavily against her. For a beat Luke stood very still. He wanted to take her in his arms but he was not sure if she would welcome comfort from him. Hell, maybe she blamed him and the entire Wells family for putting Bea in harm's way.

Feeling helpless, he grabbed some tissues off the dressing table and thrust them into Sophy's fingers. Without a word she gave him the pyramid crystal and took the offering and blotted her eyes.

"Sorry," she mumbled. "I realize you lost your uncle, too. Your poor grandparents. They've lost a son. I can't imagine—"

He gave up trying to resist the impulse to hold her. He set the crystal on the table and reached down to grip her shoulders. She did not try to draw back when he pulled her close. Instead, she sobbed into the fabric of his shirt.

For a timeless moment he held her, and while he did, he found himself contemplating a couple of dots out on the psychic plane.

"You—we—should not leap to conclusions," he said finally.

Sophy sniffed and raised her head. There were teardrops on the lenses of her glasses but hope sparked in her eyes.

"What do you mean?" she asked.

"Nothing has changed as far as the data is concerned. We just have more information now. Yes, it's possible Bea and Deke didn't make it out of the compound alive. But this is Deke Wells, action hero of the Agency, and Bea Harper, a woman with a talent for channeling crystals. They are smart people and they knew they were surrounded by danger. They would have had a backup plan."

"They did. They left clues for us. We are their backup plan."

"I'm not saying they're alive, just that we can't rule out that possibility. Deke has a talent for disappearing, and if he did go off the grid, he would have taken Bea with him. For whatever reason, they handed the assignment to us, and Deke made it clear we're on a tight timeline."

"You're right—we have a mission." Sophy sniffed, angled her

chin in a determined way and took a step back. "We have to find the source of the unstable energy in the area and call in the Foundation."

"There's nothing more we can do tonight. It's been a long day. We both need sleep."

She glanced around. "Maybe we should take shifts so that one of us can stand guard at all times."

"No need. We've got Bruce."

Bruce's ears twitched at the sound of his name.

Sophy smiled a little. "We do, indeed."

"We've also got the latest in Wells, Inc. security tech," Luke said. Relieved that she was no longer crying and hoping like hell that he had not given her false assurances, he went to his duffel and took out two small devices. "One for the balcony door and one for the front door. If anyone tries to open either, an alarm will sound and they'll get a stiff jolt of electricity."

"Good to know," Sophy said. She looked weary but committed.

He contemplated the bed. They were two adults. A few pillows down the center would ensure they did not accidentally come in contact with each other during the night.

Unfortunately.

"Do you mind if I ask why your uncle thinks you're reluctant to take control of Wells, Inc.?" Sophy asked.

The question caught him off guard. He had been focused on the sleeping arrangements. It took him a beat to recalculate.

"It's a long story."

She held up a hand, palm out. "Never mind. It's none of my business."

"It's okay."

He lowered himself into a chair, leaned forward, braced his forearms on his thighs, and loosely linked his fingers. He took another moment to think about what he was going to say. For the first time since the disaster he wanted to talk to someone. No, not someone—Sophy.

"I come from a long line of psychically talented physicists, engineers, and inventors. But I didn't get that kind of ability. That's why I was chosen to become the next CEO of the company."

"I, uh, have heard that rumor. It seems odd, though."

He smiled wryly. "No one with a lot of engineering talent wants the job and the family doesn't want to turn it over to someone who isn't a Wells. That leaves me."

"But you do have a talent."

"I can see some light from beyond the spectrum. That gives me good night vision but that's about it. They call me No-Talent Wells for a reason."

She frowned. "You said you were good when it came to connecting dots."

"I am, but that's hardly a psychic-grade talent."

"Says who? No one knows where the line between intuition and psychic talent is."

"It's just the way my brain works."

She tilted her head slightly and narrowed her eyes. "What about your ability to manipulate someone's aura the way you did mine when I came out of that vision trance at the cabin?"

"The situation with you was . . . unique."

"Seriously?"

"I was acting on the old principle that two auras are stronger than one. I didn't expect the resonance thing. That was a shock."

"A shock?" she asked a little too politely.

He'd screwed up. Again. "A surprise. A *good* surprise. It's just that I've never had that happen before, so I was—"

He decided to stop before the hole he was digging for himself got any deeper.

Her smile was as cool and polished as the silvery sculpture on the pedestal.

"You were shocked," she concluded.

He looked at her.

She waved one hand. "Forget it. If it helps, I was just as shocked as you were."

"Okay. Yes, that helps."

Not really, he decided. It didn't help at all, because she was making it clear she was blowing off the resonance incident. He was not going to be able to pretend that it wasn't important. He had a feeling he was doomed to dream about it for the rest of his life.

"I think you are underestimating the value of your ability to connect dots," she said.

"I told you, the problem with that skill set is that sometimes you convince yourself you can see connections that don't actually exist."

"I understand. I'm the one who wonders if she's seeing ghosts, remember?"

He frowned, trying to parse the distinction. It wasn't the same thing. Was it?

"Call me psychic," she continued briskly, "but I sense that at some point in the recent past there was an unfortunate incident related to dot connecting."

"Something like that."

"It shook your faith in yourself. In your judgment. Who was she?"

He straightened and sat back in the chair. "How did you know there was a woman involved?"

"The guilt trip you've put yourself through combined with the fact that you've concluded you're no longer the right person to take control of Wells, Inc. It doesn't take any psychic talent to figure out that the source of the problem is a relationship gone bad."

"Her name was Victoria. Victoria Ellsworth. She worked in the company library. Everyone liked her. She was smart, gracious, helpful."

"Pretty?"

"Very," he admitted.

"Professionally dressed at all times? Neat little suit. Pumps. Serious glasses. Hair in a bun?"

He frowned. "How did you know?"

"Red hair or blond?"

"Red. What is this?"

"I assume she was creative in bed?"

The rush of heat to his face alarmed him. "What the hell?"

"I'm just looking for connections between dots. You know how that works."

"Look somewhere else, damn it."

"Relax. It's clear what happened. You fell for the secretly sexy librarian fantasy."

"What?"

"It's a staple. Sweet, innocent librarian takes off her serious glasses, lets down her hair, and transforms into a passionate sex kitten who tells you that you are a sex god. It's not as popular as the nurse and dominatrix fantasies, but it's a standard."

"This conversation has gone off the rails." He gripped the arms of the chair and started to push himself to his feet. "I'm going to bed."

"Never mind." Sophy flapped a hand in a sit-down gesture. "Get to the good part of the story. You two had an affair?"

To his amazement, he sat down. Or maybe he dropped back into the chair. Hard to tell the difference.

"We were sleeping together," he said. "Not that it's any of your business."

"Hey, we're partners. You met one of my exes and you know I've got another who is a stalker. Seems only fair I hear more about Victoria." She frowned in disapproval. "I assume there are no rules against fraternization between management and employees at Wells, Inc.?"

"I wasn't working for the company at the time, so technically it wasn't an issue."

"You were still employed at that agency your grandmother mentioned?"

"Yes, but that's not important. What matters is that I was wrong about Victoria and I still don't know how or why I didn't see the truth until it was almost too late."

"What happened?"

"I got back from closing an Agency case and I was in a mood to celebrate. We had dinner at her place and spent the night together. Toward morning, I woke up from a dream."

"A dream?"

She sounded surprised. As if he wasn't a normal man. Maybe he wasn't a normal Wells, but that didn't mean he wasn't human.

"I dream just like everybody else," he said. *Sort of,* he added silently.

"No need to get mad. I wasn't criticizing. Tell me about your dream."

He should stop talking, he thought. But for some inexplicable reason he kept going.

"I was walking through a hall of mirrors and Victoria kept appearing in the looking glasses. But her image was blurry. I knew it was her but I couldn't make out her features. Every time I tried to focus on her reflection she disappeared and moved on to the next mirror."

"Hmm." Sophy tapped one finger on the hassock, evidently pondering what he had said. "In your dream did you try to talk to her?"

"I asked her why I could not see her clearly. She said, '*Because you don't know who I am.*'"

"And?"

"And I woke up because I knew the answer to my question. My intuition was trying to tell me that I had only seen her reflection, not the real person. I finally started asking the questions I should have asked all along. I talked to the Boss and told him I'd really screwed up. He launched an internal investigation. Turned out Victoria was a freelance industrial espionage thief who specialized in paranormal tech. She was after some of our black box R and D secrets."

Sophy's eyes widened. "There's a market for that kind of stuff?"

"It's a small one, but there's a lot of money sloshing around in it. Most people think the interest in paranormal research went out of fashion in the twentieth century, but you'd be surprised to find out who is still involved in that kind of work. A couple of small government agencies, a few billionaires like Trent Hatch, the odd mad scientist, and some low-profile organizations of people who actually do possess psychic talents, like the Arcane Society and the Foundation."

"I've never heard of the Arcane Society. Never mind. Was Victoria arrested?"

"No. She vanished as soon as she realized her cover was blown."

Sophy watched him for a moment. "Did you ever *want* the job of running Wells, Inc.?"

"Up until the Victoria episode I did. You could say I've been training for it all my life. For the past year I've been working on a strategy for taking the company into the next decade. Until now we've focused on government contracts. We need to expand into the consumer market. Regular people need better private security options in this age of relentless online fraud. And then there's the small-scale corporate security market. We've ignored it for too long."

"You were set to move Wells, Inc. forward into the future and then, wham, you were run down by a failed experiment. Trust me, I understand. That first disaster shakes you. Makes you question your judgment. It's also downright embarrassing."

"A failed experiment? Now what are you talking about?"

"The way I see it, your problem is that your first serious failed experiment happened relatively late in life. No wonder it threw you. My first took place back in college, and I had the advantage of Bea's advice and guidance afterward, so I was able to process the whole sorry mess. But it sounds like you went merrily along without any major setbacks until the unfortunate incident with a librarian gone rogue."

He was starting to know how it felt to be a deer caught in the headlights.

"Rogue?"

"It happens," Sophy said. "Not often, thank goodness, but once in a while an otherwise excellent librarian goes bad. It's always a shock. I don't blame you for being caught off guard. Speaking as a proud member of the profession, I am well aware that society expects sterling behavior from librarians. The bar is set very high."

He stared at her, fascinated. "I've never thought about it."

"Exactly. That's because we take librarians for granted. They are expected to stand strong in the face of censorship, intimidation, and threats. Their mission is to maintain balanced collections and put credible information into the hands of their patrons. Furthermore, they are obligated to make sure that everyone in their communities has access to that information. Without libraries there is no democracy. And libraries are nothing without dedicated librarians."

He did not know whether to be amused, confused, or simply floored.

"I can see you take your profession seriously," he said, trying for a politely neutral comment.

"Absolutely." She paused, eyes tightening a little. "Every librarian I know takes it seriously. Which makes me wonder if Victoria Ellsworth lied about her career path along with everything else."

"I'm not sure where to go with that. As usual, I have no idea what happened to the logic in this conversation."

"Never mind. I was just thinking out loud. But to return to the main topic, my advice to you is the same as the advice your uncle gave you. Stop kicking yourself for the screwup. Deke was right. Mistakes get made. Once you realized what had happened you did everything you could to repair the damage. It may have been a close call, but obviously the company survived just fine. Now I'm going to get ready to go to bed." She gave Bruce one last pat and stood. "First claim on that magnificent bath. I'll be in there awhile, so I'm tasking you with the job of figuring out the bed arrangements."

She started across the room.

"Sophy?" he said.

She stopped at the door of the spa-like bath and looked back. "What?"

"I might be able to deal with my failed experiment, as you call it, if I understood why I didn't see the disaster coming until it was almost too late. I'm not an exotic, high-end talent but I'm good at connecting dots. Why did I miss all the signals?"

She gave him a long, considering look. "Aside from the primal appeal of the secretly sexy librarian fantasy?"

"Aside from that," he said, trying not to grind his teeth.

"Well, I can't be absolutely positive—my aunt is the expert when it comes to identifying exotic talents—but have you considered the possibility that your rogue librarian was a reflection talent?"

She might as well have hurled a bolt of lightning at him. For a moment he was dumbstruck.

"Well, shit," he finally managed.

"They make very successful con artists because they figure out what you want and then make you think they can fulfill your deepest desires. All they have to do is say the right words. Their auras do the real work. Add to that the element of sexual attraction and it's hard to resist someone with that kind of psychic ability."

He shoved his fingers through his hair and shook his head. Disgusted. "I never considered that possibility."

She smiled benignly. "Perfectly understandable. You were looking for love, not trouble. Afterward you were too busy blaming yourself for your poor judgment to do a routine failure analysis." She disappeared into the bath. "Don't forget to fix up the bed."

The door closed.

Bruce padded across the room and rested his head on one of Luke's legs.

"You heard the lady," Luke said. "We need to engineer the bed."

TWENTY-SEVEN

SOPHY EVENTUALLY EMERGED FROM THE BATH. HER HAIR WAS LOOSE AROUND HER shoulders, her face was scrubbed of all makeup, and she was swathed neck-to-ankle in a fluffy white robe emblazoned with the inn's logo.

It struck him that she looked adorable—soft and warm and incredibly sexy.

She considered the bed with a judicious air, taking in the neatly arranged row of pillows that formed a barrier straight down the middle.

"Excellent," she said. "That will work."

She didn't have to sound so enthusiastic, he thought.

He retreated to the bathroom and came out wearing one of the robes and was relieved to see that the lights were off. Sophy was snugged up under the covers. Maybe she wouldn't notice him climbing into bed beside her wearing only his briefs and a T-shirt. In hindsight, it was clear he should have bought some pajamas before the long drive to the art colony, but they had been in a hurry and it had never crossed his mind.

When he was settled on his side of the massive bed he folded his arms behind his head and gazed up at the shadowed ceiling. Connecting a few dots.

"We need to get up very early in the morning," he announced.

"Why?" Sophy mumbled into the pillow.

"I want to check out the natural radiation levels in the area at sunrise. To do that, it will be necessary to get as far away as possible from the lights here in the compound. They are on night and day."

There was a short silence from the other side of the pillow barrier.

"Why do we have to check out the rad levels at dawn?" she asked.

"I want to see if the natural currents feel unstable or if the problem is just in the center of the compound. There are times during the twenty-four-hour solar cycle when paranormal currents oscillate in a way that allows for observations of stability. The transition from night to day is one of them."

"I didn't know that. Interesting. Good night, Luke."

"Good night, Sophy."

It was, he thought, going to be a long time until dawn. He turned onto his side and saw Bruce curled up on the carpet next to the bed. Aware that he was being watched, the dog raised his head and opened his molten gold eyes in an inquiring expression.

"No, you can't sleep on the bed tonight," Luke said softly. "There's no room."

"What?" Sophy said, her voice muffled by the pillow.

"Nothing. I was just informing Bruce that he's sleeping on the floor tonight."

"Mmm."

Sophy went silent again.

Luke switched his attention to the doughnut sculpture, going over the message Deke had held up in the hologram.

Deke was one of the Agency's most successful agents, a true professional. That meant that every word he had written on the lined yellow paper was important. So much to ponder.

But the handwritten warning was not the last thing he thought about before drifting off the sleep. Instead, he contemplated the concept of failed experiments. It was not an unfamiliar notion. After all, he came from a family of engineers. Failure analysis was embedded deep into the culture of Wells, Inc. But he had never considered using the technique to examine a relationship disaster. Until now.

There were, he thought, a lot of things he had not contemplated before meeting Sophy. He had a feeling that, going forward, his life would be divided into the pre-Sophy era and the post-Sophy era.

He did not want to think about a post-Sophy time.

TWENTY-EIGHT

Meanwhile, in the underground safe room . . .

"WE SHOULD HAVE MARRIED FIVE YEARS AGO," DEKE SAID.

"It would not have worked out well for either of us." Bea walked across the floor of the cave and sat down on a chair-sized boulder at the edge of the narrow, crystal clear underground river. "You were still blaming yourself for Irene's death and you were still hooked on the adrenaline rush you got from your Agency assignments."

The cave was a prepper's dream home, she thought. The use-by dates on the MREs and canned goods were far into the future, so she and Deke assumed the previous owner was the one who had discovered the old safe room and stocked it. Theoretically, thanks to the food and the endless supply of fresh water, she and Deke could survive for months or even years, depending on how long it took them to go mad from the effects of living in a cave. Probably weeks, at most.

But they did not have weeks or months, let alone years. They had a couple of days, if that. The disaster, when it happened, would devastate the entire compound and bury the secrets hidden under it. Their safe room was also their prison. If Sophy and Luke Wells did not find them and free them, it would become their crypt.

"When I think of all the time we wasted—" Deke shook his head. "I was an idiot."

"I believe I mentioned that a few times."

He groaned. "You told me to get therapy. I should have listened."

"I was wrong. If you had talked to a therapist you would have had to explain what really happened that day in Gilmartin's house. You could not take that risk. Even if you had been in a position to talk to a professional, I'm not sure you would have been open to change."

"So I talked to you instead."

"I'll keep your secrets," she said.

"I know."

"You needed time to accept that you were not responsible for what happened to Irene. She cheated on you. She had an affair with a very dangerous man who used her to get access to those files. When he had what he wanted, he killed her. She's the one who made the poor decisions, not you."

She did not add the rest out loud, but they both knew what she had left unsaid. Joel Gilmartin had been in his mansion on his private island, protected by state-of-the-art security and armed guards, when Deke had tracked him down. The two men had confronted each other in Gilmartin's study. Deke had walked out alive. Gilmartin had died at his desk. Natural causes, according to the authorities. No one had seen Deke arrive and no one had seen him leave.

He'd had his revenge, she thought, but it had exacted a heavy psychic toll.

"I didn't really come to terms with things until I realized that

Luke was going down a similar road," Deke said. "That shook me. Gave me a different perspective."

"He'll either accept that he will make mistakes and learn to deal with those mistakes or he won't," Bea said. "And if he doesn't learn, then he isn't qualified to become the next CEO of Wells, Inc."

Deke snorted. "That would be really bad news for the family, because we don't have a backup. The Boss says we're going to need a very special kind of talent to take the company into the future."

"What kind of talent?"

"Whatever it is that Luke's got, according to the Boss. No one knows how he does what he does. It's a little scary, to tell you the truth." Deke glanced at his mechanical watch and pushed himself to his feet. "I'm hungry. How about you?"

"Can't wait," she said. "I'm starving."

Deke contemplated the MREs stacked on the racks. "Chef's choice tonight is chicken and noodles or tuna and noodles."

"Are we out of the cheese tortellini?"

"No, but I've decided to ration it because you've been eating it for breakfast as well as dinner."

"I can't help it if I happen to like cheese tortellini."

"You need more protein."

"I'll take the tuna and noodles. Don't forget the extra veggies. MREs are not known for their fiber content."

He selected two MRE kits and moved to the rack of canned goods. "Green beans or asparagus?"

"Asparagus. I'm tired of green beans."

"Aren't we all?"

He added the asparagus to his collection and joined her at the edge of the underground river.

She watched him open the pop-top can. He moved with a masculine grace and coordination that made everything he did look easy. But under the surface things got complicated, because he never went easy on himself.

"I would like to clarify one point," she said. "The past five years were not entirely wasted, at least not as far as I'm concerned. The ten days we spent in that little Mediterranean village were incredible. And I loved the South Pacific cruise. I'll never forget the week in that hotel in the Alps. We hardly left the room."

"Fair point. We've had some good times. But I want the regular, routine things of life. I want to go to bed with you every night and wake up with you every morning. Eat breakfast together. I want evenings in front of the fire. I want to hear about your weird clients."

"That sounds lovely, but we both know you need a job."

He opened one of the boxes of MREs. "I'll figure it out. I want a normal life."

"Neither of us is normal," she said. "Actually, I don't think anyone qualifies as normal, but that's another conversation. I repeat, now that you're retired, you need to find something that amounts to more than a hobby. As it happens, I've been thinking about that. I have an idea."

"Yeah?" He opened the heater bag and slipped the packet of tuna and noodles inside. "What's that?"

"It has occurred to me that my consulting business could use the services of a talent who knows how to take photographs that can pick up paranormal radiation."

"Huh." Deke dipped his hand into the river, scooped up a palmful of water, and dumped it into the bag. "You're talking about me going to work for you?"

"It's just an idea."

He smiled. "I like it." He folded the top of the heater bag and slid the bag back into the cardboard box. "I like it a lot."

He propped the box against a nearby chunk of stone to let the meal heat and went to work on the second MRE.

She smiled. For the first time in the five years they had known each other she could see a future with Deke Wells. Assuming they survived.

TWENTY-NINE

SOPHY HAD NOT EXPECTED TO SLEEP WELL, BUT SHE AWOKE SHORTLY BEFORE DAWN, aware that she'd had a surprisingly good night's rest. She could get accustomed to satin sheets and luxurious comforters, she thought. But she refused to make rising before dawn a habit.

Belatedly she became aware of the weight of a warm, heavy body lying next to her. Shocked, she went very still.

True, the body was on top of the quilt, not under the covers; nevertheless, Luke had no business being this close and in such an intimate position. So much for the pillow barrier. She should be outraged, and she was. Definitely outraged. She would protest the invasion of her personal space, but maybe she could pretend to ignore it for a few more minutes.

"The shower is all yours," Luke said.

His voice came from the far end of the bed, not next to her. Startled, she opened her eyes and saw him. He was on his feet and in the process of clipping the auto-injector case onto his belt. His hair was damp from the shower and he looked, she thought, extremely fetching.

But if his wasn't the warm body next to her, that left only one other suspect.

She turned her head and gazed into Bruce's deceptively innocent eyes.

"You," she said.

He tried to lick her face. She gave him her hand instead.

"You're not fooling me," she said. "That's not a real kiss. I know what you want. Breakfast. Go talk to the guy who controls your rations."

Evidently concluding there was no point pleading his case, Bruce got to his feet, bounded off the bed, and greeted Luke, who leaned down to rub his ears.

Sophy started to push aside the covers and then paused, flushing. "Excuse me," she said, putting a little ice into the words.

Luke looked up, surprised. "What?"

"I would like some privacy, if you don't mind."

It evidently occurred to him that he was standing at the foot of the bed staring at her. "Sorry." He turned and went to the balcony windows. He gazed intently into the predawn darkness. "Make it quick. The sun will be up soon."

"I'll hurry."

She got up and rushed to the bathroom.

She was out in what she considered record-breaking time, dressed in jeans, a white T-shirt, and bright white sneakers. Luke was in his well-worn leather jacket and scarred boots. Bruce wore a leather vest studded with clips and a couple of pockets.

"I'm ready," she announced, taking her trench coat out of the closet.

Luke tossed her a soft fabric bag that had some straps dangling from it. "You'll need that."

She examined the bag. "It looks like a day pack."

"It is," he said.

"Are we collecting rocks or something?"

"No, this is the desert, remember?" He selected a bottle from the carton he had brought up from the SUV. "You never leave home without water."

"It's just a short walk to the far side of the compound, right? A bottle of water is heavy."

"That's why everyone, including Bruce, carries their own."

THIRTY

"I MAY HAVE NEGLECTED TO MENTION THIS," SOPHY SAID, "BUT I'M NOT WHAT you'd call an outdoorsy person. For example, I don't go camping, and I never take long hikes while carrying a hundred pounds of bottled water on my back. This forced march had better be worth it."

"You are very hard to please," Luke said. "Here I am, giving you a scenic tour of a stunning landscape that is said to be a true natural vortex, and what do I get in the way of thanks? A lot of whining."

"I happen to be very good at whining. You could say it's a talent." She stopped to catch her breath and adjust the straps of the pack. "Are we there yet?"

Luke halted beside her. "This is far enough. We're almost a half mile out of range of the artificial lights in the compound."

She turned to view the scene below. For the last quarter mile or so they had been hiking up a small but steady incline. They were now at the far northern edge of the valley, close to one of the canyon walls. The sky was illuminating rapidly, but the sun was not yet visible. The red rock cliffs were still shadowed with the remnants of night.

She stilled and cautiously heightened her senses. At first she heard only a few birds greeting the predawn light. But in the next moment she was aware of the deep chords of an ancient music.

The currents that stirred her senses would never be mistaken for human-generated energy. She knew she was listening to the beating heart and the lungs of the earth itself. Currents of power strong enough to generate earthquakes, cause volcanoes to erupt, and control the tides that oscillated just beneath the surface. That same power made it possible for life to thrive in the deepest ocean trenches and on the highest mountain peaks. It thrilled and chilled, leaving her awash in wonder and awe.

"Oh, my," she said in hushed tones. "Do you feel that?"

"You don't need any talent to pick up that kind of energy," Luke said.

"This really is a vortex site."

"No doubt about it," Luke said. "Which makes Hatch's efforts to mask the background vibe even more interesting. Why bother if the whole point of establishing an art colony on the site was to use the energy to inspire artists?"

She glanced at him and saw that he was studying the compound in the distance with rapt attention. Focused. Probably connecting dots, she thought.

Bruce had been investigating the scents around a nearby rock. He lost interest, sat down, and yawned.

"Looks like the only one who isn't impressed with the vortex energy is your pal," Sophy said.

Luke took his attention off the compound long enough to glance at Bruce. "Maybe that's because animals have a closer relationship with the natural world. They don't try to control it. They accept it and live with it."

"That's a very philosophical insight."

"For a CIA assassin? Thanks. I'm taking an online class in philosophy."

"If you keep throwing that CIA thing in my face I may be forced to hire my very own hit man."

"Noted." Luke turned to examine the canyon wall. "There it is. I knew there had to be one."

"One what?" she asked.

"A perimeter fence. I told you, the art colony is a fortress. It is only logical that Hatch would control all access points."

She swung around. "I don't see a fence . . . Oh. Right."

The barrier was little more than a nearly invisible wire strung along the canyon wall.

"Not much of a fence," she said. "Think it's electrified?"

"No, but if you go beyond it you should assume alarms will be triggered somewhere back in the compound. You can bet some of Hatch's people will be out to investigate before you get very far."

"Are we going to set off the alarms?"

"No. What we're looking for is back in the compound, not out here."

"Understood." She paused, hearkening once more to the beat of the planet. "The vibe does explain why people have been drawn to this place over the years. And probably why they don't hang around. Energy like this is exhilarating for a while but it's also disturbing. I'm sure that over time it would affect the senses."

"How?"

"I don't know," she admitted. "Maybe it would cause anxiety. Insomnia. Restlessness. The vibe in these canyons is just too powerful for humans to tolerate for an extended period of time. People might not be aware of it on the conscious level, but deep down they couldn't help but react to it."

"Hatch is aware of it. That's why he's using all the high-tech lighting to mask the vortex energy. There's only one reason why he would blow a fortune on a third-rate art colony staffed with teenagers and retirees."

"He needs the vortex energy for whatever he's working on, doesn't he?"

"Yes, and that is not good news. The connection is the weapon—Kaleidoscope—not art."

"What about the hypnotic suggestion tiles?"

"I'm not sure where they fit in yet."

She adjusted her glasses. "We know the Kaleidoscope program got its name because the weapons were constructed with mirrors and crystals."

"You're thinking of those polished tiles."

"Yes. They look a lot like mirrors." She paused. "There was a crystal behind the one in the doughnut sculpture."

"I know." Luke turned back to watch the morning sun top the canyon walls and flood the valley. "This answers one question—the natural energy currents in the area feel stable. The instability we sensed in the art colony is localized."

"Do you really think Hatch is trying to build some new Kaleidoscopes?"

"More likely they are trying to scale up the basic concept and make a much more powerful version of the guns."

"But according to your grandfather that wouldn't be possible without the six crystals—" Sophy broke off, shocked by her own words. "Wait. Do you think that Hatch and his pals have Pandora's box?"

"It would explain why Bea went missing. Anyone trying to use those crystals would need a strong talent from the Harper bloodline to unlock them."

The terrible irony of the situation struck her like an ice bath.

She clapped a hand over her mouth because she did not know whether or laugh or cry.

"Oh, shit," she got out. "I don't believe it. I mean, I do believe it, but this whole thing is unbelievably screwed up."

"What am I missing?" Luke asked.

She managed to pull herself together. "You're right, if they have Pandora's box it explains why they went after Bea. But they must have been downright thrilled when I showed up."

"Why?"

"Bea is a Harper in every way that matters, but not by blood. She has no DNA connection to the family. She was adopted at birth. She doesn't have the family talent required to unlock the crystals in Pandora's box."

THIRTY-ONE

"I DID NOT SEE THAT COMING," LUKE SAID. "I NEVER THOUGHT TO VERIFY THE HARPERS in the genealogical records at the Foundation. Didn't think it was necessary. Our families have always kept an eye on each other."

"You wouldn't have found anything in the official records. No one outside the family knows the truth about Bea. She's a Harper. To her and the rest of us that's all that matters. You know, if Wells, Inc. had taken stronger security measures to protect those old Kaleidoscopes and the documents, none of us would be in this mess."

"Are you going to bring this up on a regular basis?"

"Probably."

"Let's go back to the inn. You can continue the lecture on the way."

"Okay," she said. "But before we leave this place I want to try something."

"What?"

"Humans have always found ways to connect with the forces

of nature. One of the techniques is with music. I may never have another opportunity to experience vortex energy like this."

She unzipped a pocket and took out the chimes and the mallet. Luke and Bruce watched, very intent, as she went still and prepared herself. When she was ready she tapped one of the metal bars.

The clear, bell-like note went out into the world. She listened, waiting for the tone to fade. But for a time it grew stronger. The clarity became crystalline-sharp. The purity was exhilarating and almost painfully intense. There was nothing fragile or delicate about it.

The note began to resonate with the currents of the vortex. A shock of desire ignited all her senses. Luke's eyes heated. With a soul-deep groan he reached for her. In that moment she knew she had been waiting for him for a very long time. She threw herself into his arms.

His mouth came down on hers in a dark, primal kiss. Without warning they were locked in the embrace. Their need for each other could not be denied. It was elemental, vital, a force of nature.

Luke's hands were inside her trench coat and under her T-shirt, tightening around the bare skin of her waist, gliding upward to find her breasts. She slipped her hands inside his leather jacket. Her fingers brushed the small case that held his auto-injector. And then she was tugging the black pullover out of the waistband of his trousers.

He broke free of her mouth and worked his way to the curve of her throat.

"I could come just thinking about how good you feel," he rasped.

He shifted his hands to her hips and pulled her lower body tight against his fierce erection.

She flattened her palms against the muscles of his chest. "You're not afraid of me."

"You're wrong." He took the edge of her ear between his teeth and nipped lightly. "I'm afraid of losing you."

"You won't. Not today. I'm not going anywhere."

He sucked in a harsh breath, unfastened her jeans, slid one hand inside her panties, and cupped her with his palm.

"Wet," he said. "Soaking wet. For me. I need to be inside you."

"Yes. *Yes.*"

She moved against his hand, seeking more. No failed experiment had ever brought her to this level of desire. Everything inside her ached for the joining.

Somewhere a wolf howled, an ancient song that needed no words.

Not a wolf, she thought. Bruce.

She was vaguely aware that the note she had struck on the chimes was no longer resonating. It had disappeared into the dawn but she was still clinging to Luke and he was using his hand, bringing her to the edge of a very high cliff.

She went over so quickly and so intensely, she could no longer stand. She gripped his shoulders in a desperate effort to keep from falling.

"I won't let you go," he vowed.

He held her close, one finger sliding inside her as the tension in her lower body continued to release in waves.

"Yes," he said into her hair. "Just like that. But next time I'll be inside."

She half collapsed against him.

Slowly, reluctantly, he withdrew his hand and held it close to his mouth and nose. He inhaled deeply. "You make me so hungry."

Reality slammed back with the force of the fast-rising sun.

She held her breath, waiting for him to say, *My turn.* He had every right. She owed him an orgasm. She did not want to be in debt to a Wells, not for anything—especially not sex.

But he released her and absently wiped his hand on his pants. "Let's go back to the compound."

Right. He wanted to find a bed for the second act. That made sense. He probably assumed that they would be having sex on a regular basis for however long they were together.

She had to make him understand that the kiss was a mistake. It was, wasn't it?

Maybe she should apologize? *Hey, I accidentally tapped into the forces of the vortex when I fooled around with my chimes and we both got a rush* didn't sound quite right.

"I've got a plan for taking a look around the gallery tonight," Luke said.

Talk about whiplash. He was working on a plan to search the gallery while she was still trying to catch her breath and deal with the fallout of the kiss.

He had evidently decided to put the scorching embrace behind them and act as though it had never happened. That was the smart thing to do. The mature thing. The sensible thing.

It was also the logical thing to do, because the incident had been a complete aberration. Their senses had been influenced by the powerful natural forces in the vicinity. She understood that, and apparently Luke did, too. He was moving on. She needed to do the same.

They were halfway back to the compound when she could not stand the suspense any longer.

"Just to be clear," she said, "what happened back there when I made the mistake of running my little experiment with the chimes wasn't real."

"Felt real."

"Well, maybe it felt real, but it was artificially induced, if you see what I mean. For a brief time our senses were overcome by the heavy energy in the area. It could happen to anyone."

"Maybe, but it happened to us."

"You're going to be difficult about this, aren't you?"

"Just trying to take a logical view of the situation. Connecting dots."

"Don't get the wrong idea," she said. She took a deep breath and forged on. "Our relationship has not changed in any fundamental way. We hardly know each other, for heaven's sake."

"Don't worry, I'm not going to crawl over the pillow wall tonight. I just told you, I've got other plans."

It would be ridiculous to take that personally. Absolutely ridiculous. But the air suddenly went out of her sails.

She reminded herself that she was dealing with a man who knew how to focus. She needed to follow his example.

When they reached the sculpture garden she glanced briefly at the Maze Gallery. Even in the clear light of the desert morning, the windows were dark.

"I assume we're going into the gallery tonight," she said, aiming for a professional tone.

"You are not going in," Luke said. "You and Bruce will stay in the honeymoon suite while I take a look around the gallery."

"Going in alone is a bad idea. You may need backup."

"It will be easier for me to get in and out if I don't have to worry about you and Bruce. He has many talents, but as far as I know, he wasn't trained for professional-grade B and E work."

"But I am. I'm a Harper, remember? It's a truth known to every Wells that in my family we start training for illegal B and E work in the cradle."

"I've heard that," he said. "And I do admire talent of any kind. However, in this case I think you will be most useful if you remain in the suite with Bruce and make it look like I'm in there with you. Hang the privacy sign on the door. Everyone will assume we're doing interesting things in our private spa."

"Are you telling me that you are good enough to slip out of the room without anyone noticing?"

He smiled. "The first rule in the security business is figuring out how the bad guys operate. Then you come up with ways to stop them. So yes, I've learned a few tricks of the trade."

"What do we do the rest of the day?"

"We mingle. Attend the workshop lectures. Chat with the other guests. Most of all we make sure we attend the Meet the Artist event this afternoon and the aurora show in the sculpture garden this evening."

"Mingling is a good idea. It will give me an opportunity to see if I can spot Vincent Grant."

"Yes, it will. I have a few questions for him."

THIRTY-TWO

THE MEET THE ARTIST EVENT PROVED TO BE MORE INTERESTING THAN SOPHY HAD ANTICipated. Up until that point the day had been a bust as far as she was concerned. There had been no sign of Vincent Grant.

She and Luke were on their own at the event. Bruce had been left behind in the suite. He had not seemed to mind. When they left, he had been stretched out on the rug, evidently preparing to take a nap, but she was pretty sure he was planning to move to the bed as soon as they were gone.

Once she concluded that Grant was not at the Meet the Artist reception, she decided to take a closer look at the creators. Five of the six artists in residence were present. They milled around the buffet table with expressions that ranged from morose to irritated. In between downing canapés by the handful they muttered to each other and checked the time.

Sophy leaned over the small table where she and Luke sat, cups of coffee in front of them. "Artists are notoriously temperamental," she said, "but this lot looks way beyond moody. They really do not want to be here."

“The creative type isn’t always good at making nice with strangers, especially if those strangers are potential customers,” Luke observed. “We probably make them nervous.”

“True, but something tells me there’s more going on. I’ll see if I can corner one of them and do some chatting.”

Luke put down his empty coffee cup and got to his feet. “I’ll come with you.”

They made their way toward the buffet table. As they neared their objective, Sophy sized up the small herd.

“I vote we go for the young woman with the ponytail,” she said. “She looks annoyed enough to talk.”

Luke considered the artist Sophy had selected. “Works for me. You’re right. She’s definitely pissed.”

The artist’s name tag announced that she was Anna. There was no last name. She was not pleased when she realized that she had been cornered.

“Hi,” Sophy gushed. “We’re the Ainsleys. I’m so excited to talk to one of the artists responsible for the amazing light art we’ve seen here at the colony.”

Anna managed a resigned nod. “Are you going to bid on any of the pieces at the auction?”

“We’re considering it,” Luke said, reaching for a canapé. “Depends how high the bidding gets. We don’t consider ourselves experts in light art so we don’t want to get carried away and make a major investment mistake.”

“It’s never a good idea to buy art as an investment,” Anna said, clearly bored. “Buy it because it speaks to you.”

Luke looked as if he was about to argue the wisdom of that old advice but Sophy managed to plant the heel of her right shoe on the toe-end of one of his low boots before he could speak.

“You are absolutely right,” she said to Anna. “That’s what I keep telling my husband. But he comes from the business world.

To him everything is either a good investment or a bad one. I seem to recall your name on one of the pieces that was on display in the Maze Gallery last night."

For the first time, Anna brightened a tad. "*Midnight in the Vortex.*"

"I remember that one," Sophy said. "You certainly caught the vibe of this canyon. You know, I didn't believe there was such a thing as a vortex before I came here."

"This one's real—or real enough." Anna shuddered. "It gets to you after a while. It freaked me out a little when I first arrived but I thought it was my imagination. I've changed my mind. The weird vibe is getting worse by the day."

"How long have you been here?" Luke asked.

"Three weeks. I've been thinking about leaving. The problem is that under the terms of the contract we each signed, we're supposed to stay a full month. If you leave early you don't get the honorarium."

"I take it that's large enough to make artists want to stay," Luke observed.

"Oh, yeah. Ten thousand dollars. I'm going to use the money to take a trip to Europe and immerse myself in old-world art. I've had enough of light art. Turns out it's not my thing."

"I thought the local vortex was supposed to be inspirational, artistically speaking," Sophy said.

"Inspirational, my ass. I've heard that a lot of the artists haven't made it to the full month. They left without getting the big check. I didn't believe that at first but now I do."

"Hatch must be disappointed when the artists in residence don't feel like they are flourishing here," Luke said. "After all, he spent a fortune creating his new version of the old art colony."

Anna made a face. "I don't know why he bothered. It's not as if he cares about art. A while back all the artists were invited to his private quarters for a welcome reception. There wasn't a single piece of art anywhere in the house. Nothing on the walls. No sculpture. Nothing."

Sophy widened her eyes. "Then why did he go to all the trouble of building the colony?"

Anna gave an elaborate shrug. "Who knows? Rich guys are weird. Maybe the vibe in this canyon is eating his brain or something. Look, I've gotta go. We're under orders to socialize with the guests every fifteen minutes."

"I understand," Sophy said.

Anna drifted off into the small crowd. Sophy watched her for a moment.

"This place gets freakier and freakier," she said. "What's the point of paying desperate artists ten thousand dollars just to stick around for thirty days?"

"They are probably window dressing to make the place look like a real art colony. But if I'm right that a hypno talent is running experiments with the hypnotic suggestion tiles, it's possible they are test subjects like the rest of us."

She started to respond but stopped when she caught a glimpse of the figure hovering in the shadows of a doorway. "He's here."

Fury surged through her. She started toward the doorway.

THIRTY-THREE

LUKE WAS SURPRISED BY HOW FAST HE HAD TO MOVE TO CATCH UP WITH HER. HIS FINgers closed around her upper arm.

"Is that Grant?" he asked softly.

"Yes."

"You don't want to confront him, Sophy. Not here. Not now."

She stopped but he knew she hadn't done so willingly. He could feel the rage in the charged energy around her.

"Give me one good reason," she said, staring at the man in the doorway.

"I gave you one earlier. We need answers."

"Damn it to hell. He's gone."

Luke checked the doorway. Grant had vanished.

"Yes, but we now have more data," he said. Satisfied that Sophy wasn't going to do anything rash like grab a knife off the buffet table and go after Grant, he released her arm. "We know for sure he's here at the colony."

"We had already figured that out."

"We also know it's a good bet he's the sixth artist, the one who didn't show up for the meet and greet today."

"So?"

"Now I know where to look for him. He'll be staying in one of the casitas."

She frowned. "You've got a new plan, don't you?"

"I need to know more about him before I go into the gallery."

She accepted that. "How are you going to figure out which casita is Vincent's?"

"That won't be difficult. The aurora show is the big event this evening. You and I and Bruce will join the crowd in the sculpture garden to watch it. I'll disappear for a few minutes to search Grant's place. You and Bruce will be safe as long as you stay with the crowd."

"I'm not sure I like this plan," Sophy said.

"Got a better one?"

"No, unfortunately." She brightened. "I'll use the time at the event to chat with the other guests. I may be able to pick up some more information."

He got a familiar frisson on the back of his neck—the equivalent of a flashing yellow light—courtesy of his intuition. "The idea is to keep a low profile, remember?"

"Don't worry, I can be subtle."

"Really? When was the last time you tried subtlety?"

"I didn't scare Vincent to death this afternoon, did I?"

"Only because I stopped you."

She smiled her brilliant smile, the smile that made him catch his breath. "Bruce and I will be fine tonight while you play cat burglar."

The flashing yellow lights went red.

He thought he heard a faint voice saying something along the lines of *What could possibly go wrong?* but he told himself to ignore the warning. It wasn't like he was a real psychic. He just had some good night vision and he could connect dots.

THIRTY-FOUR

IT WASN'T DIFFICULT TO FIGURE OUT WHICH OF THE CASITAS WAS GRANT'S. ONE OF THE other resident artists, a moody twentysomething man named Mark, was happy to point out the small house. He did not bother to conceal his disdain for the occupant.

"The one at the end of the garden, closest to Hatch's place," he said. "The guy doesn't hang with the rest of us. He never shows up in the studio. Seems to be pals with Hatch, though."

"His *Succubus* struck me as rather cartoonish," Luke said.

Mark grunted. "It's a piece of shit."

"Think anyone will bid on it?"

"Who knows? When it comes to art you can never predict what people will buy."

"How long have you been here at the colony?"

Mark grimaced. "Nine days, five hours, and twenty minutes—not that I'm counting. I'm not going to make it to the end of the contract. Hate to ditch the ten grand but I haven't been able to sleep much for the past few days. When I do, I have nightmares. Worse yet, the vibe is interfering with my work."

"What's the vibe from?"

"The canyons," Mark said. He gestured to indicate the red rock walls around the compound. "Between you and me, I didn't believe in the vortex thing when I first arrived. All I cared about was the cash. But after a few days in this place I'm convinced there's something going on."

"Like what?" Luke asked.

"I dunno. Maybe this is one of those places we humans don't belong. You know, like an ocean trench. Okay to visit but you don't want to build a town there."

"I slept fine last night. But I'm not an artist. You're probably more sensitive to that kind of thing."

"Nah," Mark grunted. "The reason you didn't have a problem is that the hotel sits a couple of blocks away from what the rest of us call the hot zone. The casitas are a lot closer to the strongest vibes."

"Where is the worst spot in the compound?"

"That damned gallery," Mark said. "No question. The guests never seem to notice it much but they aren't here for more than a few days. Also, I'm starting to think that all the high-tech lights in the area dampen the freaky sensations."

"An interesting theory."

"What do I know? I'm an artist, not an engineer."

"Like Hatch?"

"Give me a break. Hatch is supposed to be some kind of genius when it comes to lights, but between you and me, he doesn't know fuck about art."

"I see. Thanks for the information. I'd better get going. My wife wanted me to find Grant."

"Don't tell me she's thinking of buying that *Succubus*."

"No, she studies mythology. She wants to ask Grant what inspired him to create the installation. I told her I'd try to track him down and see if he'll agree to sit for an interview."

"Good luck, but I'm pretty sure the inspiration was a bad horror movie." Mark started to turn away, but he paused long enough to give Luke a head-to-toe look. "I like the leather jacket. Are you into motorcycles?"

"No, they make me nervous. I'm risk averse."

THIRTY-FIVE

HE USED THE WELLS JAMMER TO OPEN THE BACK DOOR OF THE SMALL RESIDENCE. ONCE inside he paused for a moment, absorbing the atmosphere. He could feel the ominous pulse of the vortex energy all the way to his bones. Mark was right. The casitas were sitting close to the hot zone. With the lights turned off inside Grant's place and the shades closed, the vibe was very noticeable.

He heightened his senses. His night vision kicked in. The small space was now illuminated in colors that emanated from the far end of the spectrum, shades for which there were no names. He thought of them as ultra colors—ultraviolet, ultragreen, ultrablue.

He went about a fast, methodical search.

The closet was crammed with shirts, jeans, and a tux—all in black. What was it with artists and black clothes? Then he thought about his own closet. Okay, it wasn't *entirely* filled with black, but there was a hell of a lot of it. Maybe he should get an aloha shirt.

He shut the closet door and continued the search, moving quickly. He was beginning to think he was going to come up empty when he found the collection of sketchbooks under the bed.

The books were dated. He opened the first one and flipped through it. He was the first to admit he didn't know much about art, but it seemed to him that Grant had some genuine artistic ability and an eye for revealing the unexpected details in an otherwise ordinary scene.

He also had a taste for the macabre. There were a number of floral sketches and watercolors, but the plants were all carnivorous. Tiny insects were shown struggling to escape the jaws of flowers. One sketchbook was filled with pictures of elaborately decorated crypts, coffins, and graveyards. Another contained highly detailed, extremely gory crime scenes. Evidently Grant had not lied to Sophy about that aspect of his work, although there was no way to know if the drawings were official police sketches.

The succubus images started appearing in the most recent sketchbook. And then the bodies showed up—three of them. They all looked like down-and-out street people. There were no signs of wounds but their faces were contorted death masks, as if they had died confronting horror.

He studied the drawings for a few minutes, trying to comprehend what they were telling him. It wasn't just the evolution of the subject matter that sent a chill through him. There was something else going on, as well. Something ominous.

A shock wave flashed across his senses. He had to get back to Sophy. Now.

He shoved the sketchbook under the bed with the others and headed for the door.

THIRTY-SIX

THE NIGHT SKY OVER THE SCULPTURE GARDEN WAS AWASH IN ARTIFICIAL AURORAS GENerated by strategically placed machines. The ebb and flow of the colorful waves did a good job of masking the vortex vibe, Sophy thought, but the display could not entirely conceal the disturbing pulses of energy, at least not to someone who was naturally sensitive to paranormal currents.

Most of the audience appeared unaware of the buzz in the background but she knew they were unconsciously reacting to it. Some laughed a little too loud. A few were unsteady on their feet. A handful appeared anxious or uneasy. The free cocktails that were being handed out with abandon intensified the reactions of individuals in the crowd.

The scene felt uncomfortably volatile, she thought. And on top of everything else she was worried about Luke. Yes, he was in the security business, and yes, he probably knew what he was doing. But still. From time to time she glanced down at Bruce, because she had a feeling he would be the first one to sense that Luke was in real trouble. So far he seemed unconcerned.

The two of them were drifting randomly through the crowd. Thus far, Bruce had resisted the urge to pee on the sculptures. He probably didn't think any were worthy of his marker. She shared his opinion. If you looked beyond the dazzling lights, the artwork wasn't exactly captivating.

She was checking the time yet again, wondering how long Luke would be gone, when she heard the chillingly familiar voice behind her.

"The new boyfriend doesn't know the truth about you, does he?" Vincent said.

She turned quickly, fury sweeping through her. She forced herself to remember Luke's words: *The idea is to keep a low profile.* But at her side, Bruce was on high alert, golden wolf eyes focused on Vincent.

Vincent glanced at Bruce. "Does he bite?"

"He's a dog," Sophy said. "Of course he bites. He'll tear your throat out without a second's thought if I say the word."

Bruce glanced up at her with a hopeful expression.

"Not yet, Bruce," she said.

Bruce turned back to Vincent and grinned, showing a lot of fang.

Vincent took a nervous step back.

"I saw you skulking around the reception this afternoon," Sophy said. "I've been wondering if you would have the guts to show up tonight. I thought maybe you would be too embarrassed by that horrible cartoon sculpture in the Maze Gallery."

Rage twisted Vincent's handsome features. His eyes blazed with heat and something else. Something scary.

"That sculpture reveals the truth about you," he hissed in low tones. "You're a monster."

Bruce rumbled.

Ice touched the back of Sophy's neck. "You are mentally ill, Vincent. Something has happened to you."

"Yes, something has happened. I've changed in ways you can't even imagine. I'm stronger now, more powerful."

"Where did you get the new strength? Have you been watching late-night infomercials? Taking supplements? Is this where you say, '*But wait, there's more*'?"

"You stupid fucking bitch."

Bruce growled, louder this time. Distracted, Vincent flinched and looked down.

Sophy smiled. "Like I said, he bites. And so do I."

"That makes three of us," Luke said behind her.

Sophy breathed a sigh of relief. He was safe.

Bruce growled again.

"Bruce, no," Luke said quietly. "Not here. Not now."

Bruce looked disappointed but he did not go for Vincent's throat.

"This isn't over," Vincent snarled.

He turned and disappeared into the crowd. Sophy took some deep breaths in an effort to quiet her pulse.

"It's okay," she said, trying for cool and professional. "Bruce and I had the situation under control."

"Good to know," Luke said. "Because for a minute there I had the impression that maybe things were not under control and that our low-profile strategy was about to be blown to hell."

She glared. "You can't blame that little scene on me. I didn't go looking for Vincent. He just showed up."

"We don't have time to argue, but we do need to talk about Grant."

"He really has changed, Luke. I don't know what's going on, but he's not the man I met a few months ago."

"I believe you. I'm pretty sure I know what's happening to him. Let's head back to the inn. I'll tell you what I found in Grant's casita."

THIRTY-SEVEN

"VINCENT IS *DETERIORATING*?" SOPHY STOPPED PACING THE SUITE AND LOOKED AT LUKE, who was sprawled in one of the chairs, legs outstretched. "What does that even mean?"

"I think his psychic senses have been destabilized," he said. "Pretty sure the process can't be reversed, not at this stage."

"That's a breathtaking diagnosis, given how little we know about him or his paranormal senses."

"It's all there in his sketchbooks, Sophy." Luke rested a hand on Bruce's head. "His drawings look normal—competent, maybe even good, I think, although I'm no judge—up until three months ago. After that, they rapidly become less refined. Bizarre. Amateurish. There was a dark side to his choice of subject matter from the start, but the violent element is much stronger in the recent drawings."

"He first contacted me about three months ago." She went to the window and looked out into the night. "Are all the violent images variations on the succubus theme?"

"Most of them look like sketches for that sculpture we saw in the gallery. But there are others. At least three were of dead bodies."

"What?" She spun around. "Are you talking about autopsy drawings?"

"No," Luke said. "The drawings in his sketchbook look like they were done at the scenes of the crimes. The victims appear to have been living on the streets. There is something personal about the images. I don't know how to explain it. I think Grant is the one who killed them."

"Oh, shit."

"If I'm right, he's become a serial killer. The drawings are his souvenirs."

She folded her arms tightly around her midsection, trying to absorb the horrifying information. "I can't believe I dated a serial killer. Surely I would have picked up some kind of warning vibe."

"You said you haven't seen him since that date in the San Francisco alley."

"That's right." She sighed. "I assumed he was just another failed experiment."

"The sudden deterioration seems to have set in around that time."

A sickening thought struck her. She stared at Luke, horrified. "Maybe it was seeing me coming out of the trance that caused him to go insane. Maybe my energy field shattered his senses. Maybe he developed some form of PTSD because of me? What if I really am a dangerous talent?"

"Don't go there, Sophy."

It was a command. She ignored it.

"Do you think I might have damaged any of my other experiments?"

"Nope. No need to worry about that. You might have scared the hell out of some of the others but that's about it."

She froze. "You're not taking this seriously, are you?"

Luke was out of the chair and standing directly in front of her, watching her with heated eyes before she realized what was happening. He clamped his hands around her shoulders.

"I'm taking the business of finding Deke and Bea and stopping Hatch and his pals very seriously," he said. "That's why we're here, remember? But, no, I am not worried that you are a monster or that you are in any way responsible for what's happening to Grant."

She was torn between wanting to believe him and what logic was telling her. "But how can you be sure of that?"

"There are two very good reasons. First, psychic energy has to be focused in order to be used as a weapon. It might—and I emphasize the *might*—be possible for you to do some damage to another individual's aura if you got seriously intentional about it. You'd have to *want* to mess with someone's energy field and you would probably need physical contact to do it. You can't accidentally use your talent to drive someone insane or to commit murder. Paranormal biophysics doesn't work that way."

"You're certain?"

"Trust me, the Foundation has a library that contains decades of research on the subject. All of it backs up what I'm telling you."

"That is reassuring," she allowed.

"Good. Because it's the truth."

A new thought hit her. "But what if the Foundation *thinks* I'm a violent, unstable talent? They'll make sure I disappear into that private psychiatric hospital they operate. Halcyon Manor. Everyone knows it's really a prison for deranged psychics."

Luke tightened his grip on her shoulders. His eyes burned a little hotter. "Anyone who tries to take you away to Halcyon Manor or anywhere else will have to go through me."

Bruce rumbled and pressed against her leg. His amber eyes were molten hot.

"And Bruce," Luke added.

She managed a shaky smile. "I believe you guys. Thanks."

Luke took his hands off her shoulders. "That said, in the course of my work I've had a few opportunities to investigate some cases of sudden-onset deterioration of the psychic senses. Most of the victims went insane and died soon afterward. Most had one thing in common."

She tensed. "What was that?"

"The damage usually occurred when an individual was exposed to repeated doses of a dangerous form of paranormal radiation." Luke began to pace the room, very intent. Very focused. "The aura was gradually warped and destabilized. The subject might have survived the first or second or even a third dose, but repeated exposure over time proved lethal. Given the data we have, we can assume that Grant has been firing the old Kaleidoscope weapons that were stolen from my family's vault."

"He is involved in whatever is going on here," Sophy said. "That means he didn't come looking for me because a police detective happened to mention that I was good at reading crime scenes."

"We knew it was not a coincidence that the succubus sculpture showed up in the Maze Gallery. Grant targeted you."

"But it was Aunt Bea who went missing a few days ago. If I hadn't terrified him maybe he would have grabbed me instead. I'm the reason he took Bea."

Luke came to a halt, turned, and walked deliberately toward her.

"Listen up," he said. "You will stop blaming yourself for this situation. Tobias Harper and Xavier Wells are the people responsible for this mess. We're stuck dealing with the fallout, but we did not cause the problem in the first place."

She blinked a couple of times, thinking. "You know what? You're right."

"That's because I applied a little logic to the problem."

"Your ability to focus and connect dots can be a little irritating, but I've got to admit it comes in handy at times."

"I can't tell you how much that means to me. I'm grateful to know that I am occasionally useful."

She widened her eyes. "You're angry, aren't you?"

"What gave me away?"

"Well—"

"On second thought, don't answer that question."

His mouth came down on hers with stunning force. Startled, she froze. She knew he intended the kiss to silence her, but the heat flared without warning. It caught him off guard, just as it did her.

Like the vortex-fueled kiss that morning, she thought. But this time she couldn't blame it on the canyon energy. She wasn't transitioning from a trance, either. There was no logical explanation for what was happening. The thrilling rush swept through all her senses. She could feel their auras seeking resonance.

She wrapped her arms around his neck, parted her lips, and returned the kiss with fierce abandon. Luke muttered something she did not understand, something that came from somewhere deep inside. And then he was tightening his grip on her, lifting her off her feet.

A moment later she was vaguely aware of falling. She landed on the bed. Luke came down on top of her. For a few wild, glorious moments they fought each other for the embrace.

"Shit," Luke planted his hands on either side of her shoulders and lifted himself off of her. He sat up abruptly, breathing hard, his eyes molten. "We do not have time for this."

She watched him for a couple of seconds and decided he seemed genuinely regretful. "I know. Duty calls. The mission comes first. We are here because we are bound by the old pact between our great-grandfathers. Anything that gets in the way—sex, for example—is a distraction. Blah, blah, blah."

He gave her a wary look. "Blah, blah, blah?"

"Never mind. You're still planning to go into the Maze Gallery tonight, aren't you?"

"We can't waste any more time."

Inwardly she winced but she managed a cool smile. "Absolutely not. Go forth and do what must be done. Bruce and I will be okay. We also serve who only stand and wait. Blah, blah, blah."

THIRTY-EIGHT

HIS LIFE HAD BECOME A LOT MORE INTERESTING LATELY, LUKE REFLECTED. ALSO, MORE complicated. He wondered if the *blah-blah-blah* thing should worry him. Not that he had time to analyze it now.

He stood in the shadows of the side door of the Maze Gallery, one of the few areas of the compound that was not awash in bright lights. Unlike Grant's casita, the entrance was protected with a high-end electronic alarm. It was good tech but not the best. The Wells jammer would have no trouble silencing the system long enough for him to slip inside. This was what happened when customers insisted on going with the lowest bidder.

Anything that gets in the way—sex, for example—is a distraction.

What the hell did that mean? Did Sophy think that the attraction between them was nothing more than a brief distraction?

On the plus side, there was no longer any doubt that she was aware of both the physical and psychic bonds that connected them. She couldn't blame the wild kiss in the honeymoon suite on post-trance energy or vortex currents.

He'd experienced psi-heavy environments in the company labs

and in the course of his work for the Agency. The family vault reeked of the stuff. So did the Foundation museum. Some of the effects had been mildly intoxicating. Others had delivered a stiff adrenaline jolt. A few had induced hallucinations. But none had given him the rush he got when he was with Sophy.

He let himself into the gallery, closed the door, and stood quietly for a moment, absorbing the feel of the deep darkness.

The old house was drenched in night. The floor lights that had guided viewers through the gallery had been turned off. Someone had pulled the plugs on all the art installations. There were no hypnotic vibes coming from the mirror tiles.

He jacked up his night vision and suddenly his surroundings were steeped in an eerie radiance that emanated from somewhere beyond the visible spectrum. The walls, ceiling, and floor were now an impossibly deep shade of violet. A nearby display pedestal glowed an otherworldly blue.

He slipped the jammer back into his jacket and considered how to proceed. The biggest risk was that he might accidentally blunder into one of the sculptures and send it crashing to the floor. That would probably bring a thundering herd of armed security people. He wondered if Hatch's bodyguards would be among the first responders or if he would find himself confronting a handful of armed retirees. Probably the blondes. He had the feeling they were the ones in charge of protecting the real secrets of the art colony. The retirees were for show.

Satisfied that he could see clearly enough to move through the maze without crashing into the artwork, he started down the first hallway. There was a variety of methods for navigating a maze, including the classic technique of planting one hand on a wall and never lifting it off until you reached the exit point. But that approach, like the other strategies, was time-consuming. He needed to move quickly tonight. He didn't like the idea of leaving Sophy alone in the room. Bruce would protect her, but there was only so much a dog—or any guardian, for that matter—could do when confronted by an armed intruder.

He studied the violet floor. Pools of phosphorescent energy marked layers of footprints—the tracks of visitors who had toured the gallery. It was unlikely there were answers to be found on that route.

If there were secrets in the gallery, they would be concealed in one of the branching corridors that had been roped off during the exhibition. That meant he was looking for a path that was used on a regular basis by relatively few people: Hatch and those who were privy to whatever was going on inside the compound.

The first two blocked hallways showed no indications that anyone had taken those paths in a very long time. There were, however, plenty of radiant footsteps in the third corridor.

He examined the heavy velvet rope, careful not to touch it. He had to assume that it was alarmed. He took out the jammer and ran a check. The device lit up like a Las Vegas slot machine. That told him he was on the right path.

Disarming the security system took only seconds.

Once he was on the other side of the rope he followed the iridescent pools left by human feet. The pattern of the energy tracks showed no hesitation at any of the branching corridors. The people who had come and gone through this section of the maze had been very sure of where they were headed. That was a strong indication that there was something interesting at the other end of the hallway.

He went forward cautiously, using the jammer to search for hidden security traps. The path took him around an extraordinary number of corners and past the inviting entrances to several deceptive branches.

He was making progress. The familiar ping of *knowing* that he always got when he was on the right track was growing stronger. He headed toward another intersection . . .

. . . and stopped when an electric frisson hit his senses. This was not a good-news-ahead ping. This was a claxon warning him to leave. Now.

But he was closing in on something important.

Just one more corner . . .

He turned and went down the well-traveled hallway and stopped again when he found himself confronting a solid wall. There were no more intersections or branching corridors. No obvious exit. But the footsteps he had been following disappeared beneath the barrier.

The jammer pinged, indicating a nearby security device. That was promising. But he was still getting the warnings from his intuition.

He sensed the presence in the hallway and turned to confront whoever stood there. The piercing lights of a strobe shot out of the darkness, dazzling and blinding all of his senses.

The shadowy figure spoke.

"You cannot have the succubus. Her power is mine to control."

THIRTY-NINE

"OKAY, OKAY, I GET IT," SOPHY SAID. "YOU'RE WORRIED. SO AM I."

Bruce whined and gave her a *do something* look. He was pacing back and forth in front of the door. Until a moment ago he had been content to sprawl on top of the bed beside her. Until a moment ago she had been studying Tobias Harper's journal.

Now they were both on their feet, restless. The sense that Luke was in danger was growing stronger. Frisson after frisson of nervous energy was lifting the hair on the back of her neck.

"Aunt Bea says that it's a bad idea to ignore your intuition," she said.

Bruce whined again.

"All right, I agree. We can't just hang around here and wait until Luke returns. Let's go see if we can find him."

Bruce raked the door with his claws.

"Management is not going to like that," Sophy warned.

She pulled on her trench coat and started to pick up Bruce's leash. "Never mind. You can move a lot faster without me," she said. She opened the door. "Go on. I'll try to keep up with you."

Bruce bounded forward, heading for the stairs, but he stopped when he realized she was several steps behind him.

"It's all right," she said, picking up her pace. "I'll be okay. Go find Luke."

Bruce uttered a short, sharp bark. He made no move to descend the stairs. She realized he was still in guard mode. He was trying to do his job even though he was convinced that Luke needed him.

A door down the hall opened.

"Keep that dog quiet," a woman shouted.

Sophy ignored her and dashed to the stairs. Bruce went back into action, vaulting down the steps. She seized the railing and followed him. They made it to the lobby and headed for the front door.

"That dog is supposed to be on a leash, ma'am," the young man at the front desk said.

"Oh, I didn't know that," Sophy said. "Sorry. Don't worry, I'll put him on a leash just as soon as we're outside."

A voice spoke from the depths of a wingback chair. "Tell your dog that if he wants to lift a leg on any of the sculptures out there in the garden, it's fine by me. Might add a little artistic interest to some of them."

Sophy recognized the voice of the art critic who had introduced himself on the gallery tour. She searched her memory for his name. Marlon Whitley. That was it.

He was ensconced deep in the big chair, one leg crossed over the other. There was a notebook on his lap. A glass of brandy sat on the side table.

"Good evening," she said.

He picked up the glass and raised it in a casual salute. "Perhaps you'll join me for a drink when you return with your dog?"

"Thanks. I'm afraid I have plans."

"Right. Newlyweds." He winked. "I almost forgot."

"Please excuse me."

She raced through the glass doors, Bruce leading the way. She brushed aside the little rush of fake cheerfulness she got when she went past the fountain, and then followed Bruce into the glowing night.

FORTY

"DOES IT BOTHER YOU THAT YOU'RE STARTING TO SOUND LIKE YOUR ARTWORK, GRANT? Like a cartoon?"

"Shut your fucking mouth," Grant ordered.

"When it comes to art, everyone's a critic, right?" Luke said. "I saw your *Succubus* last night. It was derivative, garish, uninspired, and poorly executed. In short, a cartoon."

"You stupid bastard, you don't know what you're talking about," Grant snarled. "You think you're a critic? Well, you're a dead critic."

The strobe lights became more intense. They were beyond dazzling and disorienting. Luke knew that he was going under, struggling to breathe. He had to stop standing here like a target in a shooting gallery.

He could not fight the strobe. The energy of the flashing, mind-numbing lights was weakening all of his senses. His balance was off. He tried to reach inside his jacket but the leather got in his way. He flattened a hand against the nearest wall to keep himself upright.

According to the Boss, talking was a CEO's only real power. *Leadership 101. You've got to sound like you know what you're doing. Otherwise everyone panics.*

"That's a Kaleidoscope weapon, isn't it?" he managed. "I'm impressed that you were able to steal it from the Wells vault. That couldn't have been easy."

"Not my job. I'm a shooter, not a thief."

"Did you murder the man in the Mirror Lake cabin and leave the body on the side of the road?"

"That was Orston," Grant said. "He and Taylor went to Mirror Lake to get info on your uncle. But something happened. Orston said Taylor went mad and had to be taken out. Between you and me, Orston is on the way out, too. He can't handle the guns. He's not strong enough."

"Who told you that you were capable of firing the weapon?"

"The Alchemist. He's pretty smart, but he's no genius like my brother. Trent says that when the project is completed he and I will be the only ones standing."

In spite of the blinding light, a connection appeared between two more dots. Luke tried to take a step forward. He stumbled and almost went down.

"Hatch is your brother?" he managed.

"Half brother. Different fathers. Same mother. We're both fucking strong talents. Just different."

"What's your talent?"

"The Alchemist needs me to fire the light guns and keep the mood enhancers running. They don't last long."

"You screwed up the mood enhancer in the honeymoon suite, didn't you?"

"There's something wrong with the crystal in that setup," Grant shot back, voice rising. "It's dead. The enhancers don't work without a tuned crystal."

"Why not replace it?"

"It's not like those crystals are just lying around on the ground waiting to be picked up. You have to grow them in a lab. The Alchemist says it takes time, special chemicals, and the right seed crystal."

"The Alchemist grew the crystals that are broadcasting his hypnotic suggestions?"

"Nah. He found them in the old lab. He's got the formula but he hasn't been able to grow his own yet."

"How do the mood enhancers work?"

"Shut the fuck up. The only thing you need to worry about is this light gun. You're going to go mad for a couple of minutes and then you're going to be dead. This will be fun. I brought my camera so I can take photos. Don't worry, I'll show them to the succubus later."

The power level of the strobe got more intense. Once again Luke tried to reach inside his jacket; again he failed. But in that moment it dawned on him that he was not the only one who made a perfect target. Like a flashlight, the strobes of paranormal energy marked the spot where Grant stood.

"Nothing to lose," Luke said.

"What the fuck are you talking about?"

Luke mustered everything he had left and threw himself forward, hoping to stay on his feet long enough to slam into Grant. In the narrow confines of the hallway, he could hardly miss.

It was an awkward, clumsy move but it had his full weight behind it. Sometimes raw power was called for.

Belatedly Grant realized what was happening. He yelped and stumbled backward but he did not go down. Luke heard the weapon thud on the floor. The gun went dark immediately, but he was blinded by the afterimages. He went down hard.

Muffled footsteps echoed in the maze, fading fast. Somewhere in the distance a door opened and closed. A heavy silence settled on the gallery.

After a moment Luke realized that he was sprawled on the floor. He pushed himself to his hands and knees and groped blindly, searching for the weapon.

Blindly.

Luke tried to open his eyes and discovered they were already open. He pulled hard on his senses, but the dark-violet floors and walls did not reappear. He wondered if he had lost his regular vision, too.

"Shit."

He was trapped in the jet-black maze.

FORTY-ONE

BRUCE WAS SCRATCHING AT THE SIDE DOOR OF THE MAZE GALLERY WHEN IT OPENED without warning. Startled, Sophy looked at the broad-shouldered figure looming on the threshold.

"Luke?"

Bruce answered the question first. He threw himself at Luke, who reached down to accept the joyous greeting.

"Take it easy," he said. "I'm all right. Mostly." He rubbed his eyes. "What are you two doing here? I told you to stay in the room."

"So sue us," Sophy said. "We both got worried and decided you might need a little help."

"You were right." He studied her for a moment, blinking a few times. "Let's go back to the inn. I need to do some thinking and then I need to dream."

"What are you talking about?" she demanded. "What happened in the gallery?"

"I ran into one of your failed experiments."

"Grant? He was in there with you? What happened?"

"Let's just say he doesn't take criticism of his art in a positive way."

FORTY-TWO

"ANY SIGN THAT YOUR OTHER VISION IS RETURNING TO NORMAL?" SOPHY ASKED.

"Not yet," Luke said. "But my regular vision is okay. Stop fussing and let me think."

"I'm worried about your other sight."

"I appreciate that, but there's nothing you can do. It either recovers or it doesn't. We can't afford to sit around and wait to find out what happens. Meanwhile I need to connect some dots."

The impatience edging his words told her that she had asked the question about his vision too many times. She couldn't help it. She was still trying to process the realization that Vincent Grant had tried to murder him tonight with a weapon that had damaged—possibly destroyed—his psychic-grade vision.

She breathed out and centered herself. He was determined to play the mission-comes-first role. She had to respect that. Also, he was right. They really did not have any options. They had to keep moving forward.

"I still can't believe Vincent and Hatch are brothers," she said.

"Half brothers," Luke said. "It explains a few things."

He was standing in front of the silver doughnut, studying it as if it held the key to unlocking all of his questions.

To distract herself she sat down at the small table and examined the odd-looking weapon. It was shaped like a chunky pistol with a fat, round barrel and an oversized grip.

Experimentally, she picked it up.

"It's very heavy," she said.

"Be careful. I'm pretty sure it's dead, but when it comes to guns of any kind—"

"Always assume they are loaded. I know. It's also awkward and cumbersome. I would have to use both hands to hold it and aim it. You couldn't fit it into a shoulder holster and wear a dinner jacket over it like slick secret agents do with regular pistols."

"That's one of the prototypes that was stolen from the Wellses' vault," Luke said. "It was proof of concept. The idea was to refine it and make it more efficient."

"We have to assume the other prototype is somewhere here in the compound, don't we?"

"Yes. Probably in the hands of the smoking ghost." Luke paused. "Unless he's already deteriorated too much to use it. He may be dead by now."

She chilled. "What about Vincent? How long before—?"

"I don't know. Tobias and Xavier stopped the experiments as soon as they realized what was happening to people who fired the weapon more than once or twice. They assumed that a very strong talent could handle the guns but they called off the project before testing that theory."

"I guess there was no one around to warn Vincent or the smoking ghost about the danger of firing the weapons," she said.

"We can assume the man Grant called the Alchemist knows how dangerous the guns are. That's why he hired other people as hit men."

She turned the weapon carefully in her hands and opened her senses a little. The shock of awareness made her yelp. The heavy weapon clanged when she set it on the table and jumped to her feet. Bruce lifted his head off his paws and pricked his ears.

"Careful with that thing," Luke said.

She backed away from the table, eyeing the weapon as if it was a rattler. "That gun was used to murder someone recently."

"Sorry, I should have warned you. Grant said one of the guns had been used to murder the man who died in Deke's cabin. Maybe it was that one." Luke paused. "Or maybe that's the weapon Grant used to murder the three homeless men I saw in his sketchbook."

"I hate to admit it, but we may be in over our heads."

"That occurred to me," Luke said. "Unfortunately, we're not in a position to call for help. No cell service and no landlines in the rooms."

She shuddered. "Don't remind me."

"If we leave now—assuming we could get past the security gate—I doubt we'd be able to return with reinforcements in time to stop whatever is happening here. The message Deke held up in the hologram said we're on the clock."

"We have to find out what is going on behind that wall that you saw in the gallery, don't we?"

"Yes."

She braced herself. "You're going back into the maze tonight."

"I'm going to try to dream first."

"I don't understand."

He shrugged. "That's how I connect the dots. I do it in my dreams. This time around it's going to be an experiment because I don't know if I can still dream the way I did before I lost my other vision. For all I know my para-vision was linked to my dreamlight."

She widened her eyes, intrigued. "You can see connections in your dreams?"

"If I have enough data." He frowned. "Does that strike you as weird? You're the one who grew up selling crystals and chimes. You know as well as I do that lots of people take dream analysis seriously."

"Well, yes. But I never thought of you as the type to put much stock in dreams."

"I find them useful," he said. He sounded somewhat defensive. "But it always comes down to interpretation. That's where things can go sideways."

"You're thinking about your affair with the secretly sexy librarian, aren't you?"

He shot her an irritated look.

"Whatever," she said quickly. "Moving right along, after you dream, Bruce and I should go into the maze with you. Think of us as backup. I've got some talent that might prove useful, especially if your para-vision doesn't recover. I can see in the dark, remember? So can Bruce, at least to some extent. The three of us are a team. Allies. Colleagues. Three auras are stronger than one, right?"

He watched her with a brooding gaze for a long moment. Then his jaw tightened. "You're right. We'll go in together."

"With Bruce."

Luke's mouth twitched a little at the corner. "With Bruce."

Bruce raised his head again. His eyes glowed and he flapped his tail a couple of times.

Sophy got a rush of satisfaction. Luke was treating her as an equal partner. She was on a roll. "We know we're dealing with at least four bad guys," she said. "Trent Hatch, Vincent, the smoking ghost, and someone called the Alchemist."

"Don't forget Hatch's security team."

"Right. Plus the guards like the one we met at the front gate."

"I'm not too worried about them," Luke said. "They all seem to be retired people from Fool's Gold who are just padding their Social Security and pensions with some part-time work. I don't think they're involved in the Alchemist's project. The real question now is, who is the Alchemist?"

"We've got an entire art colony full of suspects."

"We can exclude the artists," Luke said. "Pretty sure they're just unwitting test subjects, like the guests at the inn."

"I wouldn't be surprised to find out that Hatch's security team is behind this whole thing. Those blondes look tough."

"It's a possibility, but they have the vibe of professionals. Got a hunch they're in it for the money. It's just a job for them." Luke paused a beat. "I think."

She watched him for a moment. "How did you find your way out of the maze without your other vision?"

"I used the classic technique. Planted one hand on the wall and never took it off until I got to the exit."

She unfolded her arms and dropped into the nearest chair. "You found your way out of that maze by touch alone. That's . . . incredible."

"Not really. It was the only option available." Luke went to the table, picked up the weapon, and raised it to eye level. He aimed it at the balcony window and gently twisted the thick barrel. "No question about it, this is old-school crystal tech. Physical contact is required to fire it." He lowered the Kaleidoscope and studied the doughnut sculpture. "Unlike the hypnotic tiles."

She lounged back in the chair and crossed her ankles. "No wonder everyone thinks you should take your grandfather's place as the CEO of Wells, Inc. Got to hand it to you, Luke, you do know how to set priorities and focus on a problem."

"I'm told the habit can be irritating."

"Who said that?"

"You may have mentioned it."

"Oh, right."

He set the weapon back down on the table. There was an icy heat in his eyes. "Time for me to find out if I can still dream."

She was intensely aware of the energy that charged the atmosphere around him.

"Okay." She was not sure what she was supposed to do or say next. "Are you, uh, going to get into bed?"

"I'll just try to take a nap." He sat on the edge of the bed and removed one low boot. "Do me a favor. Don't suck up all my bodily essences while I'm out. I'm going to need those later."

"We are not amused." She frowned. "Before you sleep, why don't we try the technique you used on me when I came out of the trance at your uncle's cabin?"

"What?"

"I was starting to go into the ice fever but you were able to stop the process."

He removed his other boot, rested his forearms on his thighs, and looked at her. "You're talking about trying to get our auras to resonate."

"Isn't that what you did when you helped me get back to normal? Maybe a similar process could restore your other vision."

"Your situation was different. Some of the wavelengths in your aura were in shock. All I did was use some of my energy to encourage the currents to resume normal oscillation."

"I understand. But what if your para-vision is just in shock? I might be able to encourage the currents back into normal rhythm."

"What the hell. It's worth a try."

He held out his hand. She took it, abruptly aware that she had absolutely no idea how to set up a state of resonance between their auras. On the two previous occasions with Luke it seemed to have happened more or less spontaneously. Maybe physical contact was all it took.

She was in the process of cautiously heightening her senses when Luke tightened his grip on her hand and drew her down across his thighs. Before she realized what was happening, he wrapped an arm around her and lowered his mouth to hers.

"What are you doing?" she squeaked in surprise.

"We don't have time to waste running experiments. This is the fastest way I know for the two of us to set up resonance."

"But—"

For a few seconds she fought to get control of the kiss; to stay in command of the situation. But he was doing the same. Their auras flared, clashed, and suddenly they were both surrendering to the excitement, the yearning, and the thrill of bone-deep recognition.

Luke fell back onto the bed, taking her with him. She tumbled across his chest, heightened her talent . . .

. . . and immediately sensed the damaged currents of his talent. She knew intuitively how to ease the wavelengths back into normal resonance. Just a little light housekeeping.

Luke looked up at her. His eyes burned. "Damn. You did it. I've got my night vision back."

She pushed herself off his chest and sat up on the side of the bed. "How do you feel?"

"Good. Very, very good. Now I'm sure I can dream."

He lay back on the pillows, straightened out on the bed, closed his eyes, and . . . dropped into sleep.

She watched him for a moment and then she looked at Bruce.

"That's a handy talent he has," she said softly.

Bruce yawned, curled up, and went to sleep, too.

"Gosh, don't feel like you have to stay awake just to keep me company," she said. "I'll find something to do."

She sank into the reading chair and picked up Tobias Harper's journal.

FORTY-THREE

"WHAT THE FUCK HAVE YOU DONE?" HATCH SAID. "WELLS IS ALIVE AND BACK IN HIS room. And that's the least of our problems. The Alchemist is going to be furious when he finds out you lost the weapon."

"I didn't lose it," Vincent muttered. "I dropped it. Don't worry, Wells couldn't have found it. He was blind when I left him in the maze. He should be dead. I don't know how he made it out alive."

The two of them were taking what was supposed to look like a late-night stroll through the sculpture garden. Even though they were outside they were keeping their voices low. The Scary Blondes were following them at a discreet distance. Theoretically they could not eavesdrop, but just to be on the safe side Hatch had turned on the scrambler he wore on his belt. It pulsed lightly, indicating that it was functioning.

Vincent shivered with rage, frustration, and an edgy sensation that he refused to label panic. It wasn't his fault everything had gone wrong tonight. Yes, he had acted on impulse. He had been watching Wells. When he realized the bastard was heading toward the gallery he had been unable to resist what had appeared to be a golden opportunity. He had unlocked the second entrance to the underground lab, the one that had been designed as an emergency exit, grabbed a weapon, and followed Wells into the old house.

It wasn't until his quarry went straight into the maze without the benefit of a flashlight that he had realized Wells had at least some para-vision. That information had increased the thrill of the hunt. He had killed three times now to make sure that he had what it took to power the weapon. The authorities had labeled the deaths natural causes and promptly forgotten about them. The Alchemist, who had accompanied him to observe, had been impressed. Told him he was a natural.

But Wells hadn't gone down the way the street people had. He had fought back.

"He made it out alive because you didn't finish what you started," Hatch said. "You failed."

"I didn't fail. I hit him hard. A full dose. I think the weapon is losing its power."

"Those fucking guns channel human psi. They are only as powerful as the shooter. Face it. You screwed up. We've got to get a handle on this situation, and fast."

"It wasn't my fault," Vincent said. But he knew Trent didn't believe him. Fuck, he wasn't sure what to believe himself. Wells should have gone down and stayed down. "One thing's for sure. The rumors about No-Talent Wells are wrong. At the very least he's got psychic-grade night vision."

"Not surprising. The ability to see a little beyond the normal spectrum is common in the psychic community, and he comes from a long line of strong talents. Stands to reason he's got a minimal vibe. Forget him. You need to retrieve the gun before the Alchemist realizes it's missing."

Another panicky tremor raised the hair on the back of Vincent's neck. "Order the Scary Blondes to get rid of Wells. They're your security team. I'm sure they know how to make people disappear."

"What am I supposed to tell them? That you followed Wells into the maze and tried to murder him because you thought he was standing between you and your *Muse* but you fucked up? Do you realize how delusional that sounds?"

"The Alchemist will be pissed. What can he do about it?"

"He might decide you can be replaced," Hatch warned.

Vincent snorted. "He says Orston and I are the only ones with the talent required to fire the weapons, and Orston is fading fast. Besides, who else is he going to get to recharge his mood enhancers? He needs me. You heard him."

"I've been playing games with very smart people like the Alchemist ever since I was a kid, Vincent. And if there's one thing I've learned it's that you can't trust any of them."

Vincent looked at a nearby sculpture, a brightly lit bouquet of surreal flowers. Talk about uninspired and derivative. He wondered which of the so-called artists in residence had produced it—you couldn't use the word *created*, not for those childish flowers. It was a cartoon.

Before the succubus had drained his energy field he had been a thousand times more talented than any of the artists in residence. He had to get control of the bitch so that he could recover his talent.

"Vincent, are you listening?" Trent said.

"Yes, I'm listening. You can't trust very smart people. That's not news. I don't trust anyone. What's your point?"

"My point," Trent said grimly, "is that we can't trust the Alchemist. He may decide he doesn't need you now that he has another Harper woman."

"The first one didn't work out well."

"He's convinced the niece has the right talent. Once the project is completed, the Alchemist might decide he doesn't need either of us."

Vincent glanced at him. "You've got a plan, don't you?"

"The Alchemist is brilliant, but he's borderline insane. That makes him dangerous. It also makes him manageable. He thinks he's manipulating us but the opposite is true. Yes, I've got a plan. But first you have to recover the weapon."

FORTY-FOUR

LUKE FELL INTO THE DREAMSCAPE STAGED WITH THE CHARACTERS AND DATA HE HAD assembled and let his intuition tell him a story.

Sophy has vanished into the maze. He tried to follow her but now he is lost. He can see in the way that one does in dreams, but he has nothing to guide him. The walls of the narrow corridors tower upward into nothingness. The intersections are endless. Every time he turns a corner he is met with a blank wall.

He must find Sophy.

He turns another corner. For the first time he is not confronted with a wall. Instead, he sees the silvery doughnut sculpture. The polished finish of the alloy is blindingly bright. It's like looking into a sun-splashed mirror. There is a reflection in the bright surface but he cannot see it clearly.

The one thing he's certain of is that he is not seeing his own face in the mirror. He sees someone else, someone he knows but can't quite recognize.

"Who are you?" he says. "Where is Sophy?"

The reflection laughs.

Before he can ask any more questions he senses a presence behind him. He turns, hoping to see Sophy. But she is not there. He is facing Hatch's personal security team. The twins are wearing their stylish tuxes.

"You have become a problem," one of them informs him.

"I get that a lot," he says.

"Grant has also become a problem," the other blonde says.

"I know, but he's your problem, not mine."

"Your uncle is a problem, too."

He turns back and tries once again to focus on the sculpture. He must figure out why it is significant, because if he doesn't he will lose Sophy forever . . .

He came out of the dreamstate on a rush of knowing. When he opened his eyes, he saw Sophy standing beside the bed, regarding him with an anxious expression. Bruce was beside her. He did not appear anxious—he looked as if he was anticipating action.

"I thought you might be having a nightmare," Sophy said. "I didn't know whether to try to wake you or not. I've never been around a lucid dreamer when they are actually in a dreamscape."

He frowned. "What did you call me?"

"A lucid dreamer. Why? Do you have another term for your talent?"

"No." He swung his legs over the side of the bed and sat up. "I don't have any particular word for it. I just . . . dream."

She smiled. "You dream to order and you make connections in your dreams. That's the working definition of a lucid dreamer. It's certainly a useful talent for a CEO who has to make decisions that will affect people and a business far into the future."

Behind the lenses of her glasses, her brilliant eyes glittered with a little energy. He could feel the tension shivering in the atmosphere and knew her senses were slightly heightened. The reading lamp next to the recliner was on and Tobias Harper's journal was open on the table. It was clear she had spent whatever time had passed reading.

"Tell me about your dream," she urged.

"You were lost in the Maze Gallery."

"You dreamed about me?"

"Indirectly. There was a lot going on, but now I have to interpret it. That's the hard part. How long was I out?"

"Not long." She glanced at her watch. "Maybe fifteen minutes."

Evidently concluding the situation was under control, Bruce pushed his nose against Luke's hand, waited until he got an ear rub in exchange, and then padded across the room. He settled on the carpet, head up, ears alert, eyes intent. *Eager for the hunt to begin*, Luke thought.

"Not much longer, pal," he said.

"What?" Sophy asked.

Bruce grinned.

"Never mind," Luke said. "About my dream."

"Right. You said it has to be interpreted."

"Dissecting a dream is like working with a deck of tarot cards. So many possible ways to read them."

"I understand."

"I think my intuition was trying to tell me something important about the doughnut sculpture."

"Maybe I can help."

"How?"

"By doing what we librarians do when we talk to patrons—ask the right questions so that we can point them in the right direction."

"Go for it."

She went back to the reading chair, sat down, picked up a notepad and a pen, and adjusted her glasses. "Let's start at the beginning. What do you remember about the dreamscape?"

She was in professional mode, he thought. He almost smiled.

"I was in the maze, looking for you," he said.

She looked up, frowning a little. "Did you find me?"

"No." He studied the sculpture. "I found the doughnut. It was mirror-bright. Glaringly bright. I wasn't able to look directly at it. There was a reflection but I couldn't identify the person. And then the twins showed up."

"Hatch's personal security team?" Sophy tapped the pen against the notepad and narrowed her eyes. "If you're going to tell me that you were having a hot sex fantasy involving that pair, I'm rescinding my offer to help you analyze your dream."

"Trust me, there was no sex involved. They said I had become a problem. Then they said that Vincent Grant and my uncle were problems. The only thing all three of us have in common is a close connection to a Harper woman."

"My aunt in your uncle's case. Me as far as you and Vincent are concerned."

"Which tells me that you and Bea are the critical factors in this situation. And there is only one reason for that."

Sophy took a breath. "Someone really does have Pandora's box. They want the crystals unlocked."

"Yes. But we have already considered that possibility. It's the other two elements in the dream that need to be interpreted."

"Which ones?"

"The reflection in the mirror-finish surface of the doughnut that I couldn't see clearly and the blinding brilliance of the sculpture."

"Do you think the reflection might be the Alchemist?"

"Maybe."

Sophy tapped the pen against the notepad again. "We have already concluded that the Alchemist is someone here in the compound."

"So, my dream was trying to tell me that he is someone I've seen here? That is logical but not helpful. As you said, we already knew that much."

"What is it about the overbright doughnut that is important?" Sophy asked.

He looked at her reflection in the polished metal sculpture. She was perched on the reading chair, pen in hand, the notepad on her lap. Very intent. Very serious. She watched him through the lenses of her black-and-crystal glasses, her eyes fierce and beautiful . . .

. . . Eyes that she concealed behind mirrored sunglasses when she worked a crime scene. Mirrored glasses that hid her secrets.

And suddenly a few more connections appeared.

"The mirror-finish," he said.

"We know that the Kaleidoscope weapons work on mirrors," Sophy said.

"Yes, but that's not what's important here. I think my dream was trying to tell me that it's the alloy that's key."

"Isn't that sculpture made of polished stainless steel?"

"Looks like it, but I'm not talking about the doughnut. It's the mirrored tile embedded in it that is important. It's not stainless steel. It's a very different material but it is mirror-bright and it is hiding secrets."

"What kind of secrets?"

"I think they are actually batteries. The hypnotic message is infused into the crystals but the battery is the power source. It stores human psychic energy, at least for a time. Someone has to recharge it periodically. That's evidently Grant's job. But once it's on, it activates the crystal. Someone is using the crystals and the batteries to broadcast hypnotic suggestions, but that's not nearly as significant as the technology of the tiles."

Her eyes widened in understanding. "You said the lack of a

battery that can store paranormal power is a major reason why that kind of energy hasn't become mainstream."

"Exactly. The mirror tile batteries aren't very strong—the range is only a few feet and I'm sure they drain quickly. But that's partly because human-generated energy isn't very powerful. Pretty sure the Alchemist thinks he can store serious vortex energy in them."

"In those little tiles?" Sophy shuddered. "That can't end well."

"He's been running experiments somewhere here in the compound. That's why the para-rad levels have been climbing."

Sophy put down the pen and the notepad and picked up Tobias Harper's journal. "According to my great-grandfather, the third engineer involved in the Kaleidoscope project, Maxwell Coburn, was obsessed with his theory that mirrors were the key to creating paranormal batteries."

"Did Harper have a problem with that?"

"Yes. Tobias wrote that it would be extremely dangerous to store a large amount of paranormal energy inside mirrors, given our lack of understanding of the physics involved."

"No shit."

"But evidently Maxwell Coburn was convinced that the six crystals in Pandora's box were capable of channeling large amounts of paranormal energy into the mirror batteries and releasing that energy on demand. Coburn never got an opportunity to test his theories, of course, because of the disaster that destroyed the Fogg Lake lab."

Luke flattened a hand on the surface of the sculpture. "Now Hatch and the Alchemist and their buddies are not only trying to construct Coburn's batteries, they intend to charge them with vortex energy."

"So foolish," Sophy whispered. "No one can control that kind of raw power."

"When has the risk of trying to control the forces of nature ever stopped people from attempting to do just that? Think nuclear energy, dams, solar power, hydrocarbons. In Iceland they tap into the energy of volcanoes. One way or another, all the power we use comes from nature."

She took a long breath. "Yes, but this is different. We know almost nothing about vortex energy. We don't even have a way to measure it. If it's possible to tap into it, I doubt if it could be controlled. There's a theory that all the various vortices around the planet are connected by ley lines. If that's true, attempting to channel the energy of one vortex might lead to a chain reaction."

"I think it's safe to assume that the Alchemist, who seems to be pulling the strings on this project, is not entirely sane."

"And Vincent Grant isn't what anyone would call stable now, either," Sophy said. "I wonder if his brother is."

"Hatch? No way to know if he qualifies as sane, but judging by his personal security team, he has a skill set that is required for the project. Someone wants him protected, at least as long as he's useful. We need to go into the maze. Now."

"Wait. Let's slow down and think this through in a logical manner."

"That's supposed to be my line," Luke said.

"You weren't using it, so I am. I came across something else in Tobias's journal that might be important."

"Go on."

"There were three engineers on the team—Xavier, Tobias, and Maxwell Coburn. But there was also a fourth person."

FORTY-FIVE

HE HATED THE GALLERY, ESPECIALLY AT NIGHT. THE MAZE THAT FILLED THE INTERIOR OF the old house made him think of the inside of an Egyptian pyramid—a structure designed to be both trap and tomb.

But Trent was right, Vincent thought. He had to retrieve the weapon. The Alchemist would be furious if he found out it was missing, and the guy was already semi-insane. The problem of Luke Wells could be handled later.

He stood unmoving for a moment, collecting his nerve and heightening his talent. Thanks to his psychic senses, his vision was keen enough to allow him to make out some of his surroundings, and he had one of the little locators Trent had designed to navigate the maze. But neither provided much comfort. The sensation that the walls were closing in on him was getting more intense by the second.

Earlier, when he had followed Wells into the maze, he had been powered by rage-induced adrenaline and the thrill that came with the anticipation of the kill. The weapon made him invincible. The takedowns gave him a rush like no other.

During the training process, the Alchemist had explained that every time he fired the Kaleidoscope, the weapon adapted a little more closely to his aura. It was a tuning process. The better the tuning, the more energy he could generate through the gun.

But the failure to kill Wells tonight had shaken him. For the first time he wondered if the Alchemist had lied. What if the weapon was not aligning with his aura? What if it was damaging his energy field instead? Maybe that was what had happened to Orston and Taylor.

No. The Alchemist had assured him that he was much stronger than those two.

He would worry about that later. He had to focus on what he had come here to do. His first priority was to recover the weapon.

He clicked the locator and aimed it at the floor. The otherwise invisible green line glowed in the darkness, marking the path through the maze to the door of the old lab. As long as he could see it, he would not get lost.

He shivered. The unnerving sense of dread was growing more intense. He forced himself to follow the radiant green line.

Relief spiked briefly when he reached the wall. This was where he had found Wells. He had dropped the weapon somewhere in the vicinity. He didn't spot it with his psychic vision, so he took a penlight out of a pocket and methodically searched the floor.

There was no sign of the weapon. Another wave of panic lanced through him. What if Wells had made it out of the maze with the gun?

He made himself search a little while longer, but reality was setting in. The weapon was gone. Wells must have found it. This was not good news. But Trent would know how to handle the situation. Trent always had a plan. Trent would take care of everything.

He reached the intersection where the route to the lab met the path the test subjects used to tour the installations. He hesitated, and then, unable to resist another look at his masterpiece, he hurried through the gallery.

He stopped when he reached *Succubus* and aimed the penlight at the sculpture. It was *her*. He had captured the monster in all her terrifying power. She had tried to destroy him but she had failed. Thanks to the weapon, he was the stronger one now. Soon he would conquer her. Control her.

He was enjoying the little rush of anticipation when he heard the slight movement in the shadows behind him. Startled, he almost dropped the penlight. He spun around to see who had followed him into the maze.

"Is that you, Wells?" he asked, trying to sound strong.

The figure stepped into the light. It wasn't Wells.

"What are you doing here?" Vincent asked, bewildered.

He never got an answer. The paranormal strobe lights sparked, riveting him to the spot. Somewhere outside the gallery a siren wailed. He vaguely recognized it as the emergency evacuation signal. Back at the start, Trent had insisted that it be installed. But it was supposed to go off only if something went wrong in the lab.

Before he could begin to understand what was happening, he started the dark slide into unconsciousness. He had a flash of awareness and knew he was dying. Trent would not be able to fix things this time.

The darkness overwhelmed him.

FORTY-SIX

SOPHY GRIPPED THE BALCONY RAILING AND WATCHED THE COMMOTION DOWN BELOW IN front of the inn.

"Why is the siren going off?" she asked. "I don't see any smoke."

She and Luke and Bruce stood together, looking out over the brightly lit compound. The alarms blared into the night. People spilled out of the casitas and the hotel lobby. A handful of uniformed security personnel were attempting to organize the situation.

Luke studied the confused crowd. "There are two possibilities. Either there really is an emergency of some kind—"

The alarms ceased and an authoritative male voice boomed over a loudspeaker.

"Attention. My name is Sam Grayson; I'm in charge of security. This is not a test of the alarm system. I repeat, this is not a test. We have just received word from the weather service that a lightning strike in the mountains has ignited a fast-moving wildfire that is headed in our direction. If it reaches us, this valley has the potential to become a trap. We must evacuate immediately."

Anxiety rolled through the crowd.

"There is no need to panic, but for your own safety, please move quickly. Hotel guests, return to your rooms. Pack your bags and then wait out in front of the lobby. Your cars will be brought to you. That way we will avoid congestion in the garage. Employees and resident artists will gather up only what they can carry and leave immediately. I repeat, do not panic."

"Way to get people to panic," Luke said.

Sophy looked at him. "You said there were two possible explanations for this evacuation. One was that it was for real."

"The other is that Hatch and the Alchemist decided to clear out the compound so they can move forward with their project."

"You think that is what is happening, don't you?"

"Yes. Mostly because there is no sign of Hatch or Grant or the Tuxedo Twins. They should be out here helping the guards organize the evacuation."

Sophy watched vehicles driven by security personnel begin to line up in the hotel driveway.

"Think they'll bring your car around to the front of the inn?" she asked.

"No," he said. "You and I are not meant to leave the compound."

"I was afraid you were going to say that. This is the part where they try to grab us, isn't it?"

"Yes." Luke turned away from the railing and headed back through the glass doors. "But they won't do it in front of an audience, and we're not hanging around to see what they have in mind. We're going to disappear."

"As I recall, those were among the last words your uncle wrote on his hologram note."

"And they are the reason I think Deke and Bea are still alive. My uncle has a talent for disappearing. It's one of the things that made him good at his job when he worked for the Agency."

"One of these days you're going to have to tell me the full name of that agency."

"One of these days I'll do that. But we've got work to do. Take this." Luke tossed a day pack to her. "Grab your phone and a bottle of water."

"If we're going on the run, water is excess weight."

"This is the desert," Luke said.

FORTY-SEVEN

SHE DUTIFULLY STUFFED A BOTTLE OF WATER INTO THE DAY PACK AND MADE SURE SHE had her phone. By the time she was ready, Luke and Bruce, wearing their own packs, were waiting at the door. Tension shivered in the atmosphere around them. Their eyes were molten gold. A couple of hellhounds, she thought, but they were her hellhounds—for now.

She was about to join them when she remembered the books. She grabbed *An Investigation into the Fool's Gold Canyon Vortex* and Tobias Harper's journal and added them to the pack. *Talk about excess weight*, she thought. But she was a librarian. The books held dangerous secrets. She could not risk leaving them behind.

Out in the hall, chaos reigned as most of the guests rushed for the elevator or the lobby stairs with their suitcases. Several opted for the emergency exit at the end of the hall.

"We're using the emergency stairs," Luke said. "It empties out into a service lane, not the front entrance."

He headed toward the fire escape. Bruce and Sophy dashed after him.

They reached the first floor along with a handful of other people and moved out into the service lane. The guests who had chosen the emergency exit rushed down the lane and disappeared around the corner. A few minutes later Sophy, Luke, and Bruce found themselves alone.

"All clear," Luke said. "Let's go."

The desert night was filled with the rumble of cars coming and going in front of the inn, but the narrow strip of pavement in back was empty. It was also unlit except for a dim light over the exit door. In the shadows it was easier to detect the vortex energy that shuddered in the atmosphere.

"The levels are still rising," she said quietly. "It's as if we're sitting on top of a volcano that is getting ready to blow."

"That is a visual I could have done without." Luke reached the end of the service lane and stopped. Bruce halted beside him. "I don't see anyone in the sculpture garden. Looks like everyone, including security and the staff, is heading for the front gate."

Man and dog went forward. Sophy followed.

"In hindsight, we should have called in the Foundation back at the start," she said.

"In hindsight, that might have been a good idea. But back at the start we were just trying to find Deke and Bea and retrieve some old Bluestone artifacts."

No one tried to stop them when they crossed the sculpture garden. As far as Sophy could tell, there was no security left.

By the time they reached the Maze Gallery they appeared to have the entire art colony to themselves. Sophy looked back at the main gate and watched the taillights of the last vehicle disappear.

"This is just so weird," she whispered. "The place is deserted. We're the only ones left."

"Don't bet on it," Luke said. He stopped in front of the main entrance of the dark house and tried the door. It opened easily.

"Unlocked," Sophy said. "Someone left in a hurry."

"Looks like it." Luke pushed the door wider.

Sophy expected a sea of night inside the house. She had been prepared to heighten her other senses. But the lobby was illuminated in the subdued light of a wall sconce, just as it had been on the night of the exhibition. The doors that separated the entrance from the antechamber where she and the others had been hit with the first hypnotic suggestion were open, and so was the second set of doors. The floor lighting was on, marking the path into the display area.

Bruce rumbled softly. His attention was focused on the gallery path.

Luke studied the dog for a few seconds. "Find."

Bruce went forward at a quick pace. Luke followed. Once again Sophy found herself rushing after them. She reminded herself that they were the experts when it came to security matters.

"You know, maybe one of us should have brought a gun," she whispered.

"I don't think Bruce is warning us of a threat," Luke said. "This is his *there's something interesting up ahead* look."

To Sophy's surprise, it wasn't just the path into the gallery that was illuminated. So were the installations. But the mirror tiles were silent.

"The tiles have flatlined," she said.

"Evidently Grant hasn't recharged them." Luke rounded a corner. "Maybe he can't."

"Because he's deteriorating?" Sophy said.

"Yes." Luke followed Bruce around another corner and stopped. "Or because he's dead."

"What?" Sophy turned the corner and froze when she realized they were in the hallway where Vincent's *Succubus* was displayed.

The witchy female figure was illuminated just as it had been on the night of the exhibition. The eyes glittered with a demonic light. *Succubus* loomed, triumphant, over her victim. But the original sculpture figure at her feet was no longer visible. Vincent Grant was sprawled across the base of the installation and he was very dead.

FORTY-EIGHT

SHOCK CAUSED SOPHY'S SENSES TO FLARE. SHE SLAMMED INTO HER TALENT BUT THERE was no clear note from her chimes to guide her and help her focus.

The result was a disorienting trance. It was as if she had been tossed into a nightmare. Currents of madness, panic, and violence emanated from the walls, the floor, and the sculpture. They flooded the small space, swirling around her, threatening to overwhelm her.

Just an uncontrolled trance, she thought. *You've been here before. You know how to escape. Breathe.*

"Sophy?"

Luke's voice came from outside the dream. She was suddenly aware of Bruce leaning heavily against her leg. She seized on the lifelines and collected her senses. The trance energy steadied. She got control.

The first ghostly figure appeared. She knew it was Vincent. He stood in front of *Succubus*, glorying in his creation. The second ghost arrived, madness shivering in the energy around him. There was a surge of panic from Vincent. A dazzling blast of light. Vincent collapsed.

She heard herself speaking in her trance voice. "*Vincent was killed by the smoking ghost.*"

"That explains the cigarette butt that Bruce just found," Luke said.

She took a couple more breaths and came out of the trance. Back in control. She realized Luke was holding her hand. She remembered that she was wearing her regular glasses, not her mirrored shades. But once again Luke was unfazed. Focused.

"Are you okay?" he asked.

"Yes." And she was. The familiar shot of adrenaline was pulsing through her but not in the hot, wild way that led to the ice fever. This rush she could handle. For the first time she wondered if maybe some of the disturbing aftermath of her trances was caused by the fear of how onlookers would react. She'd been burned so many times.

But Luke was different.

He released her hand and started back toward the intersection, Bruce at his heels. "We need to keep moving."

She adjusted her pack and followed him.

"You really were born to take charge," she grumbled.

"What?"

"Nothing. You were right. Poor Vincent became a problem for someone."

"Poor Vincent?"

She ignored the sarcasm. "If I read the vision correctly, he was murdered with one of those Kaleidoscope weapons. That means Orston, the guy I called Smoking Ghost, has fired the light gun at least twice that we know of and probably more often."

"Count on it." Luke stopped in front of a darkened hallway that was closed with a velvet rope. "Here we go. This is the corridor that leads to the wall."

"How can you tell? It looks like all the other hallways." She paused, raising her talent a little so that she could see the dark passageway. A stream of footsteps, old and new, glowed faintly on the floor. "Oh, right."

Bruce followed Luke unhesitatingly into the hall. Once again she found herself bringing up the rear. It was getting old.

"This path has been in use for decades," Luke said. "Probably since the house was built."

"Yes, I can see that." She stopped and managed, barely, to swallow a small screech. "Damn. Another one."

Luke halted and looked back. "Another body?"

"Not a body but, yes, another murder scene." Warily, she heightened her senses and caught a glimpse of a figure standing over a dead man on the floor. "*Not Smoking Ghost this time. And not Vincent. I don't see any signs that the killer used one of the Kaleidoscope weapons. It's hard to estimate times but I think this murder took place about two years ago.*"

"That would put it at approximately the time the last owner of the house was said to have gone mad and died in here. He was probably murdered because the Alchemist wanted control of the property. Even if he had been willing to sell, he had to be taken out."

She slipped out of the light trance. "Because he knew the secrets of the house."

"Yes. Are you okay?"

"What?" Then she realized he was worried she might be on the edge of an ice fever attack. "Yes, I'm fine."

And she was, she thought. Or at least as fine as a person could be while discovering murder scenes in a maze.

"Let's keep moving," Luke said.

It was a command, not a suggestion. She resisted the temptation to fire back with a snappy, *I'm on it, Boss.*

She stopped a moment later because Luke and Bruce had halted in front of what looked like a steel wall.

"This is it," he said.

She watched Bruce trot forward and lower his nose to the nearly invisible line that marked the lower edge of the wall. The dog sniffed and then scratched at the metal.

"There's something on the other side." Sophy said. "But I don't see a lock or a security code panel."

"That's because someone went to a lot of trouble to hide it."

Luke took a small device out of one of the pockets of his jacket and moved it methodically around the edge of the steel plate. He paused when a tiny green light blinked.

"Here we go," he said.

He did something to the gadget and a small, concealed plate opened, revealing an illuminated control panel.

"I can probably unlock that for you," she offered.

"Thanks, but believe it or not, some of us can still get by the old-fashioned way—with good tech."

"I was just trying to be helpful."

Luke flashed one of his rare, fleeting smiles. "Nobody likes a show-off. Stand back. Bruce doesn't seem to be alarmed, but we don't know what's on the other side."

She obediently retreated a couple of steps and glanced at Bruce, who was intent on whatever was on the other side. Luke was right; he did not look as if he was sending a warning. But maybe that was because, like Luke, he didn't scare easily.

She flinched when a low, grinding rumble sent tremors through the wooden floorboards. The steel panel slid slowly aside, disappearing into the wall.

"Impressive," Sophy said. "Even though you were showing off."

"Just demonstrating the bleeding-edge technology that defines the Wells brand."

"Bleeding edge?"

"One step beyond cutting-edge."

"You may not want to use that line in your advertising. It's a little off-putting."

Luke didn't respond. His full attention was on the staircase in front of them. It was lined with subway tiles that glowed with a faint blue radiance. Bruce looked interested but showed no signs of alarm.

"Great," Sophy muttered. "A basement. What could go wrong? Where is the light coming from?"

"It's paranormal energy," Luke said. "Can't you sense it in the atmosphere? The tiles on the walls have been absorbing it for decades."

"Like the house itself," she said. "But what is the source of the energy? It doesn't feel like vortex power."

"We just walked into one of the old Bluestone labs."

FORTY-NINE

"A BLUESTONE LAB." SOPHY GAZED DOWN THE GLOWING STAIRCASE. "OKAY, THAT EXplains the paranormal heat. Still, it's hard to believe, isn't it?"

Luke understood her astonishment. Based on the isolated location, the strong vortex energy, and the age of the house, he had begun to suspect that the original art colony had been established as an elaborate cover for a Bluestone lab. Nevertheless, walking into one of the legendary facilities was a unique and darkly thrilling experience. So much power. So much mystery. So many secrets.

"Luke? Are you okay?"

He shook off the shock and awe. Time to focus. He slid the pack from his shoulder and unzipped it.

"Nobody knows for sure how many labs were involved in the Bluestone Project," he said. "Best guess is that, like the Manhattan Project in World War II, there were four, maybe five. Three have been located so far. This looks like number four."

He reached into the pack and took out a plastic baggie.

Sophy watched him. "What is that?"

"One of Deke's T-shirts." He slipped the garment out of the baggie. "I took it out of his dirty clothes hamper."

He offered the shirt to Bruce, who sniffed it. "Find, pal. Please."

Bruce gave him an *easy-peasy* look and promptly went down the stairs.

Luke slung the pack on his shoulder. "He's picked up the scent. Let's go."

Sophy caught up with him. "Talk about old-fashioned search and rescue techniques. I was expecting you to whip out another bleeding-edge gadget."

"Sometimes the tried-and-true ways work best. In addition to having a great nose, Bruce also functions as an excellent alarm system. He'll let us know if we've got unwanted company."

The staircase ended at the entrance of a large, tiled chamber furnished with rusted steel workbenches, broken glass beakers, and clunky-looking lab instruments that clearly dated from the mid-twentieth century. Two typewriters sat atop vintage government-issue desks. White metal cabinets inset with glass lined one wall. A calendar featuring a buxom blonde in a microscopic bikini dangled from a thumbtack stuck in a corkboard. The hands of an old analog clockface were stopped at five thirty-three.

Logbooks, file folders, and miscellaneous desk accessories were piled in a corner, as if someone had used a broom to sweep them out of the way.

"*Something bad happened here a long time ago,*" Sophy said.

It took him a beat to realize that she was in her trance voice.

FIFTY

THE TRANCE HAD STRUCK OUT OF NOWHERE, THE WAY IT DID WHEN SHE WAS IN HER teens and coming to terms with the fact that she was stuck with a truly annoying talent. She had taken one step into the old laboratory . . .

. . . and fallen straight into the ghost world.

A terrible sense of panic and chaos swirled in the room. Most of the ghostly shadows appeared to be male, but her senses registered two of the figures as female. The secretaries who had been sitting in front of the typewriters, she thought.

Several people in the fleeing crowd ran for the door at one end of the room. A few dashed in the opposite direction and vanished down another tiled hallway.

The intense and disorienting visions threatened to overwhelm her. She seized on her crime scene reading skills to make sense of what she was witnessing.

". . . *The energy levels are too high*," she said in her other voice. "*A miscalculation. Shut down the machine. Too late. Too late.*"

"Where is the machine?" Luke asked.

His voice came to her from outside the trance.

You can do this, she thought.

She felt the weight of Bruce's body pressed against her leg. He watched her with his amber eyes. She touched his head and then she fumbled in the pockets of her trench coat, desperate for the chimes and mallet.

She found both and struck a clear, high note. It steadied her senses, allowing her to concentrate on reading the scene.

"The machine is not in this room but it is nearby. Some think they will find safety at the far end of the lab. Others are desperate to escape through the door. They've had very little warning."

She struck another clean, clear note and rode it out of the trance. The adrenaline hit her bloodstream, but this time it was charged with the residual energy of the fear and desperation that had soaked into the floor and walls and ceiling so long ago.

She dropped the chimes and mallet back into a pocket. "We're standing in the middle of an old disaster zone."

"You said something about a machine?"

"Yes, I picked up that much."

"Probably an earlier attempt to tap into the vortex forces."

"Idiots."

Her nerves settled back into what passed for normal these days. She reached down to pat Bruce on the head. Evidently satisfied that she wasn't going to fall apart, he left her side and went back to investigating the room.

He picked up a scent almost immediately, dashed off, and disappeared into the hallway at the far end of the chamber.

"That's the direction several of the people in this lab ran all those years ago," Sophy said. "They thought they would find safety there."

Luke went after him. "Stay close."

"Trust me, I'm not going to run off and explore this place on my own," she said.

They followed Bruce around the corner and down a short, glowing hallway. At the far end was a steel door set into a wall of thick glass blocks.

"Looks like a safe room," Luke said.

Bruce plunked himself down in front of the door and looked at Luke with a triumphant expression.

"I don't understand," Sophy said. "Why is he—?"

She broke off when a figure moved into view behind the glass blocks. She recognized him from the hologram—Deke Wells. But it wasn't until a second person appeared that her spirits soared.

"Aunt Bea." She rushed to the glass brick wall and flattened both hands against the surface as if she could shove it out of the way. "You're alive."

FIFTY-ONE

"THEY CAN'T HEAR US AND WE CAN'T HEAR THEM," LUKE SAID. "THEY'RE TRAPPED INside that room."

On the other side of the glass wall, Deke pointed toward the steel door and mouthed a word that looked a lot like *key*.

Luke studied the large, old-fashioned iron padlock that secured the door. "We've got a problem. It's not a keypad or a smart lock. My jammer is designed to handle modern security systems. That lock takes a key or a set of bolt cutters."

Sophy examined the lock. "Hmm."

He raised his brows. "I know you can handle crystal locks. Is this where you demonstrate the Harper family talent for old-school breaking and entering?"

She shot him a severe look. "Do I insult your family?"

"On a regular basis. But I try to rise above it. Please tell me you can deal with that lock."

"You call that a lock? It's not a lock. It's a toy."

She reached up and unclamped the large clip that secured her hair. He watched, intrigued, as she opened the clip and withdrew what appeared to be an old-fashioned steel hatpin.

She went to work on the lock. On the other side of the wall, Bea smiled proudly. Deke winked and grinned.

Luke wanted to share the upbeat moment but his intuition suddenly kicked in, stomping out all positive thoughts.

Bruce had been exploring the scents in the hallway. He abruptly stiffened and growled a warning. Sophy went very still.

Deke and Bea were no longer smiling. They were focused on the hallway behind Luke. He slipped the auto-injector out from under his jacket, palmed it, and turned.

Smoking Ghost stood in the opening, a Kaleidoscope weapon in his hands.

"The Alchemist said that if you got inside the lab you'd probably show up here at the old safe room," Smoking Ghost said. He aimed the weapon at Luke. "Looks like he was right."

"You do realize that weapon is making you insane," Luke said. "Every time you fire it, you get another hit of psychic recoil. It's warping your paranormal aura."

"That's a fucking lie." Smoking Ghost's face twisted with fury. "The gun is still tuning itself to my aura. I'm the only one left who can fire it now that Hatch's brother is gone. Grant couldn't handle the weapon, you see. I had to put him down like you would a mad dog."

Bruce growled but Smoking Ghost ignored him.

"Not yet," Luke said very softly.

"You're next, Wells," Smoking Ghost said. "We need the Harper woman but we don't need you."

He tightened his grip on the weapon. His eyes flared with a sick lust.

Luke aimed the auto-injector and pressed the trigger mechanism. A dart containing a powerful sedative shot across the short distance, tore through the fabric of Smoking Ghost's shirt, and embedded itself in his chest.

Smoking Ghost yelped in surprise. He dropped the gun and tried to yank out the dart but it was too late. The drug hit him hard and fast. His eyes rolled back in his head. He went limp and collapsed on the floor.

Luke rearmed the auto-injector, tucked it back into his pocket, and went forward to retrieve the Kaleidoscope weapon.

"Is he dead?" Sophy asked.

"No, but he'll be out for a while."

She went back to work on the lock. "So, just to be clear, you *could* have been a CIA assassin."

"Disappointed?"

"Nope."

He watched her wield the hatpin, probing gently. The padlock sprang open. She removed it and got to her feet. Deke was already pushing the door open. He and Bea spilled out.

Sophy tucked the hatpin back into her hair clip and wrapped Bea in a huge hug.

"I've been so worried," Sophy said.

"So have I," Bea said. "I knew that old hatpin would come in handy someday."

"Gotta love the Harper talent," Deke said. He glanced at the motionless man on the floor and then looked at Luke. "What kept you? Bea and I were getting damned tired of MREs."

"Sorry for the delay," Luke said. "What the hell is going on?"

"Long story." Deke stepped over the unmoving Smoking Ghost. "But first things first. We need to get out of here."

"Deke is right," Bea said. She pulled free of Sophy's arms. "The fools running this project are trying to tap into serious vortex energy. They have no idea what they're doing."

Luke led the way toward the hall that would take them back

into the old lab. He glanced at Deke. "Any chance you know where your pistol ended up?"

"No, and we don't have time to look for it. Is that wimpy little tranq pen all you've got on you?"

"Afraid so."

"How many times have I told you to carry a backup?"

"I worked in data analysis, not in the field like you. Dots. I'm good with dots."

"Luke is an off-the-charts lucid dreamer," Sophy said to Bea.

"Is that right?" Bea sounded impressed. "That will be a very useful talent for a CEO."

"What the hell?" Deke shot Luke a concerned look. "Are you still having those weird dreams like you did when you were a kid?"

"I never stopped having them," Luke said. "I just stopped talking about them."

"Why?"

"Take a guess," Luke said.

"Your parents weren't serious when they talked about sending you to a shrink because of your dreams."

"Yes," Luke said. "They were."

Bruce growled another warning before Deke could respond.

"Freeze or the women die first."

Luke recognized the voice of a professional in the security business—someone who knew how to use a gun and would not hesitate to pull the trigger. He knew Deke did, too.

Both of them stopped. Bea and Sophy did the same.

"Turn around. Slowly. Control the dog or I'll take him out."

Bruce shivered with anticipation.

"No, Bruce," he said quietly.

Bruce obeyed but he did not shed any of his battle-ready tension. He was ready to defend his pack.

They all turned around to face Hatch's private security team.

The blondes were armed with high-powered pistols. They wore head-to-toe black—matching uniforms, black caps, and black boots.

"Damn," Bea muttered. "It's those two again."

"Meet the armed Barbies," Deke said.

"No offense," Sophy said to the team, "but the tuxes were a better look for both of you."

FIFTY-TWO

"WE DON'T HAVE TIME FOR THIS," BEA SAID IN HER SOOTHING PSYCHIC-KNOWS-BEST voice. "We must get out of here immediately. Surely you can feel the energy levels rising. There's going to be an explosion and we'll all be buried under the rubble."

The twins ignored her. Sophy wasn't surprised.

"Forget trying to talk sense into them, Bea," she said. "The Alchemist has probably promised them that they will be fantastically rich at the end of this project."

"No more talking," Blonde Number One said.

Blonde Number Two gestured with the pistol. "Through that doorway, all of you. The Harper woman is right, we don't have a lot of time. The Alchemist is waiting."

Sophy looked at Luke, who was exchanging silent messages with Deke. She knew they were planning a desperate move that would no doubt get at least one of them killed. Even if it worked it might not buy them the time they needed. There was only one hope for surviving the day.

"No," she said quietly.

The men looked at her. So did Bruce.

"She's right," Bea said firmly. "We don't have time. Sophy is our best chance."

"Shut up," Blonde Number One snapped. "Move."

Luke and Deke exchanged another look and then evidently made their decision.

They went through the door, Bruce at Luke's heels. Sophy and Bea followed.

The security team escorted them down a short, glowing passageway and into a large, circular chamber. Except for a small patch of bare concrete, the curved walls and the domed ceiling were covered in mirrored tiles. The uncovered section explained the source of the hypno-tiles, Sophy thought. They had been pried off the wall.

Ten six-foot-tall towers fashioned of the same mirror-finish alloy stood in a ring at the center of the chamber.

Inside the circle was a pedestal. Six round, faceted crystals were lined up on top. Each glittering stone was about two inches in diameter.

The mirrored chamber was bizarre, but it was the seething currents of energy swirling in the space that rattled Sophy's senses.

She caught her breath. "So much power."

"So stupid to mess with it," Bea said.

Deke looked at her.

"Still think this is the best way out?" he asked softly.

"It's the only way out," Bea said. She looked at Sophy. "Isn't it?"

Sophy met Luke's eyes. "I think so, yes."

"It's too late," Hatch said, his voice flat. "The energy levels are close to ignition point. Had them under control, or thought I did, until the fucking insane idiot decided to crank up the intensity of the light. It's amazing there hasn't been an explosion already. Just a matter of minutes now, if that."

Sophy and the others turned toward him. He was hunkered down on the floor of the chamber, his arms wrapped around his updrawn knees. He regarded them with hopeless resignation.

"Yes," he said before anyone could ask a question. "I got played. And they murdered my brother. The only thing I can say for myself is that I managed to pull the emergency evacuation alarm before the Scary Blondes showed up. At least the staff and the test subjects had time to get away."

Marlon Whitley stepped out of what appeared to be a control room. His shaved head gleamed in the light. There was a feverish energy around him.

"Welcome to my little project," he said.

Sophy looked at him. "And you wonder why nobody likes a critic."

FIFTY-THREE

WHITLEY CHUCKLED. "IF I WERE A REAL ART CRITIC I WOULD TAKE OFFENSE, MS. HARPER. But I'm an engineer. I specialize in rare earths, a subject about which I'm sure you know nothing, so your opinions are of no interest. You're probably wondering why I invited you here today."

"I'm here because you kidnapped my aunt," Sophy shot back. "And Deke Wells, too," she added somewhat belatedly. "You belong in prison, you asshole."

"Uh, Sophy," Luke said quietly.

She ignored him, righteous fury igniting her senses. "You're playing with forces you can't control."

Whitley smiled. "Which is, of course, why you're here. The six crystals were created precisely to control extremely powerful forces such as vortex energy. Once you unlock the stones, I will be able to use them to channel the raw power of the natural forces in this area and store it in the mirror batteries."

She stared at him, so outraged she could barely speak. "If you think for one minute that I'm going to help you—"

"Congratulations," Luke said, smoothly interrupting her.

"You've found a material that can store vortex energy. Impressive. A rare earth alloy?"

Sophy glared at him but he did not appear to notice.

"A previously unknown element that my great-grandfather discovered after Bluestone was shut down," Whitley said eagerly. "He never gave up on the project, you see."

Deke folded his arms. "Your ancestor was Maxwell Coburn, the third engineer involved in the development of Kaleidoscope."

"Exactly," Whitley said. "He survived the explosion. In the chaos that followed, he faked his own death. But he had his logbooks and, even more crucially, he had classified information that made it clear the Fool's Gold Canyon lab had been working on the battery problem, too. He tracked down the facility and found it in ruins."

"Because the researchers here managed to destroy their own lab, apparently," Bea said.

"They didn't have a way to control the energy they were trying to harness and store," Whitley said. "But now that problem has been solved, thanks to the crystals."

"The *locked* crystals," Sophy said.

"You will unlock them," Whitley said coldly. "If you don't, the security team will start shooting people. Your aunt will be first."

Sophy glanced at the blondes. Their faces were expressionless. She couldn't tell if they would follow Whitley's order or not.

"No," she said, horrified. "You can't do such a thing."

Whitley shrugged. "Your choice, Ms. Harper."

"Grabbing me turned out to be a miscalculation," Bea said using her professional psychic consultant voice. "But I'm afraid you have made an even bigger mistake thinking you can control the forces of this vortex. There is already too much energy stored in this chamber. It's been accumulating over the decades. Your experiments have made things a thousand times more dangerous."

"She's right," Hatch muttered. He fixed Bea with a despairing look. "A few hours ago I realized that the chamber was in a very unstable condition. Don't know why I didn't see that sooner. I've tried to explain the situation to Whitley but he refuses to listen."

"*The crystals can control the forces of the vortex*," Whitley shouted.

Sophy looked at him. "Assuming I unlock the crystals, what do you plan to do with them?"

Luke answered the question. "He thinks the crystals can be used to channel the energy in this room into the battery towers and lock it inside. The crystals will then be used to release the energy in a controlled fashion on demand. Think of a nuclear reactor."

"Or a nuclear bomb," Deke growled.

Sophy looked at Whitley. "Even if I can unlock the stones, you'll need someone who is very good with crystals to channel energy through them in order to control the battery towers."

"That would be me."

A woman stepped out of the control room and walked briskly toward the group. She wore a demure, knee-length, navy blue skirted business suit, a white blouse, and low black pumps. Her copper-red hair was pulled back into a neat bun. The severe style highlighted her elegant profile. A pair of tortoiseshell glasses framed her blue eyes. She gripped a metal clipboard in one hand.

"I'm very good with crystals," she said in a warm, feminine voice that could only be described as charming. "Imagine my delight when I realized I could embed certain emotional prompts into some old crystals we found here in the lab and use the tiles to switch them on. I've learned so much from the experiments I've been running here at the art colony."

"Shit," Luke muttered.

The woman managed to look both hurt and disappointed. "Is that any way to greet the woman you were planning to marry? We had some good times together. So many memories. I still think about that night at the little inn in the wine country—"

"That's enough, Victoria," Luke said quietly. "We've got a situation here. You need to focus. We all do. This chamber is hotter than hell and getting hotter."

Bewildered, Whitley turned toward Victoria. "I don't understand. What's going on here?"

"Shut the fuck up, Whitley," Victoria said in the same charming tone. "This is my project. It has been from the beginning. You are the very definition of a useful idiot."

Sophy winced. That voice was dangerous. It carried the currents of Victoria's reflection talent.

Whitley's jaw dropped. "How dare you? This is my project."

Victoria ignored him. So did everyone else.

The chamber was hot, Sophy thought, but that was nothing compared to her temper. She flashed Victoria her most polished smile.

"So, you're the secretly sexy librarian," she said.

FIFTY-FOUR

"THE WHAT?" VICTORIA BLINKED AND THEN SHE LAUGHED. "YES, THE INNOCENT-librarian-goes-wild-in-the-stacks trope works like a charm every time, especially on a no-talent."

"This is embarrassing," Luke muttered.

Deke grunted in a sympathetic way.

Sophy paid no attention. She was focused on Victoria.

"When Luke told me about you, I knew you were almost certainly a reflection talent," she said. "You should be ashamed of yourself. You have failed to uphold the standards of our profession."

"If it makes you feel any better, I'm not a real librarian."

"I *knew* it. How did you get your fake librarian hands on the crystals in Pandora's box?"

Victoria's eyes shimmered with triumph. "Everyone remembers that there were three paranormal engineers on the Kaleidoscope program, but no one remembers there was a fourth talent on the team. My great-grandmother."

"The secretary," Sophy said. "Mildred Green. My great-grandfather wrote that he was starting to suspect she was the real Communist spy."

"There was always a secretary in those days," Victoria said. "No one paid much attention to them but they knew all of the secrets. For example, my great-grandmother discovered the combination of the safe. On the day of the explosion, she grabbed the crystals on her way out. Later she went to the trouble of faking her death, but it hardly mattered because everyone had forgotten about her."

"I understand," Sophy said. "Librarians have a similar image problem. Everyone wants help from the staff at the reference desk, or readers' advisory, or the archivist, or the rare books specialist, but no one remembers the person who helped them locate what they were looking for."

"Luke is right about one thing," Victoria said. "This place is going to explode. If you don't unlock the crystals immediately I will leave you and your friends down here. Just think—you'll have a front-row seat for the fireworks."

Sophy got a senses-jarring ping.

"Okay, this is interesting," she said. "Evidently you do realize that we're all standing in the middle of a ticking time bomb. You're scared, as well you should be, but you're going to try to force me to unlock the crystals anyway. As soon as that's done, you're going to grab them and run, aren't you?"

"What is she talking about, Victoria?" Whitley yelped.

"She's not buying your theory that the towers can store vortex energy safely," Luke said. "She's just here for the crystals. Right, Victoria?"

"They're both lying," Victoria said, putting a little extra dose of charm into the words. She kept her attention on Sophy. "We're all running out of time."

Sophy glanced at Bea, who gave her a reassuring smile. The

message was clear: *Remember the first rule of the psychic consulting business: never let the audience see you sweat.*

She turned to Luke. Cool confidence gleamed in his eyes. His message was easy to read, too: *You've got this.*

Deke winked. *I'm in.*

Bruce padded close so that he was standing next to her. Message: *You're not alone.*

She patted the top of his head, straightened, and walked toward the circle of mirrored towers. She slipped between two of the batteries and stopped in front of the pedestal. She studied the six glittering crystals and selected one. It was locked, but a frisson of awareness zapped through her senses.

She looked at Luke.

"So much power," she said.

His eyes heated. "I know."

She concentrated on the crystal, feeling her way into the complex pattern of the lock, searching for the anchor current. It didn't take long. Tobias Harper had been good with locks, but she was even more talented. She pulsed a little buzz of energy to neutralize the currents that secured the crystal.

The stone blazed to life in her hand, pulsing with vermillion flames. Her thrill level was suddenly off the charts. She was intensely aware of the wild energy flooding the chamber, aware that, with the aid of the crystal, she could channel some of it, at least for a short while.

"You did it," Victoria said, euphoric with relief. "Unlock the others. Hurry. We don't have much time."

"I can do that," Sophy said. She set the crystal back down on the glass pedestal and took the chimes and mallet out of her trench coat. "But I've got options."

"What are you doing?" Victoria demanded.

The charm had evaporated from her voice.

Sophy ignored her. She struck a pure, delicate note, releasing it into the chamber. The crystalline tone soared, growing louder and more resonant until it pealed like a great bell.

Bruce unleashed an unearthly howl.

"What's happening?" Victoria screamed. "Stop."

"The towers," Whitley shrieked. "They'll overheat."

Sophy dropped the chimes and the mallet into a pocket and once again picked up the flaring crystal.

"Here's the really interesting thing about channeling vortex energy," Sophy said. "I just realized I might be able to use it to let you see what I see."

She went all the way into her talent, pulling on the wild forces in the chamber to project her visions.

"No," Victoria shouted. "Stop."

Hatch got to his feet, his eyes wide. "What are you doing?"

The Tuxedo Twins stood frozen, open-mouthed. Luke, Bea, and Deke watched her, but they made no move to stop her.

The otherworldly fog coalesced swiftly, filling the chamber. Shadowy figures appeared in the mist. There was no sound, but the visions needed no audio. It was all too obvious that the figures were screaming, running for their lives, and in the center of the room the mirror towers burned with a terrible radiance.

"*Welcome to my world,*" Sophy said in her trance voice. "*Welcome to the past. The explosion will happen any minute now. They tried to channel the power of the vortex and they discovered too late they could not control it.*"

"Ghosts," one of the twins said. "Impossible. What's happening?"

"There are no ghosts," Victoria shouted. But her elegant features were tight with fear. "She's creating a mass hallucination. Trying to scare us."

"It's working," Hatch said.

The spectral figures moved in the fog. Their silent panic charged the atmosphere.

"Shit," Twin Number Two rasped. "We didn't sign up for this."

"No," the other twin agreed.

Both women holstered their weapons and ran for one of the two doors.

Whitley shrieked in rage and then fled into the control room. He slammed the door shut, locking himself inside.

"You stupid fucking bitch," Victoria screamed at Sophy. "You've destroyed everything. I spent two years planning for this moment. *Two years.*"

Sophy struck another pealing note on the chimes and rode the currents out of the dreamstate. She got hit with the familiar flash of fear, afraid that she might be forever trapped in the terrible in-between state . . .

. . . and then she was safely on the other side, flying on the dark wings of an adrenaline rush that was unlike any post-trance ride she had ever experienced.

Victoria froze, horrified. "Who are you? *What* are you?"

Sophy remembered that she was not wearing her mirrored sunglasses. She smiled.

"You may be the secretly sexy librarian," she said. "But I'm the librarian from hell."

FIFTY-FIVE

VICTORIA WHIRLED AND FLED. SOPHY THOUGHT SHE MOVED WITH IMPRESSIVE SPEED, considering the pencil skirt and the pumps.

There was a reverberating clang as the massive steel door slammed shut behind her. The other heavy door closed a second later, sealing the chamber. Sophy heard the muffled thuds of dead bolts sliding into place. She and the others were trapped in the battery room. The energy levels were so intense she knew they had only a couple of minutes left before the inevitable explosion occurred.

"That's enough, dear," Bea said. "Time for some housekeeping."

"Your aunt's right," Luke said. "This has all been damned entertaining but we need to move. Can you neutralize the energy levels long enough for us to get out of here and back to the surface?"

"Sure," Sophy said.

In that moment she was a goddess.

She knew at once that she would not be able to calm the seething vortex currents with her core talent alone. Human energy simply wasn't strong enough to tame the powerful forces of nature.

She picked up the unlocked crystal and set about channeling energy through the stone.

When she had identified the currents she needed she went to work. The job required strength and subtlety. No one would thank her if she accidentally triggered the explosion that was waiting to happen.

Technically the task was no different than scrubbing the psychic stains of trauma that had soaked into a residence. She just needed a lot more power.

"I really hate housework," she grumbled to no one in particular.

When she was finished an eerie calm settled on the chamber. Satisfied that she had done all she could, she lowered her talent. The crystal went dark. She relocked it, aware that her fingers were shaking. This was not a good time for the ice fever, she thought.

She set the stone on the pedestal with the other crystals, dusted off her hands, and looked around.

"We should leave," she said. "The power levels have been temporarily neutralized, but that situation won't last long. There's too much energy embedded in this place. Too much heat. Something very bad is going to happen soon."

"We'll go out the way we came in," Luke said.

The door of the control room opened. Whitley stood in the entrance. He looked thrilled.

"I knew the crystals could control the forces of the vortex," he exclaimed. "I was right."

"No," Luke said. "This place is going to blow in a matter of minutes. Your only chance is to leave with us."

"I am not going anywhere. This is my masterpiece."

"Suit yourself," Deke said. "We're leaving."

Luke took the jammer out of his jacket. The steel door slid open, moving a lot more slowly than it had closed.

A maddened Smoking Ghost stood in the way. He had a pistol in one hand.

"So much for the new sedative formula," Deke said.

"Go for it, Bruce," Luke said.

Bruce launched himself at Smoking Ghost. His powerful jaws clamped around a forearm. Smoking Ghost yelled and tried to get out of the way. The gun fell to the floor. So did Smoking Ghost. He groaned once and went still.

Bruce stood over him and looked at Luke for directions.

"Thanks, pal," Luke said. He crouched beside Smoking Ghost and checked for a pulse. He shook his head and got to his feet. "The effects of the Kaleidoscope recoil would have taken him out very soon but the sedative probably sped up the process. Let's go."

Sophy glanced back into the mirrored chamber. Whitley was standing in the middle of the circle of towers, admiring his handiwork.

"There's no point trying to convince him to leave," Bea said quietly. "He's insane."

"And he's responsible for several deaths," Deke added. "Let him go down with his ship."

They retraced their steps back through the old lab and up the glowing blue staircase. Bruce led the way through the maze. Sophy followed the others outside.

The first light of dawn was showing over the canyon walls. The illuminated sculptures sparkled in the gardens. The windows of the empty inn were warmly lit. It all would have been very serene, she thought, if it weren't for the weight of impending doom that enveloped the deserted compound.

"With luck, the SUV is still in the garage," Luke said. "If not, we'll have to use one of the golf carts."

Deke grunted. "If we end up escaping in a golf cart, we all agree that we will take an oath to never tell anyone."

The SUV was in the garage. It sat alone amid the rows of empty parking spaces. Luke unlocked it and got behind the wheel. The others piled in. Deke took the front passenger seat, reached underneath it, and produced a pistol. He lowered the side window and took up a shooter's position.

Sophy, sitting in the back seat with Bea and Bruce, met Luke's eyes in the mirror.

"You told me you weren't armed," she said.

Luke drove hard and fast out of the empty garage, heading for the gate. "I said I didn't like guns."

"The Wells family is in the security business, dear," Bea reminded her gently. "It stands to reason they have some familiarity with firearms."

"Luke told you the truth," Deke said. "He doesn't like guns. Take it from me, he's not very good with them."

"Thanks for the positive feedback," Luke muttered.

"You were born for upper management, not fieldwork," Deke said.

Sophy sat back in the seat. "Actually, Luke was born to dream."

Deke glanced at her, curiosity sparking in his eyes. "Think so?"

"No doubt about it."

The SUV roared through the open gates, but Luke braked when a figure lurched into the middle of the road and waved frantically.

"It's Hatch," Sophy said. "Looks like the others left him behind."

"As far as I'm concerned we can leave him behind, too," Deke growled.

"We need some answers and he has them," Luke said. "He can ride in the cargo bay."

They paused long enough for Hatch to clamber into the back of the SUV. He collapsed next to the case of bottled water.

"Thanks," he gasped.

Luke floored the accelerator.

The explosion occurred a short time later. The towering red rock canyons that enclosed the small valley contained most of the energy but the force of the blast sent shock waves through the desert floor. The road heaved and twisted beneath the wheels of the SUV. Pavement cracked and buckled.

Sophy put an arm around Bruce, who was not strapped in, and held him close. In the cargo bay Hatch yelped as he got tossed around. They all hung on while Luke fought for control of the vehicle.

When things settled down Deke glanced back through the rear window.

"The town of Fool's Gold will be okay," he predicted. "The authorities will probably write it off as an earthquake that, in turn, caused a fire. Luckily for all concerned, the art colony was evacuated shortly before the emergency occurred."

"Nice work coming up with a sanitized version of events," Luke said. "You might want to consider a job in the marketing division at Wells."

"No thanks," Deke said. "I've got other plans. I'm going to work for the Shop on Hidden Lane."

He reached one hand over the seat. Bea smiled, grasped his fingers briefly, and squeezed.

Luke flashed a quick grin. "I can't wait to hear what Grandma has to say about that."

Sophy gave Bea a stern look. "Just how long have you and Deke Wells been—" She broke off, aware that she was flushing. She waved one hand. "Never mind. We'll discuss this later."

"Good idea," Bea said. "Because it's a long story."

"With a happy ending," Deke said.

"Even if we almost got killed," Bea added.

Sophy looked out the rear window. The smoke was growing pale and starting to thin. "Whitley can't have survived the explosion."

"No," Deke agreed. "The lab wasn't built to withstand those forces. Nothing is."

"I wonder if the Tuxedo Twins and the fake librarian made it out of the blast zone."

"I hope not," Hatch said. He grabbed a bottle of water and opened it. "Like I said, I got played."

"Talk," Luke ordered.

FIFTY-SIX

"THE BASTARDS LEFT ME BEHIND." HATCH SLUMPED IN THE CARGO BAY, LEGS STRETCHED out in front of him, and gulped some water. "I always knew my so-called security team couldn't be trusted. Whitley insisted that I hire them. Never liked him, either, but I thought I could handle him. I guess it was his assistant who made sure the security team got hired. Shit. She was running the whole show all along from behind the scenes. She seemed so sweet. So innocent. So nice."

Sophy almost felt sorry for him.

"She's obviously a powerful reflection talent," Bea said. "The ability is a lot like a talent for hypnosis."

Hatch slugged down some water and then shook his head. "I never thought I could be conned like that."

"No one does," Luke said from the front seat.

He did not sound sympathetic, Sophy thought. He sounded annoyed—with himself.

"How did you get involved in this mess?" he asked.

Hatch groaned. "Whitley—in hindsight I realize it was the

assistant manipulating him—made me believe I was fulfilling my lifelong dream."

"I'm guessing that wasn't a dream of supporting the arts," Bea said.

Hatch grunted. "No. Whitley is borderline insane. I knew that from the start. But he and the woman hooked me when they offered me access to that old lab. Turns out that back in the days of Bluestone they were researching the properties of paranormal light in the Fool's Gold Canyon facility. They thought it was the secret to creating the batteries. I couldn't resist the opportunity. I had always wanted to explore the possibilities of using light to enhance the human lifespan, and now I was being offered an entire lab that had once been devoted to paranormal photonics."

"What did they want in return besides your money?" Luke asked.

"They told me that all I had to do was figure out how to activate an old Bluestone machine that generated various spectra of paranormal light. That didn't take long. Hell, the logbooks were still there in the lab. But it required a certain kind of talent."

"Your kind of talent?" Deke asked.

"Yeah." Hatch gulped some more water. "I got the machine up and running. Whitley was able to make it work to get the old battery towers online. He and his fake assistant were afraid the Foundation might get wind of their work. They needed a cover to explain the activity at the old art colony. I was desperate to carry out my own research. So we came up with the idea of reviving the art colony."

"Did you know Victoria Ellsworth was running experiments with her hypnotic suggestion tiles?" Sophy asked.

"Yes, but I didn't care."

"When did you realize they were trying to tap into the vortex energy?" Bea asked.

Hatch grimaced. "Not long after we started the colony I warned Whitley the forces in the area were dangerous, but he was sure he could handle them with the batteries and the crystals."

"All three of you had different goals," Luke said. "Whitley was obsessed with using vortex energy to charge the battery towers. Ellsworth wanted to get the six crystals unlocked and perfect her hypnotic suggestion tiles. You were focused on experimenting with paranormal photonics."

"That about sums it up," Hatch said.

"Did it ever occur to you that the lack of a single focus for the project might be a problem?" Luke asked.

Hatch sighed. "No."

Sophy aimed a finger at the roof of the SUV. "A failure to have a leader with a clear-eyed vision at the top of an organization will inevitably bring down an entire project."

That announcement was greeted with silence. Bruce leaned over and tried to lick her face.

"Which one of you stole the Kaleidoscope weapons from the Wells vault?" Luke asked.

"Whitley said his assistant grabbed the Kaleidoscope guns."

Deke whistled softly. "She must have used some pretty fancy tech to break in to that vault."

"The best," Hatch said. "Whitley said she used a new high-tech lockpick that she picked up while she was working at Wells, Inc."

Deke grunted. "The black box lab."

Luke winced. "Ouch."

"Obviously your family vault is not as secure as you think," Sophy said. "Sounds like your company labs need a security upgrade, too. More work for you, Luke."

Deke looked at Luke. "Is she like this all the time?"

"You get used to it," Luke said.

Time to change the subject, Sophy decided. She twisted around in the seat to look at Hatch.

"I'm sorry about your brother," she said.

Hatch nodded morosely. "Thanks. We weren't that close, but before Mom died, she made me promise I'd take care of him. I didn't do a very good job."

"He was doomed when he started firing the Kaleidoscope weapons," Deke said. "Those old guns are too dangerous for anyone but the strongest of talents. The psychic recoil is a killer. Literally."

Hatch looked back down the road. The last wisps of smoke still swirled into the sky.

"Those damned weapons won't be a problem for anyone now," he said. "Nothing could have survived that explosion. Same with the crystals."

Sophy saw Deke and Luke exchange silent messages again and knew the crystals had survived. They were probably in Luke's or Deke's pack. She looked at Bea, who winked.

AN HOUR LATER DEKE ANNOUNCED THAT THEY HAD CELL SERVICE. "I'LL CALL VICTOR Arganbright at the Foundation. What's left of the Fool's Gold Canyon lab is his problem now. He can take Hatch off our hands, too."

Hatch stirred in the back of the SUV. "What's this about the Foundation?"

"We'll let Arganbright figure out what to do with you," Luke said.

"Huh." For the first time, Hatch brightened. "I wonder if they are doing any work in the field of photonics."

"Probably," Deke said.

Sophy cleared her throat. She met Luke's eyes in the mirror. "You're calling in the Foundation?"

"There's no other authority that can handle this," he said. "If we go with the FBI, the CIA, or any of the other alphabet agencies, we'll have an even bigger mess on our hands."

"I see," Sophy said. "Will it be absolutely necessary to mention Aunt Bea and me?"

"Don't worry," Deke said. He grinned at her over his shoulder. "It will be like you and Bea never existed."

"Are you sure Arganbright will go along with that?" Bea asked.

"Wellses and the Foundation have worked together for a long time," Luke said. "Arganbright knows when to stop asking questions."

"I hate to say this," Sophy said, "because I am not a fan of the Foundation. But *if* those crystals somehow survived the explosion and *if* they were to be recovered, it would probably be best if the Foundation took charge of them. I'll bet Arganbright and his crew have a really secure vault."

"Sophy is right," Bea said. "The Foundation should take responsibility for those crystals." She coughed discreetly. "If they happen to show up again."

"Great idea," Deke said. "I hear they've got first-rate security at the Foundation."

Luke met Sophy's eyes in the mirror. "Wells, Inc. designed the Foundation vault."

FIFTY-SEVEN

"AT LEAST IT'S NOT THE HONEYMOON SUITE." SOPHY SURVEYED THE HOTEL ROOM. "BUT it's hard to believe that this was the only room left in the entire resort."

She set the shopping bag containing new underwear, jeans, a white shirt, some essential toiletries, and a slinky little nightgown on one of the double beds. She had bought the gown on impulse when she and Bea had hit the lingerie section of the department store. The plan was to buy only the necessities they needed to hold them over until they got back to Mirror Lake, but she had been unable to resist the sexy little garment. Bea had made no comment but she had smiled a very knowing smile.

"Don't blame me," Luke said. He dropped the bag containing his new clothes and shaving gear on the other bed and unsnapped Bruce's leash. "Deke booked the rooms while I was dealing with the people from the Foundation. He just assumed we were a couple."

Sophy sniffed. "I wonder where he got that idea?"

"You'll have to ask him. But you can stop fretting about your virtue. I'm exhausted. I need a shower. After that we are going to meet Deke and Bea for drinks and dinner downstairs and then I'm going to fall into bed and sleep. Do you realize how long it's been since either of us has had any serious sleep?"

"No," she admitted. "I've lost track."

She looked at him across the width of the two double beds. They were all exhausted, she thought. Well, except for Bruce. He was eagerly investigating the room.

It had been a long drive through the desert to the regional airport where the Foundation agents had met them. After some discussion with Victor Arganbright on the phone, Luke and Deke had transferred the six crystals into the custody of the Foundation team.

"We can always recover them if necessary," Luke said after they were all back in the SUV and heading for the resort. "We know the Foundation's security system inside out."

Bea chuckled. "You think like a Harper."

"He thinks like the next CEO of Wells, Inc.," Deke said.

Hatch had seemed relieved, even enthusiastic, about being handed over to Arganbright's people. He was certain he could talk his way into a position at one of the labs. He was probably right, Sophy thought. Research into the paranormal was one of the core missions of the Foundation, second only to protecting the secrets of Bluestone. But it was annoying to know that he would go free.

Deke must have guessed her feelings on the subject. "If it makes you feel any better, I can promise you that even if he succeeds in talking Arganbright into putting him on the Foundation staff, Hatch will be under the equivalent of house arrest," he said.

"He may have all the money in the world, but he'll be wearing a psychic ankle bracelet."

"Well, that's something, I suppose," she muttered.

"It's the least Arganbright can do," Luke said. "Hatch was responsible for a lot of really bad art."

The Foundation had taken charge of what was left of the Fool's Gold Canyon Art Colony. The experts could not wait to start excavating the scene. There was, Deke said, nothing like the discovery of a previously unknown Bluestone lab to get Victor Arganbright excited.

Agents were dispatched to search for the Tuxedo Twins and Victoria Ellsworth.

It had been late afternoon when Luke pulled into the resort parking lot. They had all headed for their rooms with the gear they had picked up at the shopping mall.

This was, Sophy thought, the first time she and Luke had been alone since they had found Bea and Deke in the old lab. Well, make that the first time she and Luke and Bruce had been alone.

She looked at the new nightgown in the shopping bag. "I wasn't fretting about my virtue."

Luke paused in the act of taking a package of briefs out of his own shopping bag. He watched her from the far side of the room. In spite of his exhaustion there was a lot of heat in his eyes. Energy shifted in the atmosphere.

"Just to clarify," he said, "are you not fretting about the safety of your virtue because I'm too tired to be a threat tonight?"

"You will never be a threat," she said.

He winced. "That squishing noise is the sound of my ego being squashed flat."

Horrified, she stared at him. "I didn't mean it that way."

"How did you mean it?"

She felt the heat rise in her face. "I meant I know you would never hurt me. I trust you."

"Since when?"

She thought about that. "I'm not sure. From the start, I think."

His mouth kicked up at the corner. "So you've trusted a Wells for a little more than three days?"

"That sounds weird, doesn't it? I told myself I shouldn't trust you because you're a Wells, but somehow I knew that if you made a promise, you would keep it. What about you? Do you trust me? I know you're not afraid of me or my talent, but do you *trust* me?"

"From the start."

"Even though I come from a long line of psychics who have a talent for lockpicking and safecracking?"

"That doesn't worry me because I come from a long line of engineers who invent state-of-the-art security equipment."

She wasn't sure how to decipher that, so she plunged ahead. "I guess we don't have to worry about the stupid feud anymore."

"I'd say Deke and Bea took care of that issue for us."

"Yes, they did." Her spirits rose out of the depths and soared into the stratosphere. "Do you realize what this means?"

"I have a feeling you're going to tell me."

She swept out her arms. "You and I can try dating."

Laughter flashed in his eyes. "Okay, but can we skip the crime scenes in dark alleys? Maybe go to some nice restaurants instead? For the sake of variety?"

"Absolutely," she said.

"Can I assume I am not a failed experiment?"

She was mortified. "Of course not. Don't be ridiculous. Our relationship was never like that."

She had a feeling she was starting to flail.

"How would you define the status of our relationship?" he asked.

"Well—"

"Let me know when you figure it out. Meanwhile, I suggest we both get cleaned up and go downstairs. I don't know about you, but I need a drink."

FIFTY-EIGHT

THEY GATHERED IN THE RESORT'S OUTDOOR BAR. THE LONG LIGHT OF THE SETTING SUN bathed the sparkling pool and the luxuriously green golf course beyond in a golden glow. Sophy found the scene oddly surreal. It was hard to believe they were all safe.

The establishment was only lightly crowded. They found a booth that promised privacy and ordered drinks. Bruce took up a position under the table, alert for any bar snacks that might be coming his way. Sophy slipped him a pretzel.

Bea raised her wineglass. "To happy endings."

Sophy and Luke and Deke followed suit and swallowed fortifying doses of medicinal alcohol.

Luke lowered his glass of whiskey and looked at Deke. "About this particular happy ending."

Deke groaned and drank some of his whiskey. "I was afraid you were going to go there."

"In the hologram message you wrote that you and Bea were planning to check out the Maze Gallery and that if you disappeared, Sophy and I should not waste time looking for you. What went wrong?"

"My fault," Deke said. "I'm getting too old for fieldwork."

"It was not his fault," Bea said firmly. "The plan went perfectly, right up until it didn't."

"That happens a lot with plans," Luke noted. "Start from the beginning."

"Not much to tell," Deke said. "A month ago, Bea got an invitation to consult at the Fool's Gold Canyon Art Colony. The proprietors wanted to verify the existence of the vortex forces. A large honorarium was offered plus a room at the inn."

"It sounded interesting because of the money, of course," Bea said. "But it was the location that intrigued me. How could I resist the chance to explore a little-known vortex site that had a lot of mysterious history? I accepted the offer, but then Deke decided to retire, so I changed my mind. I was getting ready to decline, but Deke got a ping and said maybe we should go together if I could get a ticket for a plus-one."

"What was the ping?" Luke asked.

"I remembered coming across something about the Fool's Gold site in the Agency files," Deke said. "Bea and I did some serious digging in her library and came up with a vague link to Bluestone. I was curious, too. I was also getting suspicious. The art colony people approved the request for a plus-one."

"What could possibly go wrong?" Sophy said.

Deke grimaced. "I figured that if something did go wrong, it would be Luke who would come looking for us, and Bea said you might be with him, Sophy. I had a contact hack the art colony website and print out a second set of reservations for a couple named Ainsley. I made sure you would get the same room we had been booked into, just in case. Figured it would give you a starting point."

Sophy narrowed her eyes. "Did you know it would be the honeymoon suite?"

"Nope." Deke shook his head. "Cool, huh? The sad part is that we never got a chance to enjoy it. As soon as we arrived at the art colony we knew something was way off. Found the mood tile in the sculpture in the room and decided to do some serious investigating. As a precaution we took the holographic photo with the message and Bea locked it into the crystal. We started with the gallery. Found the door to the old lab. Ran into the armed Barbies, who made it clear they wanted Bea but didn't need me."

"They tried to kill him," Bea said. "He escaped, managed to find me, and together we made it into the safe room. It was our only option at that point."

"We were safe in that prepper's cave," Deke said. "They couldn't get at us. But after they put that padlock on the door, we couldn't get out. So we sat back and waited for you to find us, Luke."

"Sorry for the delay," Luke said. "Things got complicated after you left Mirror Lake."

"Yeah?" Deke cocked a brow. "How?"

"One of the Kaleidoscope shooters, Orston, murdered his partner in your cabin. They were there to get some background on you. Evidently Orston claimed his partner went insane and had to be put down."

Bea frowned. "Someone was killed in Deke's cabin? There will be a lot of very bad energy."

"I did some housekeeping," Sophy said. "But you know how it is with that kind of stain. You can't scrub it out entirely."

FIFTY-NINE

BACK IN THE ROOM SOPHY YANKED THE NEW NIGHTGOWN OUT OF THE SHOPPING BAG and forced herself to walk—not run—to the bathroom.

When she emerged some time later she was securely wrapped in a hotel robe. Luke brushed past her.

"I'll be out in a few," he said.

He vanished into the bathroom and closed the door. Firmly.

Sophy looked at Bruce, who was curled up on one of the beds.

"This is starting to feel very awkward," she said.

Bruce yawned and went to sleep.

She selected the bed that he was not using, slipped off the robe, turned out the lights, and settled under the covers—careful to stay on her side of the bed. Leaving the opposite side open. Available. Just in case Luke wanted to climb in on that side.

There was a heavy thump and the mattress sagged as Bruce took her up on the offer.

"Not you," she whispered. "You've got a whole bed to yourself. You don't need this one."

Bruce blinked his amber eyes a couple of times, curled up, and went back to sleep.

The bathroom door opened a short time later. Luke went to the window and drew the curtains aside. A wide swatch of silver moonlight slanted into the room. Sophy half closed her eyes and watched Luke shed his robe. She held her breath.

"Move, Bruce," he muttered softly.

Bruce got to his feet, turned around a couple of times, and re-settled on the foot of the bed. Luke got in beside Sophy and pulled up the covers. She was intensely aware of the weight and heat of his body. He was so close.

A deep thrill stirred her senses. Anticipation tingled through her. She waited for him to say something or to reach out for her.

Nothing happened. After a moment she levered herself up on one elbow and looked down at him.

His eyes were closed and he was already breathing slowly and steadily.

She flopped back down on the pillows and gazed up at the deep shadows overhead. Probably for the best, she thought. They were at a crossroads. They had not even had a real date. Sex at this point would complicate things even more than they already were. Sex would be a really big mistake.

Total mistake. Especially in front of the dog.

"We need to sleep," Luke said without opening his eyes. "At least, I need sleep. However, if at some point you wake up and decide to suck my vital essences, let me know. I wouldn't want to miss the experience."

"That is not funny."

"CEOs are not known for their sense of humor."

"In that case, you are certainly qualified for the job." She blinked and then propped herself up on her elbow again. "Wait. Does that mean you've decided to take control of Wells, Inc.?"

"Yes."

"Why?"

"You convinced me that the rest of the family is right. I need to accept my mistakes, learn from them, and move forward."

"Like a shark?"

"What?"

"Never mind."

"Looking back, it was our conversation about my relationship with Victoria that helped me make the decision."

"Glad to be of assistance. We librarians are here to serve."

SIXTY

SOPHY AWOKE TO THE SOUND OF A FEW SHORT, SOFT RAPS ON THE HOTEL ROOM DOOR. Bruce leaped off the bed and rushed to greet whoever stood on the other side.

"I'll get it," Luke said. He rolled out of bed and grabbed a robe.

"You ordered room service," she mumbled into the pillow. "Brilliant."

"Unfortunately I wasn't thinking that far ahead last night."

He unlocked the door and opened it a few inches, careful to shield their early-morning visitor from the view of the bed.

"This had better be important, Deke," he said.

"Thought you'd like to know the Foundation people took the helicopter up at dawn. I got a call a few minutes ago. They picked up the twins and Victoria Ellsworth. They are all on the way to Foundation headquarters as we speak."

Sophy sat up in bed, holding the sheets to her breasts. "What's going to happen to them?"

"Probably not much," Deke called from the other side of the door. "The three people who committed murder—Orston, the guy he killed in Mirror Lake, and Vincent Grant—are dead. So is Whitley, the man who put the weapons in their hands. As for the others, the Foundation and the Agency are obsessed with burying the truth about the Bluestone Project, so there probably won't be any official charges. The real threat to all of them is that they know the Foundation will be tracking them closely from now on."

"What about Hatch?" Luke asked.

Deke snorted. "Arganbright couldn't wait to offer him his own lab at Foundation headquarters in Vegas. But he will be wearing an ankle monitor."

"I'm surprised by how quickly the Foundation agents picked up the fake librarian and the Tuxedo Twins," Sophy said.

"That was the easy part," Deke said. "Ellsworth and the twins waved down the helo."

"They were on the run," Sophy said. "Why would they do that?"

"Their vehicle broke down in the middle of nowhere and they didn't have any water," Deke said. "They figured out fast that they wouldn't survive for long."

"This is the desert," Luke said.

"I'm getting tired of hearing that," she grumbled.

"He's right," Deke said. "Out here water is more valuable than gold."

"Whatever," she said. "So I guess the only one who won't get closure is poor Mack Rivington. He'll never know for sure that he was right about the murder in Mirror Lake."

"He won't get to make an arrest," Deke said, "But the Foundation is sending agents to Elk Cove to take possession of the body and the case. Your friend Rivington will at least have the satisfaction of knowing that the Feds were concerned enough to take over the investigation. He'll be told it's a matter of national security and that will be that."

Bruce whined, evidently bored with the conversation.

"I'm up and dressed," Deke said. "Want me to take him for a morning walk?"

"Thanks," Luke said. He picked up the bag of dog food and handed it to Deke. "After the walk, do me a favor and feed him. Keep him busy until I call you."

"No problem."

Luke tossed the coiled leash to Deke. "You won't need this unless one of the hotel staff sees you and gets upset."

"Right. Ready to go, Bruce?" Deke said.

Bruce pushed his nose through the opening. Luke widened the door. The dog disappeared out into the hall.

Luke closed the door and turned to look at Sophy.

"About last night," he said.

She chilled and clutched the sheet more tightly. "It's too soon to have that conversation. We haven't had a real last night."

"What the hell?"

"You know what I mean." She waved her free hand. "Nothing happened last night. Or the night before. Or the night before that."

"A couple of hot kisses don't count?"

"They were artificially induced."

He nodded in somber comprehension. "Got it. No sex involved so no about-last-night conversation." He stalked to the side of the bed and looked down at her. "You know, it's damn lucky for both of us that I'm learning how to follow your jumps in logic. Some men might be intimidated. A lot of men would feel like they'd been left behind in a cloud of dust. Confused and disoriented."

Relief and a glorious sense of certainty swept through her. She was so happy she wondered if she might possibly be glowing. "But not you."

"The trick is to connect the dots," he said. "Then I can fill in the missing bits."

"Luckily you're good at connecting dots."

"Got a talent for it." He headed for the bathroom. "I'll be right back."

When he emerged a short time later he had a couple of foil packets in one hand. He tossed them down onto the bedside table. She took the opportunity to race into the bathroom.

He was in bed waiting for her when she returned. The black T-shirt and briefs he'd had on earlier were in a heap on the unused bed along with the robe. He watched her with smoldering amber eyes.

A thrill of certainty went through her. Luke knew her secrets and he wanted her. She knew his secrets and she wanted him. They trusted each other. That was enough. For now.

He held out one hand. "I like the nightgown."

"I'm glad."

She went to the bed, took his hand, and got in beside him. He came down on top of her, easing her back onto the pillows. She thrilled to the weight, heat, and strength of him. His rigid erection pressed against her thigh. Everything inside her softened in response.

He brushed his mouth across hers, inviting her to join him in the sensual dance. With a low moan of wonder and delight, she flattened her palms on his sleekly muscled back and stroked downward to his waist.

It was his turn to groan. "The first time I saw you, I knew we were going to be good together," he said into the curve of her throat. "I just didn't know how good."

"That is so not true. The first time you saw me all you cared about was getting me to read the scene in Deke's cabin." She raked her nails lightly up his back and wrapped one of her legs around one of his. "You were very, very focused, but not on me."

He nipped her ear, letting her feel his teeth. "That's where you're wrong. The second you opened the door I knew you were the most important piece of the puzzle."

"So I was just another dot to be connected to the other dots?"

"You were the most spectacular dot of all." Luke slipped the dainty strap of her nightgown off one shoulder. "The most exciting dot." He lowered the other strap and freed her breasts. "The sexiest dot."

He took one nipple between his lips. His palm flattened on the sensitive skin of her belly. She arched into him.

After a moment he raised his head and looked down at her. "I also knew you were the dot that was going to give me the most trouble."

She started to laugh but his hand shifted to her hip and his mouth tightened on her other breast. She gasped instead.

"Is that how professional dot connectors talk dirty?" she managed.

"Depends." His fingers slipped between her thighs. "Is it working?"

"I think so." She gasped when he found the tight, sensitive place above her soaking wet core. "*Yes.*" She caught her breath. "Yes, it's working. My first impression of you was that you were going to be a very difficult client."

He eased one finger into her. "Obviously we were made for each other."

She clenched around his finger. Her insides tightened. "Obviously."

A deep, sensual hunger ignited her senses. This was passion, she thought. The real thing. She wanted him in ways she had never wanted any other man and she was not afraid to take the risk of letting go. With Luke she was free to fly.

She reached down and wrapped her fingers around the hard, full length of him.

His reaction was a fierce, husky groan. He eased another finger into her and pressed her sensitive clitoris with his thumb. She shuddered and began to stroke him, learning the feel of him. Discovering how he responded to her touch.

He rolled onto his back, taking her with him. For a moment she was tangled up in the sheets. She succeeded in freeing herself in time to see him reach for one of the foil packets on the nightstand. She sat up astride his thighs and scowled as she watched him sheathe himself.

"You just happened to have those handy?" she said. "And here I thought we were both yielding to spontaneous combustion or something."

"According to the Boss, a smart CEO is a prepared CEO. I picked up the condoms at the mall yesterday while you were shopping for a very sexy nightgown."

She smiled, smug and happy in the knowledge that they had both been scheming to achieve the same outcome.

"A smart librarian is always prepared, too," she whispered.

He crumpled the silky nightgown up around her waist. In the morning light his half-closed eyes burned.

He guided himself into her, taking his time at first, as if he wanted to savor the process. That was fine, she thought, because as badly as she wanted him deep inside, she needed time to adjust—not only to the size of him, but to the intuitive realization that sex with Luke was a risk in ways she could not explain, even to herself. She knew only that her life would be different afterward.

They were probably moving too fast. Yes, she trusted him and yes, he was not afraid of her or her talent and yes, there was some kind of bond between them—but they had known each other for less than four days. What if the attraction was a temporary bond generated by proximity and shared danger? What if . . . ?

"I love you, Sophy Harper," Luke said.

She stilled and looked down at him.

"I love you, Luke Wells," she said.

And then he was all the way inside, filling her, stretching her, urging her toward satisfaction. She tightened herself around him as the tension built deep within her.

In the next moment she was riding the waves of a release unlike anything she had ever experienced. She felt Luke thrust into her one more time, heard his exultant roar as he followed her over the edge.

Somewhere out on the psychic plane a perfect, crystalline note sounded. They held each other close and rode the music into the warm, damp aftermath.

SIXTY-ONE

LUKE CAME OUT OF THE BATHROOM AND SETTLED BACK DOWN INTO THE TUMBLED BED. He could not remember ever feeling better in his life.

"Your turn," he said.

Sophy got up, pulled on her robe, and handed him the room service menu. "Order breakfast. I'm starving."

"I'm on it."

He watched her disappear into the bathroom. A sense of satisfaction welled up deep inside. They were truly a couple now—connected on a bone-deep level that he could not explain.

He studied the menu with close attention, because he was hungry, too. He placed the order and waited for Sophy to reappear. A buzz of anticipation aroused all of his senses. There were going to be more mornings like this one, mornings when he and Sophy would have breakfast together. He wanted a lifetime of mornings with Sophy. A lifetime of nights. A lifetime of dreams made real.

She emerged still enveloped in the robe. Her hair was loose around her shoulders. She looked soft and cuddly and incredibly sexy. He was getting hard again just looking at her.

"How long until room service arrives?" she said.

"Really? You're thinking about breakfast instead of ravishing me? I'm crushed."

"I'll do a better job of ravishing you once I've had some protein and a couple of cups of coffee."

"Promise?"

"Promise."

"Okay, then."

She sat on the edge of the bed and gave him an expectant look. "Tell me when you first knew that you were falling in love with me."

He smiled. "I told you. The night you opened the door of the shop and informed me that I was late and that you were going to bill me triple the usual rate for a reading."

She frowned. "I'm serious."

"So am I."

"That's very sweet but it's hard to believe."

"Yeah, I had a hard time believing it, too. I figured my brain was a little scrambled because of the long drive and the fact that I was worried about Deke. So I put the issue aside. I was planning to deal with it in the morning. But then I had an unscheduled dream."

She brightened. "About me?"

"No, about Bruce."

"Oh."

"I dreamed about the night I found him bleeding in the middle of the road. It was as if he'd been waiting for me. That was my imagination, of course. He was in shock and would have died. It was sheer coincidence that I came along. It could have been anyone."

"But it was you and now the two of you are a team."

"I think Bruce would say we're a pack, but yes. Anyhow, when

I woke up I knew I was in the same situation as Bruce had been when I found him—standing in the middle of the road, waiting for you to come along."

"Hmm." She considered that briefly. "You were on the doorstep, not in the middle of the road."

"Details."

"And you weren't bleeding from a gunshot wound."

"No, but I was in crisis mode. I had to find Deke and I had to decide if I wanted to take control of the company. On top of that my intuition was telling me that things were about to get a lot more complicated, which turned out to be true."

"Still, you hadn't been shot."

"I've explained that my dreams need to be interpreted."

"I get that, but I don't see how you can interpret that particular dream as anything other than a straight-up dream about the night you found Bruce."

"Are all librarians as unromantic as you are?"

"We prefer to deal in hard facts."

"You want hard facts? I'll give you hard facts."

He pulled her down onto the bed and lowered himself along the length of her body. She reached down and took his erection into her hand.

"That is a very interesting hard fact," she said.

"It certainly struck me that way."

He bent his head to kiss her. A series of sharp raps on the door made him pause.

"Room service."

He groaned and eased away from her warm body. "I need better timing."

Sophy scrambled out of bed. "This is perfect timing. I'm hungry. Give me a minute to hide."

He watched her disappear into the bathroom. Impulse struck.

"Will you marry me?" he called after her.

"Yes," she yelled from inside the bathroom.

He smiled, tightened the sash of his robe, and opened the door. The room service waiter grinned.

"Congratulations," she said.

"Thanks." He took the heavily laden tray from her hands. "It's been a whirlwind courtship."

"Sometimes you just know."

"Yes. Sometimes you do."

SIXTY-TWO

The Cerberus research lab . . .

"FLD NUMBER ZERO ZERO TWO IS MISSING," THE LAB TECH ANNOUNCED.

His name was Reed and he looked worried, as well he should be, Egan Ashton thought. This was very bad news, perhaps even catastrophic for the research program.

Reed had worked in the lab since the inception of the Cerberus Project. He was good with the dogs and they seemed to like him—although with these particular dogs you could never be sure. Egan was starting to suspect that they could read humans even better than the researchers knew.

"That's the second dog in the past three months," Egan said. "Any sign of a security breach?"

"No, sir. The camera feed shows FLD Zero Zero Two in her kennel all night long but when I went in to feed her this morning she was gone."

"There's no way FLD Zero Zero Two could have manipulated the lock." Egan hesitated. "The dogs are smart, but they aren't that smart."

At least, he didn't think so.

The animals were descended from dogs that had been living in the tiny mountain community of Fogg Lake when the explosion in a nearby government lab had occurred. Like the humans and everything else in the vicinity, the canines had been exposed to two days of heavy fog laced with unknown paranormal radiation. No one knew what the source of the energy was because the government had gone to great lengths to destroy all the records related to the lab.

A year ago, decades after the explosion, someone at the Foundation had noticed that the descendants of the dogs of Fogg Lake were a little different.

Egan's team had been tasked with conducting an experimental program. The goal was to examine the potential of the Fogg Lake dogs for law enforcement or military work. There were rumors that a certain intelligence agency wanted to know if the animals could be trained to serve as couriers in dangerous corners of the world.

Initial results were promising, but there had been some unexpected complications. Among other things, the litters were small—just two or three puppies at most. The real problem, though, was that the dogs did not bond easily with their assigned human handlers. In fact, Egan was starting to suspect that the animals were choosing the people they were willing to work with, not the other way around.

The dogs were not abused. They were well fed and properly cared for. No one was using them for medical experiments. The training was state-of-the-art and based on play. For the most part the animals seemed to enjoy the exercises.

Now two of them had vanished.

"Someone is stealing the dogs," Egan concluded.

"That's what it looks like," Reed said.

"I will have to report this. There will no doubt be an investigation."

"Yes, sir," Reed said.

Egan clutched his clipboard and walked briskly toward his office on the other side of the compound. Sometimes, especially after dark, when he encountered one of the animals, he thought he saw the wolf beneath the surface of several thousand years of domestication.

He shuddered, aware that the dogs were watching him with their weird amber eyes. It was almost as if they knew he was a cat person.

AUTHOR'S NOTE

Welcome back to the JayneVerse. I hope you enjoyed the ride. I know some of you have questions about Bruce, the hellhound. Hey, you didn't think the human residents of Fogg Lake were the only ones affected by that weird paranormal mist that enveloped the town after the explosion in the secret government lab, did you? Yep, the animals in the area wound up with a psychic vibe, too.

If you're new to the books featuring the human descendants of Fogg Lake, I invite you to check out the first three novels to feature it: *The Vanishing*, *All the Colors of Night*, and *Lightning in a Mirror.* Those will bring you up to speed on the history of the town.

And should you be curious about other books in the Jayne-Verse, you are welcome to visit my home on the web, www.jayne annkrentz.com and sign up for my monthly newsletter.

Oh, and before I forget, the answer to your question about Bruce is yes, we will have another adventure with a Fogg Lake dog in the next Jayne Ann Krentz novel.

Waving from Seattle,
Jayne